The Man Behind the Menu

GREG WATTS

Milestone Books, London

Copyright © Greg Watts 2018

The rights of Greg Watts to be identified as the author of the work has been asserted by him in accordance with the Copyright, Designs and Patents Act 1988. All rights reserved.

This is a work of fiction. Names, characters, businesses, places, events and incidents are either the products of the author's imagination or used in a fictitious manner. Any resemblance to actual persons, living or dead, or actual events is purely coincidental.

www.gregwattswriter.co.uk

ISBN:

978-0-9931885-2-7

Published by Milestone Books, London, 2018
Printed and bound by Book Printing UK,
Remus House, Coltsfoot Drive, Peterborough PE2 9BF

In memory of the wonderful Keith Floyd,
whose cookery programmes were not only huge fun,
but also inspirational.

1

2015, Kensington, London

As Frank Darley strolled importantly through the crowds, every so often someone would come up to him to shake his hand or ask for a selfie. Others would nod, smile, or discreetly point at him. *Look, there's Frank! Walking around on his own, like an ordinary visitor.* Frank would grin back, sometimes silently mouthing a hello. He was enjoying the attention, and he guessed that when many people returned home it wouldn't be what they had seen at the stands they would be talking about, but having seen 'Frank'.

It was his twelfth time at Hospitality UK, his twelfth year of wandering the aisles at the Olympia, which, with its nineteenth-century iron and glass arched roof, looked more like a railway station than an exhibition hall. Every January it hosted the biggest and most important trade fair in the food and beverage industry. Chefs, restaurant managers and owners, producers and suppliers from across the country, and a few from overseas, came to show off what they had to offer or to discover what was new, and there was never any shortage of novelties nowadays. They also came to network, of course, which meant to find others who could benefit their business.

At over six hundred stands, smartly dressed men and women with fixed smiles lingered, ready to answer questions about their products or services from the visitors wandering past. Many offered a free pen, keyring, a magazine, or other items no one really wanted, but took all the same. The food and drink stands tried to lure people with tiny free samples, which smacked not of generosity but of meanness. There were also talks, seminars, cookery demonstrations, pop-up bars and restaurants.

Frank, just short of forty years old, was the most famous chef in Britain; at least so he liked to think. His fame had spread beyond Britain to the United States, the rest of Europe and even the Far East. It was said, although no one could remember when or by whom, that a tribe in a remote area of Polynesia had somehow got hold of one of Frank's cookery books, perhaps *To Be Frank* or *Frank's Secret Service*, and he was now revered as a god and his book regarded as a sacred text. Another version had it that it was a tribe in a remote region of Peru. Polynesia, Peru, who cared? It was a great story, a cracker, an absolute belter. 'Never let the truth get in the way of a good story,' Zoot always told him.

Television, rather than the food he cooked, was the secret of Frank's success. Frank never cooked in the restaurants that proclaimed his name above the door, unless he was publishing a new book, making a TV programme, or doing a photo shoot. That didn't matter, at least as far as he was concerned, because his presence was there – his spirit – hovering over the teams of cooks in the kitchens, the scurrying waiters and waitresses, and the diners seated at the tables out front. No one could see him, but he was omnipresent, invisible. Almost immortal.

Yet Frank wasn't satisfied with all the fame he had achieved and with the lifestyle it bought – the house in Beckenham, the second house in Italy, the expensive cars, the holidays. He didn't know why, but something inside told him he needed to be crowned the most brilliant chef in the world. That idea had become an obsession with him.

In previous years, he had given talks or cooking demonstrations at Hospitality UK. However, this year, he was just a visitor – but one on a mission: he needed an idea, a big idea, if he was going to win the Golden Pan award. The Golden Pan was an annual international award, regarded as a kind of Nobel prize for the culinary arts, that went to the chef judged to be the most innovative in the world, one who had done something with food that no one had ever done before. As a member of the International Culinary Academy, Frank would be attending the awards ceremony later that year in San Sebastián in Spain. And he was determined that it would be him stepping up to the podium to receive the trophy. No English chef had ever won the award. He wanted to be the first.

In his more reflective moments, he wondered why he had become so obsessed by winning the Golden Pan. He'd won all sorts of other awards over the years – Best Young Chef, Celebrity Chef of the Year, British Onion Council Food Hero (twice), British Food Awards Champion (four times), Cookery Book of the Year (three times). Why had the Golden Pan come to dominate his thoughts? Why was it so important? He didn't know. And this realisation nibbled away at him and posed awkward questions about who he actually was. 'Don't become a stranger to yourself,' his dad had once said to him. Frank wondered sometimes if indeed he had.

It wasn't just the idea of winning the Golden Pan that whirled around his mind all the time. There was something else, something much deeper, something more troubling. It surfaced at unexpected moments, stirring dark thoughts in him. And this was happening more and more often lately.

Strolling around a corner, Frank came upon a panel discussion, with several people engaged in animated chat on a sofa encircling a glass table. Each clutched a microphone. The moderator was the mayor of London, Asif Venkataraghaven, a small man with a weaselly voice, often referred to as Venkat. Frank thought he was more concerned with ticking politically correct boxes than with promoting healthy food. He was one of those politicians always on the lookout for the latest bandwagon to climb aboard to signal how politically correct or virtuous they were. That was why some sections of the media called him 'Rentacaravan'.

Frank peered ahead at the names of the panel members on the screen behind the sofa: the head of the charity Vegetable Attack; the deputy director of NHS England's Nutrition, Diet and Obesity Strategic Partnership Task Force for Community Engagement; the professor of fast food at the University of South-East London's Institute for Contemporary Food Studies; the chief engagement and awareness officer of the Joint Department of Education and Skills and Health Service Executive Schools and Colleges Forum for Promoting and Delivering Healthier Eating in an Inclusive and Equal Society; the head of marketing for the Campaign for Real Cabbages; and the head of campaigns at the Council for Organic and Sustainable Produce.

A self-important woman wearing long earrings and a colourful scarf draped around her neck was droning on. She wore a brooch in the shape of what Frank presumed was meant to be a banana, but could easily be mistaken for something else. He groaned inwardly as he listened to the soundbite words tumbling out of her mouth: nutrition, diet, obesity, epidemic, childhood, junk food, fizzy drinks, scandal, crisis, environment, sustainability.

Eating healthily was, of course, important, but he was against the kind of food puritanism that was emerging. He saw nothing wrong in occasionally buying James a Happy Meal in McDonald's, or taking him as a treat to that shop where the shelves were lined with old-fashioned glass jars full of the kind of sweets he'd eaten as a child. There were people out there – self-proclaimed liberals – who seemed to want to ban everything ordinary people liked. These moral crusaders who were marauding through the culinary world reminded him of religious zealots.

He continued through the exhibition, browsing among the suppliers' stands – water coolers; restaurant paging systems; slip-resistant footwear; video walls; lighting; menu designs; organically produced staff uniforms; glassware; disposable prayer mats; mannequins sitting at tables for restaurants struggling to attract customers; robots that can cook fries; and fries that cook themselves. At one time, going to a restaurant for a meal had involved interacting with the staff. Now, though, apps were available that meant customers never had to speak to a waiter. They could order their food and pay for it by simply tapping their mobile phone.

His attention was caught by a stand with display panels featuring photos of motorcyclists wearing white helmets and red leather jackets with gold crosses emblazoned on the back. Out of curiosity, he wandered over. It turned out to be a company called Christian Pizzas on Wheels. A caption above the photos proclaimed, 'Hungry for something? Want a home delivery pizza? Then why not contact Bible Bikers and feed your soul.'

'Hello,' said a man with a bushy grey beard, who was wearing the same outfit as the bikers in the photos.

'Christian pizzas? What's all that about then?' said Frank.

The man, with an earnest expression on his face, went on to explain that his company delivered pizzas – sourdough, of course – which came with short biblical texts printed on cards in the boxes. Once a customer had ordered their pizza from the website, they could then choose from a menu of spiritual food.

'It's a bit like adding extra toppings. Instead of mozzarella or mushroom, you can choose unemployment, addiction, depression – you know, all sorts of things that the Word of God can help with.'

'Much take-up, then?' asked Frank, looking for something to say.

'Oh, yes, we're growing very fast. You see, it's all about if people won't go to church, then the church must go to them. Jesus would have done this.'

'What, get on a bike?'

'Yes.'

'How do you know?'

'The Lord told me to do this,' said the man matter-of-factly.

'You reckon?'

'The Bible tells us that Jesus used unleavened bread at the Last Supper. But this was just a cultural thing. Pizza hadn't been invented then – and anyway it's only another form of bread. If it had, Jesus might well have used it instead.'

Frank looked at him in astonishment, trying not to laugh. 'What, you mean God told you to set up a pizza business?'

'It's the Lord's business, not mine. He's the one in charge.'

As Frank turned away from the stand, out of the corner of his eye, he saw Johnny John, in his trademark gold baseball cap with two red Js on the front, coming towards him. They hadn't spoken since the soufflé challenge they had taken part in on breakfast TV to mark World Soufflé Day a few months before. When Frank had taken his soufflé out of the oven and it had collapsed, Johnny had mocked him, saying he'd heard his business was going the same way. Frank had been unable to conceal his anger at the remark and replied by calling Johnny a wanker, a term you didn't usually hear on TV at half past eight in the morning as you buttered your toast or checked your child's school bag.

'Hey, how you doing, Frank? You busy?' said Johnny, shaking his hand.

'Yeah,' said Frank flatly. 'What about you?'

Johnny grinned. 'Busy, busy, busy.'

'Same here.'

'So you got any more openings coming up, then?'

Frank knew that Johnny also had his eye on the Golden Pan award. He shook his head. 'You?'

'Nah, just concentrating on what I've got, mate. It's been crazy since the last book. Sold nearly a million, you know. And that's just in the UK.'

'Really,' said Frank coldly.

'The reason it's so popular, you see, Frank, is that I don't complicate recipes.'

'Yeah, neither do I.'

Johnny smirked. 'Not saying you do, but you should try including less ingredients. You've got to remember people haven't got time nowadays.'

Frank glared at Johnny. 'What are you on about?'

'The thing is, *Johnny Seasons* only has five or six ingredients. You should take a leaf out of my book.'

'My books sell well.'

'Yeah, yeah, course they do, course they do. Anyway, Frank, better get going. Got an interview with *What the Chef?*'

What a pompous arsehole, thought Frank, as Johnny swaggered off. Too many ingredients. Who did he think he was? What a load of rubbish!

Frank moved on to the section where the food and drink producers were located.

There was artisanal organic candyfloss cheese from Blackpool; chicken in doughnuts with dairy-free cream; sourdough pizzas in a sachet; handmade chocolate cucumber crisps; Iranian vegan burgers; gluten-free cupcakes with icing made from Mexican edible flowers; kale and blueberry smoothies with Aleppo pepper; Norwegian-style cauliflower gluten-free bread; Russian tacos filled with minced crocodile; Chinese kangaroo noodle burgers; Bolivian southern fried squirrel fritters in panko breadcrumbs; haggis and dehydrated cactus powder curry; Devon crab ice cream free from milk; single estate Arabica heirloom Ethiopian coffee made from beans grown on a farm at an altitude of 3,000 feet that has no electricity; Shropshire craft non-alcoholic pale ale made from hand-picked hops and water from the Welsh mountains;

and vodka-flavoured brandy with organic juniper aged in natural oak barrels for two years in a cave off the B3276 in north Cornwall.

To make your product sound appealing, you had to tack on an adjective before it. So everything was 'heritage', 'natural', 'artisanal', 'organic' or 'handcrafted'. Frank had been a chef too long to take any of this seriously. He knew these words were nothing more than marketing ploys. He knew of one restaurant that advertised their asparagus as 'locally grown' when in fact it was shipped in from Peru. Yes, technology might be shrinking the world, but that was taking things a little too far. The word 'artisanal' was a particular favourite of his. It was meant to conjure up an image of someone working away with their hands in a rustic kitchen when in fact the product being sold was produced by people in white overalls and disposable caps in a strip-lit industrial unit on the edge of a nondescript town. For Frank, all that mattered was whether the food was good or not.

Dishes and drinks were judged nowadays not by what went into them, but what was left out. The buzz phrase was 'free from', as if a product had somehow escaped some terrible fate: free from sugar, free from gluten, free from dairy. Such was the free from frenzy that it would be only a matter of time before some new restaurant opened and proclaimed that it was free from diners.

Most of the display boards on the stands featured smiling photos of the business owners and some text about how and why they started the business. It wasn't enough to come up with a new concept in food; you also had to have a story, or if you didn't have much of one, then you had to make one up. If you were running a new pizza business, then, to emphasise how authentically Italian it was, you needed to tell your audience that you'd travelled around Italy exploring the local cuisines and discovered an amazing type of pizza, which had been life-changing for you. You might have only gone on a budget weekend break to Florence, but that wasn't the point. The point was to persuade your audience that you were an expert and bringing them something unique.

'Would you like to try some?' said a voice with a thick accent.

An attractive young woman in bright red lipstick was holding out a silver tray containing pieces of a soft-looking cheese on cocktail sticks.

Frank smiled at her. 'Yeah, don't mind.'

'It's made from a combination of milk from cows, goats, sheep and mothers.'

'Mothers?' said Frank, picking up a piece of the cheese.

The young woman beamed at him. 'Yes, young mothers. Usually under thirty. Their milk is very good for you. It's not just the land in Spain that is fertile.'

'You mean ... women's ... breasts?' said Frank, not sure if he had heard the young woman correctly.

'Yes. Try it.'

Frank hesitated and then cautiously popped the cheese into his mouth and began to chew on it. It was surprisingly creamy and sweet. 'Yeah, not bad.'

'We are a new company. Based in Barcelona,' said the young woman.

At her mention of Barcelona, the uneasy feeling he had been experiencing lately returned again. He tried to dislodge the image from his mind.

'Have you been to Barcelona?' she asked expectantly.

'Some years back,' said Frank in a low voice.

'Did you like it?'

He nodded and turned to walk away, murmuring, 'Anyway, thanks.'

'You're welcome.'

He passed more stands: takeaways delivered by drones, an outdoor catering company delivering gourmet meals to cemeteries and crematoriums, traditional Irish pubs with sushi bars, a company called Womenu providing non-sexist menus, another where customers could order a chef online and have him or her delivered to their front door to cook a meal. When he reached the demonstration area, a large crowd was watching a chef wearing a headset showing how to make triple-fried locusts with organic crispy nettles and a tree bark sauce.

Frank stood there, wondering if locusts might actually be quite tasty, and then opened his brochure and impatiently flicked to the section headed Talks and Seminars. He ran his eyes down the list of topics:

**The Customers Are Always Right – Except When They Are Wrong
Turning Bad Reviews into Good Ones**

Dirty Burgers – Clean Eaters
Writing a Menu like a Movie
Forty Allergies You Need to Know About
What Your Loos Say About You
Teach Your Staff Vegan-Friendly Language
Reducing Your Food Miles
What to Do When a Wheelchair Arrives
Size Matters: The Portion Debate
How to Make No Shows Pay
Should You Tip Your Customers?
How Automation Can Help Your Handmade Food Business
The Future of Restaurant Street Food
Hal AI or Not Hal AI? That Is the Question

None of these topics ignited his interest.

Then he spotted a title that intrigued him: 'Eating is not about food.' The speaker listed was Professor Edward Bumgarner, a neuroscientist at the Center for Science and Innovation in California. The talk was about to begin, so Frank hurriedly consulted the exhibition plan and set off towards the live theatre on the floor above.

Around fifty people were seated on rows of plastic chairs in front of a small podium on which Professor Bumgarner, a tall, thin man with a pointed beard and glasses, was being introduced by a glamorous woman. Frank slid into a seat at the back.

'So what is food?' began the professor, looking out at the audience. 'It might seem a simple question, right? But what I want to present to you today is a new way of understanding what we eat. To some of you this might sound off the wall; others might think it's a revolutionary way of understanding what happens when we eat. When we taste food – a piece of fish, a steak – it's not about something that goes into us. Food is an experience you construct from all of your senses, and as with all of your senses, your perception is driven by your brain. What we see sends signals to our brain. We have a relationship with food. An intimate relationship.'

He began pacing backwards and forwards. 'Food is about hopes, aspirations, dreams. It's about what you want to be. It's about who you think you are. And if we think about nutrition, it comes from the objects you eat, but it's also something that comes out of your knowledge and expectations. Sure, we hear a lot about obesity, people eating too much or eating the wrong things. Most people don't understand that what they are seeking when they eat that burger or that chocolate dessert is a sensation. It's not the actual food on the plate. Eating – particularly dining – is considered among the most sensory of all activities in which we participate. We draw on all our senses when we eat; sight, smell, touch, taste and sound. And colour cues alone can set all sorts of expectations. Depending on the sensory cues of a food, we make several judgments. For example, if we see a long, tubular, yellowish food that smells of isoamyl acetate – a main aroma compound in bananas – immediately we could identify that as a banana. But only as long as we have been exposed to bananas previously. Now, before eating this banana, we will have certain expectations: if the skin has strong green tones we would expect it to be unripe, while a yellow skin with a few brown spots would indicate it is ripe or perhaps overripe. If it is totally brown, we would assume it to be decaying.'

The professor paused and reached down for a glass of water on the table. 'Many people want to influence what people eat. Maybe some of you do. Sure. That's fine. But the model is wrong. The taste of things doesn't come from the ingredients. Taste comes from expectations. If you see a thing of a particular colour, you'll expect it to taste a certain way. Am I right? And no matter what's gone into your mouth, what's gone into your eye beforehand changes how it tastes. If you have the four senses of sight, touch, smell and sound present, then, as if by magic, you also have taste.'

At that moment it was as if a small fly had hit Frank's head. Wasn't this what he had always said? We eat with our eyes. Was there an idea floating around here that he could use to create a new restaurant, some kind of fresh concept that would amaze the critics and leave other chefs envious for not having thought of it first? He rubbed his chin, his gaze fixed intently on the professor, who enjoyed seeing the interest he had awoken on the faces of the audience sitting in front of him.

The professor continued. 'What about play? Do you ever think of that? Or is that something only children do?' Another pause, this one longer, as he scanned the audience for reactions. 'I would argue that we need to play with the way food looks and we need to play with the way people expect their food to look and taste.' He grinned. 'Okay, here's a big word: multisensory. Food should be multisensory. What do I mean by that? I mean we need to think not just about its taste, but about how it looks, what it smells like, what it feels like. Even what sounds it makes. Eating is a complete multisensory experience. It's about awareness of what's going on around you and inside of you. You see, it's not really about what's on your fork, as I said earlier. It's about what you experience. How your senses interact with the environment you are eating in.

'And finally I want to say something about technology. If you work in a kitchen – or you work anywhere in the hospitality industry – you will appreciate the role technology plays in making life easier. Think of a modern kitchen or restaurant and compare that with one thirty, forty years ago. Sure, some things haven't changed much, but others have. The microwave, *sous vide*, point of sale, online ordering, display screens, social media … Instagram. Even 3D printing in the kitchen. No, I'm not kidding. You can print food. In the smart kitchen of the future, your power blender may be able to link to a device on your wrist that's been tracking your diet, then check in with your freezer and your kitchen scale. It could set up the right smoothie recipe based on what's on hand, how much weight you've gained and which fruit you prefer. Your oven will be able to decide how and when to start roasting the salmon, then text the family when dinner's ready. Your fridge may be able to place a shopping order, based on a careful study of how much you like to pay for certain items, whether you want them organic and whether peaches are in season. The smart kitchen of the future might even track how much of the dish you end up throwing away, and let you know who took the last beer in the fridge – don't worry! It ordered more. So you get the picture. You see, here's the thing: creativity is shaped by what technology can do. And that's not just the case in hospitality. It's the case in any walk of life. New technology enables us to be more creative. And in the hospitality industry, if you want to survive – to thrive – then you've got to be creative.'

When the professor finished his talk, everyone applauded enthusiastically. Frank sat there, deep in thought, his mind swirling with excitement. He now had his big idea. But where was he going to find the money to finance it? The banks wouldn't help, not now that he had taken out those loans to prop up his restaurants and other businesses. Yet London was swimming with cash, with City investors eager to become part of a restaurant. Restaurants were sexy; hedge funds weren't. He brightened at the thought. There would be someone out there who would back him.

2

When Frank arrived at Castle Lodge, his father was in the lounge, taking part in the weekly chair yoga class with a dozen or so other residents. Frank stood watching as Terry sat there, moving his hands through the air and touching his knees in a childlike fashion to the instructions of a fast-talking young woman in a purple T-shirt, purple leggings and bare feet, accompanied by Rod Stewart's Forever Young. His father's white hair had become paper-thin, and Frank wondered if his own would one day be the same. From the expression on his face, Terry looked to be thoroughly enjoying every minute of the yoga.

Following his mother's death the previous year, Frank had soon noticed that his father was neglecting himself. Ever since his National Service days, Terry had been someone who always wore a tie and whose shoes were so shiny that you could almost see your reflection in them. 'Cleanliness is next to godliness' was one of his favourite sayings. But lately, he had stopped ironing his shirts, only shaved every few days, and his flat began to look untidy. And, worryingly for Frank, he had started to forget things, such as names of places and people he knew, and he had begun to stumble.

Frank had invited Terry to come and live with him and Annalisa, but he'd refused, saying he would feel in the way. So Frank suggested he move to a good care home, and offered to pay for it. Initially Terry rejected the idea. However, after tripping over in the street one day, fracturing his arm and collarbone, which led to him spending two weeks in hospital, he reluctantly agreed to the idea.

Frank took him to view half a dozen care homes around the outskirts of south London, and each time Terry turned up his nose. They were either too gloomy, too institutional, or too dirty. Frank had to admit that some of the homes left a lot to be desired, not least with the prices they were charging.

However, when his father visited Castle Lodge, he immediately liked it. Castle Lodge was a former nineteenth-century convent, set in attractive parkland in north Surrey, where you could just hear the roar of the traffic on the M25. It looked and felt more like an upmarket hotel than a care home. The reception had a small coffee bar, comfortable chairs dotted around, and, on the wall, Frank's father noted with delight, a giant Scrabble board. To add to the homely feel, a screen behind the reception desk listed the names of residents who had birthdays that month.

Frank hadn't expected his father to adapt so quickly to living in a care home, thinking he would miss his independence. But Terry loved it. Castle Lodge had two restaurants; a small cinema; a library; a swimming pool; a spa and therapy suite; a hair salon; and its own shop, where residents could buy essentials. Visiting speakers came in regularly and the home's two minibuses took residents on weekly shopping trips to Sutton, or to the theatre and concerts.

Frank admired the staff at the care home. They were kind, thoughtful, and cheerful. Most were Eastern European or African. He knew their work wasn't easy, especially as some of the residents had dementia and others could only get about in a wheelchair. His father could be short-tempered and awkward at times.

In his two years there, Terry had struck up a close friendship with another resident, Jill, who had been a well-known film actress from the 1950s to the 1970s and had appeared in a number of West End shows. The two of them spent much of their time together and attended tango classes and ballroom-dancing evenings. Even though Terry was seventy-five and Jill was eighty-three, Frank wondered if their relationship was more than a friendship, but that wasn't the kind of thing his father would ever discuss.

After the class ended, Terry eased himself out of the chair and, leaning on his walking stick, came slowly towards Frank. 'Makes me feel young again,' he said.

'Yeah, it's that attractive young woman that does it, Dad,' said Frank.

'Well, you might as well have an attractive one rather than an ugly one.'

Frank smiled. 'I brought you these,' he said, holding up a plastic carrier bag.

'You get some midget gems?'

'Yeah, and a bottle of Teacher's.'

'Lovely.'

Frank climbed the stairs behind his father to the first floor. Terry preferred the stairs to the lift, as he felt the exercise did him good. Frank followed him as he shuffled along the carpeted corridor to his apartment at the end. Each corridor was named after a famous film. Terry lived on White Christmas Way. On the walls were prints of impressionist paintings and framed photos of actors and comedians from once-popular TV programmes. Several members of staff, all in blue uniforms, were busy vacuuming, cleaning, or delivering clean linen to rooms. They all smiled or said a cheery hello as Frank and his father passed them.

Terry's apartment, like all the other forty-three apartments, had a proper front door with a number on it and a letterbox. It consisted of a kitchen/diner, bedroom, and bathroom, and was spacious and tastefully decorated in pastel colours. Frank had asked the care home company to put in a section of extra shelving to accommodate his father's CDs, which numbered over 1,000, and his equally large DVD collection. There was a small balcony with a table and chairs, where Frank and his father sometimes sat in the summer.

Frank pushed aside a slippery heap of magazines and pill-bottles on the coffee table and placed the tea-tray next to his father, who was slumped heavily on the settee.

'How many restaurants is it that you've got now?' asked Terry, unsteadily picking up his cup.

'Four, Dad. And a café,' said Frank wearily. His father always asked this question. He had never been to any of Frank's restaurants, something that niggled away at Frank. Terry dismissed them as serving 'fancy food'. Frank couldn't understand why his father was lukewarm about his career. At times, he wondered if, in fact, Terry was jealous of his success. He had never really praised him, like fathers were supposed to praise their sons.

Yet he was always quick to tell Frank how well his older brother, Michael, was doing. Michael had emigrated to the United States ten years before and had become the head of a Miami construction company that built shopping malls and offices. In all of that time, Michael had come back to London to see his father only once. Yet it was always Michael this, Michael that. It had been the same when Frank was growing up. Michael was always the golden boy. Michael had gone to university, landed a job as an engineer with a top company, and then, as his father put it, got snapped up by the big boys in the States.

'Only four? I thought it was more.'

'Four's enough, Dad. I don't need to tell you how hard the restaurant business is.'

'It's all different to my day,' said Terry.

'So you always say, Dad.'

'In the 50s, the celebrities were film stars. Frank Sinatra, Elizabeth Taylor, John Wayne. They were real stars – not like today.'

Frank nodded, glad to have found some common ground with his father. 'Yeah, Annalisa and I both love watching the old films.'

'Then in the 1960s, it was photographers and hairdressers, then you had all the rock stars with long hair in the 1970s, those fashion designers in the 1980s – never did understand all that stuff. And now it's cooks! Cooks! I'd never have believed it.'

'Things change,' said Frank, his attention momentarily caught by the framed newspaper cutting of his father standing outside his bistro with the French chef Pierre Limogne. He remembered, when he was a child, how Terry used to speak with such reverence about the man.

Terry continued. 'When I got into catering, you were just stuck in the kitchen. No one had a clue who you were. There was no glamour about cooking. None of these TV shows and all that carry on.'

'There's nothing wrong with TV shows,' said Frank, feeling himself tensing up.

'Some of these restaurants nowadays are ridiculous. I read about one that's opened in Hampstead or somewhere. And you won't believe it. It's for dogs.'

'How do you mean?' Frank hadn't heard about this.

Terry bit into a digestive. 'You take your dog with you and they give you a menu for it. I'm not joking.'

'Yeah, but, that's probably just one of these dog grooming places trying to get publicity.'

'Listen …' He paused to swallow the digestive. 'They even have wine for dogs – have you ever heard anything like it? Then all the dogs eat in a separate dining room. Who on earth comes up with these ideas?'

While he'd been driving to Castle Lodge, Frank had contemplated, briefly, telling his father about his big idea. He wanted to say, Dad! Guess what? He wanted to see Terry's eyes light up and hear him say, 'Frank, you have always had such a brilliant mind …' He was glad now he hadn't. Terry would only have poured cold water on it. So, trying to put an end to the things-were-better-in-my-day routine, Frank said, 'How are things, Dad?'

'A few aches and pains, but what do you expect at my age?'

'Did you see the osteopath last week?'

'He wasn't able to do much,' Terry grumbled.

'What about a massage?'

'Nah, I gave it a go, but it's not for me.'

Terry stretched his right leg out, grimacing as he did do. 'So how's that new book selling, then? Going like hot cakes, is it?'

'I haven't seen the figures, but, yeah, it's probably doing okay.'

'Okay? What do you mean okay? Half the country buys your books.'

'They sell well,' replied Frank, knowing that his father wasn't applauding him but actually criticising him.

Terry shook his head. 'I've never understood this craze for cookery books. It's beyond me.'

'People want to learn,' said Frank.

'If you ask me, it's just a fad. I bet most people never look at them once they get them.'

'You don't know that.'

'Take your mother. She had all your books, but the only cookery book Sue ever looked at was one by that John John chap or whatever his name is.'

'Johnny John?' He hated having to mention his name, especially in a conversation with Terry.

'That's him. Quite funny. Your mum had watched his series about India. She loved it.'

'Yeah, well,' murmured Frank. He could remember Sue enthusing about Johnny John and how he'd had to prevent himself from criticising him. Those cheesy asides to the camera, the exaggerated smile, and all that false bonhomie. Frank couldn't stand it. And that was before his public falling out with Johnny over the soufflé. Sue had followed every step of Frank's career, though, and had always encouraged him to aim high and be the best.

Terry took a sip of his tea and continued. 'She reckoned his recipes were easy to follow. She said yours had too many ingredients.'

'There's nothing wrong with my recipes,' said Frank sharply.

'But she loved the photos. She said they were very artistic.' His father chuckled. 'Terry, she said, I've never heard of half of the things Frank says you need.'

'Dad, all the things I listed, you can buy in most high streets.'

His father ignored him. 'The thing is, in my day in the restaurant business, we didn't go in for all this fancy stuff, all this decorating plates malarkey. And what do they call it? Fusion? More like confusion. In my day I just served people good honest food.'

'That's what my recipes are about,' retorted Frank. He'd heard all this from his father before. He had always wanted to do more as a cook than just serve coq au vin or mushroom risotto, like Terry had done. When he had become interested in cooking, in his teens, he had soon begun to see that his father had no ambition. Terry was content to cook the same thing day after day. Frank wanted to do much more exciting food. And he wanted to be someone in the culinary world, not just a cook slaving away in a kitchen in south-east London to feed the same old faces.

There was a knock at the door.

'Come in!' called Terry.

A plump black woman with large eyes waddled in and broke into a smile. 'Oh, hello Frank …'

'Hi,' said Frank.

'Sorry for interrupting, Mr Darley, but I wanted to know if you'll be taking Communion today.'

Frank looked at his father with raised eyebrows.

'What time?'

'At three o'clock.'

'Yes, I'll be there.'

'Okay,' said the woman. She hesitated and then said brightly to Frank, 'Giles is doing really well at college.'

'He's a bright lad,' said Frank.

'That chat you had with him really worked. He can't wait to finish and start work. He's a hard worker.'

'When he's finished, I'll see if I can find a position for him. You know, I can't promise, but we've usually got vacancies in the kitchen.'

'Oh, he'd love that! Thank you so much, Frank. God will bless you.' As she moved towards the door, she turned around and said, 'You're lucky you have such a famous and kind son, Mr Darley.'

'He's all right,' said Terry grudgingly.

'I didn't know you were religious,' said Frank, turning to his father after the woman had left.

'At my time of life you need all the help you can get. Sometimes I go to the Church of England service and sometimes the Catholic one.'

'But you're C of E, aren't you?'

'It's all the same at the end of the day. Like supermarkets. I prefer the Catholic priest, though. He's Indian – about your age. You can have a laugh with him. He knows I'm not Catholic, but he still lets me have the wine and bread. No idea if it does anything, but I like the prayers and Bible readings and that. Anyway, how's Annalisa and James? It's been a while since I saw them.'

'Dad, they were here two weeks ago.'

'Were they?'

'Remember, we went to that pub for lunch?'

Terry looked into the distance. 'Yes ... that's right ... the place with a real fire.'

'The Black Swan. You liked the lamb cutlets.'

'Oh, yes. I'd forgotten.'

'Anyway, they're both fine. How's Jill? I thought she'd be at the yoga.'

'She's gone down with something. I'm popping in to see her later.'

'Tell her I asked for her. And how you getting on with the internet?' asked Frank. He had bought his father a laptop for Christmas two years ago but had only recently persuaded him to install broadband.

'I don't use it much.'

'You know, you can buy all sorts of CDs on Amazon, and on YouTube there's probably some films of your favourite musicians.'

'I had a look at Amazon. I wrote to them to ask about a Frank Sinatra CD I was looking for. They never replied.'

'You wrote to them?' Frank chuckled. 'Dad, Amazon only works online. You have to have an account and pay by card.'

'Oh, I'm not doing that. If I can't pay by cash or cheque, then I won't bother.' Terry heaved himself up off the sofa and grabbed hold of his walking stick. 'I think I'm going to have a nap.'

'Okay, Dad,' said Frank, also standing up. 'I'll give you a ring.'

Frank watched as his father made his way towards the bedroom and then stopped. 'Oh, yes, I forgot to tell you. Guess what your brother's doing? He's going out to Kuwait to build an airbase.'

'He's done well, Dad,' said Frank flatly.

Frank's father continued towards the bedroom and chuckled. 'You can say that again.'

'But when did he last come to see you?'

'He's busy.'

'I'm busy, Dad. Everyone's busy.'

Frank watched his father disappear into the bedroom, and then he opened the door and let himself out.

As he walked back along the corridor, he found himself thinking back to when he was eighteen and his father had told him that he was going to sell the bistro. It had been Michael, with his fancy university education and big ideas about property, who had encouraged him to do this. Michael had no interest in the business. Frank had always dreamed of taking it over one day and turning it into something different. And that was what his mother had hoped would happen. He had felt hurt that his father hadn't given him that opportunity. And even though his career had taken off when he went to work at the Majestic Hotel, all these years later, his father's decision still rankled.

3

As his British racing green Bentley – CHI EF – glided effortlessly and near-silently along the South Circular Road in the sleeting rain, Frank danced his fingers on the steering wheel to Bon Jovi's I'll Be There for You. Nodding his head from side to side, he tried to sing along to it. He felt the shimmering keyboard sounds fizzing inside him.

It was just before the beginning of the rush hour, and the traffic was beginning to thicken. A red double-decker bus pulled out in front of him, so he had to crawl behind it. On the back a brightly coloured poster said:

JESUS IS HERE!
Every Sunday, 7pm
The Church of Mighty Miracles
Unit 43 Premium Business Centre, Croydon
BE PREPARED TO BE AMAZED!

What's amazing, thought Frank, is what Jesus is doing in a business centre on Sunday evenings in Croydon. Shouldn't he be somewhere in the world with really serious problems?

Frank always enjoyed the drive home to Beckenham, noting how south London gradually changed from grey to green. With its pleasant roads of well-maintained houses, its high street dotted with restaurants and small independent shops, and its parks and sports grounds, Beckenham had little in common with the landscape of sprawling council estates, minicab offices, late-night ethnic supermarkets, and takeaways in the part of south-east London Frank had grown up in. Beckenham was posh. On the noticeboard of the trendy coffee shop on the main road near his house were business cards advertising cello tutors, private Mandarin tuition, dog walkers, counselling, Spanish nannies, landscape gardeners, home carers.

When he stopped at a set of traffic lights, his eyes darting this way and that, a white van with a ladder on top and three guys in blue overalls squashed in the front seats drew level alongside him. One of them, who was wearing a black baseball cap with some sort of logo on it, started grinning and waving. The three of them broke into laughter and then gave Frank an exaggerated thumbs up. Frank acknowledged them by raising his hand regally and producing a faint smile before returning his gaze to the lights. As the lights changed to green and he pulled away, the van tooted several times and then shot forward. One of the men leaned out of the window and looked back with a big grin. Frank waved. The man gave Frank the two fingers, shouting, 'Wanker!' Frank just laughed, giving his own two fingers.

He drove on through Clock House with its cluster of dreary-looking takeaways near the railway station – Chicken 4 U, Chicken King, Bombay Nights, The Wall of China – and then past the fire station, the war memorial, and the Odeon cinema. He got stuck behind another double-decker bus. This, too, had a poster on the back:

**Don't be a murderer
BE A VEGAN!
You know it makes sense**

No, it doesn't make sense, grumbled Frank to himself. That was the problem when people found a cause. They wanted everyone else to support it. If you don't want to eat meat or fish or dairy products, fine. But don't expect everyone else to do the same. And don't try and make us feel guilty.

As he passed a new tapas bar in the high street, he wondered if it would succeed, given all the competition already in Beckenham. Like so many areas of London, it boasted a restaurant every few yards. Yet many new restaurants went under within the first three years. You could tell when they were struggling to attract customers, because they sat anyone who came in by the window ('the window trick') to make it appear busier. His own restaurants had survived, but making a profit wasn't easy, even when you were a celebrity chef and had your name above the door. He hated it when people complained in online reviews that thirteen quid was expensive for cod and chips. What they didn't consider was that the price wasn't just about the potatoes and fish. He had to pay the rent or lease, the staff, and then there were business rates, utilities, insurance, waste management, and all the tens of thousands spent fitting out a restaurant and kitchen. That was what your thirteen quid was paying for. And, oh yes, something called profit. After tax had been paid, of course. Some people didn't have a clue. If they wanted cheaper fish and chips, then they should cook it at home. But, of course, if they did that, he would be out of business.

He swung into a long, broad road bordered by chestnut trees along the neatly cut grass verge and barrelled along it, enjoying the sudden burst of speed, until he reached the set of wrought iron gates to his seven-bedroom Victorian detached house. It had two bathrooms, a conservatory, a cellar, a triple garage and a garden with plum and apple trees, flowerbeds and a pond. Its rooms were well proportioned and had high ceilings and large sash windows. Annalisa had turned the house into her project, enlarging the kitchen, creating a games room, and having a pond and waterfall built in the garden. Now, planning permission had just been given by the local council to construct an indoor heated swimming pool with a retractable glass roof and a Jacuzzi, something Annalisa had always wanted. At school she had represented the county at swimming and had won countless medals and trophies, which were displayed in the lounge. Frank had argued that a swimming pool would cost too much, when, in fact, he just couldn't face all the mayhem the builders would cause.

Silently mouthing *pow!*, he pointed his remote key fob at the gates, and they slowly began to open. He inched the Bentley forward, its tyres crunching over the gravel, and came to a halt alongside Annalisa's new silver Range Rover Discovery.

He hung up his coat on the walnut rack by the staircase in the hall and wandered down the corridor into the spacious kitchen. The radio was tuned to Capital FM. Annalisa, wearing a baggy pink T-shirt and multicoloured leggings, was standing at the island in the middle, shredding a lettuce, her auburn hair tied back. Beside her was an open copy of *Slim with Jim* by Jim Slight, one of her favourite singers. This was her latest diet book. She had got bored with *Fast Food by Rhona Gold*, winner of the Olympic gold medal in the 400 metres, and *Lose Weight in 30 Minutes* by reality TV star Nicola Vanity. Annalisa's obsession with diets puzzled Frank. With her slender figure, the last thing she needed to do was diet. He concluded that for her, dieting was a kind of hobby. He was just as puzzled by her driving to the gym down the road, a journey which took no longer than four minutes, spending 30 minutes on a motorised treadmill, and then driving back home. Surely it would make more sense just to go for a proper walk.

'How was the exhibition?' Annalisa asked, looking up.

'Brilliant! I've got my idea for the new restaurant.'

'You have?'

Frank grinned broadly. 'Yeah. It's a cracker! Christ! I don't know why I didn't think of it before.'

'Come on, then. What is it?' said Annalisa playfully.

Frank tapped his nose. 'It's a secret.'

'You can tell me, can't you?'

'I want to surprise you. Annalisa, just wait. You'll be amazed! And I'll tell you what. So will the judges of the Golden Pan.'

'Really.'

'Yeah, I'm going to open the kind of place that no one else has ever dreamed of. It will blow their minds!'

He placed his iPhone down on the island and sauntered over to the fridge freezer, which was the size of a bank vault, pulling out a bottle of beer.

'Did you see your dad?'

'Yeah.'

'How was he?'

'Seemed to be in good form. He enjoyed his yoga.'

'You know, I keep meaning to do yoga. People say it really helps you to get ... centred. Or whatever they call it. There's a class on Monday evenings at the leisure centre.'

'Yeah, you should give it a go.'

'Well, I've had an interesting day as well,' said Annalisa brightly.

'What, with Katarina at the country club?'

'We had a wonderful massage and a facial. Oh, it makes me feel so refreshed.'

'That's good,' he said, wondering if they had also gone clothes shopping in Bromley. He couldn't understand how women could spend hours wandering around clothes shops. Was it therapy, as some psychologists suggested? Or were they psychiatrists? He could never remember.

'And guess what?'

Frank took a swig from his beer. 'Go on.'

'We went to this really unusual restaurant. It was in a church. I mean, one they still use.'

'So the church is moving into hospitality,' said Frank with a chuckle. 'You know, I met a guy at Hospitality UK today selling Christian pizzas.'

'Christian pizzas? What are they?'

'Pizzas that come with Bible quotes. Have you ever heard anything like it?'

'That's weird.' Annalisa placed the lettuce in a salad spinner and took it over to the sink. 'Anyway, it was a really delicious meal! It was all vegetarian. Did I tell you Katarina's thinking of becoming a vegan?'

'Yeah, you mentioned it.'

'She's really into it. She goes to meetings, and reads up on it and everything.'

Frank gave a sarcastic laugh. 'She's always into some bloody cause or other. One week it's global warming, the next migrants or foxes or whatever. She's like a bloody walking charity.'

Annalisa turned on the tap. 'She's interested in lots of things, that's all. She just thinks killing cows and that is murder.'

'Murder!' Frank rolled his eyes. 'Gimme a break.'

'I was thinking, you know, maybe she's right. She's on a special diet of plants and nuts now.'

'Plants and nuts. What is she? A bloody squirrel? Murder. What rubbish.'

'It's not rubbish.'

Frank pointed a finger at her. 'Look at you.'

'What?'

'You're murdering that bloody lettuce. That's a living thing, isn't it?'

'It's not the same. A lettuce doesn't have feelings.'

'How do you know?'

'You're being ridiculous.'

'Listen, there's nothing wrong in eating meat. People have been doing it since the garden of Eden. Everyone needs feeding.'

'We can eat other things, though.'

'Yeah, but think about wild animals.'

'What do you mean?'

'They have to be killed. If they aren't, they destroy a farmer's crops. If you go to the States, you'll see the kind of problem they have with deer and wild boar. They're everywhere in some places.'

'Yes, but the way they kill animals is cruel, Frank. Katarina showed me pictures on her phone. Ugh! It's really terrible!'

'That's nothing to the way animals kill each other. Ever seen a lion kill a baby giraffe? I'll tell you what, that's bloody cruel.'

Annalisa picked up a bottle of extra virgin olive oil. 'Well, I'm going to eat more salads and things.'

'You're not going bloody vegan as well, are you?'

'I just don't like the idea of the way we kill animals just so we can eat.'

'Annalisa, this vegan thing is about middle-class people who live in cities having an idealistic view of the countryside. Okay, yeah, there are issues about factory farming. I'll agree. But the problem is, vegans don't see the bigger picture.'

'Anyway, before I forget, we're going to have to find a new gardener.'

'Why? What's up with Bill?'

'You mean Tom.'

'Oh, yeah. Tom.'

'He says he's getting on and it's too much for him.'

'Poor bugger's well past his sell-by date.'

'You know, he's done a wonderful job. Have you seen all those herbs in the greenhouse?'

'No,' murmured Frank, absent-mindedly checking his phone for messages. He hadn't bothered to look inside the greenhouse since it had been built.

'There's rosemary, thyme, parsley, sage, everything. Mmm, it smells fantastic when you walk in.'

Their conversation was brought to an end by the sound of footsteps coming towards them.

Six-year-old James appeared in the doorway, wearing his school uniform and holding a plastic Batman figure. He hesitated and then trotted over to Annalisa.

'Hello, darling, you okay?' said Annalisa softly, bending down.

'I'm thirsty,' James said sheepishly.

'Okay, do you want water or milk?'

'Can I have lemonade?'

'No lemonade, Little Man,' said Frank with a firm shake of the head. 'Have some milk. It's good for you. Makes you big and strong like Daddy.'

The boy nodded and Annalisa went to the fridge to get a bottle of milk.

Frank finished his beer, pressed the pedal of the recycling bin with his foot and dropped the bottle in. 'What time we eating?'

'About an hour,' Annalisa said as she shepherded James out of the kitchen.

'Okay, I've got some phone calls to make,' said Frank, walking towards the corridor that led to his study.

He sat down at his hand-dyed grey writing desk with bespoke nickel handles wrapped in black leather. On it was a phone with a high-definition touchscreen attached to it and an iMac. He logged into his company website and began scrolling through his emails: invitations to speak at the National Beetroot Festival and Expo Slow Fast Food; invitations to appear on the TV shows *Love Your Wallpaper* and *Celebrity Shoes*; invitations to appear on radio shows; invitations to endorse shampoo/camping gear/natural yoghurt/a chain of gyms.

There were invitations to lend his name to charities – save the rainforest, save the whale, sponsor a tiger, sponsor an African child, promote sustainable fishing, educate Bolivian farmers to grow crops, provide bicycles for the homeless, provide laptops for the elderly, promote vegetables in schools.

There were CVs from people – bricklayers, data analysts, teachers, heating engineers, bank managers – all star-struck and thinking there's a cooking pot of gold waiting for them if only they can get into a kitchen. Frank knew that if they got into a professional kitchen, most would quickly realise how hard the work was and how long the hours were, and they would be gone within days or, in some cases, hours. Cleaning down a kitchen at 11pm and taking out black bin-liners to the wheelie bins, or filleting plaice and cod at seven in the morning, wasn't glamorous.

And, as always, there were urgent requests for money from people he'd never heard of in places he'd never heard of.

Overwhelmed by all these requests, he leaned back in his leather chair and clasped his hands behind his head. He stared hard at the photo on the shelf above his desks of himself and Annalisa on their wedding day. Was it nearly ten years ago? He could still recall it so vividly. Him, dressed in a grey morning suit, arriving breathless at the small church in the pretty Hertfordshire village where Annalisa had grown up, after having gone with his father to check the catering at the hotel was going smoothly. The reproving look of the elderly vicar standing in front of the altar. Annalisa, looking like a beautiful flower in her white dress trimmed with lace. Walking arm in arm down the aisle, with the deep, heavy notes of the organ filling the church, and a shower of rose petals falling on them. Lining up for the photos in the blinding sunshine as the church bells rang out. Taking Annalisa's hand as she stepped into the back seat of the white 1925 open-top Rolls Royce Silver Ghost. The drive along the country lane to the hotel. The floral walkway leading into the banqueting room, where a vintage champagne fountain had been installed and two gold thrones stood at the end. The six-course meal, cutting the five-tiered chocolate cake decorated with marzipan roses, the white marquee emblazoned with violet and red Fs and As. His father dancing with Annalisa's mother and Annalisa's father dancing with his mother. Nick dancing with one of the bridesmaids, a beer in one hand, and falling over. Standing beside a karaoke machine with Annalisa at the end of the evening and belting out 'We Are the Champions'.

The ping of an email jolted him from his reverie. It was a Google alert: 'Johnny John.' Frank clicked on the email and an article from the magazine *What the Chef!* appeared.

Johnny John Brings New Dining Experience

We caught up with celebrity chef Johnny John at Hospitality UK today and heard about his exciting plan to open a restaurant on the Greenwich peninsula where diners will cook their own food.

The 54-seater restaurant, DIY, will be located in three connected shipping containers next to the O2 Arena and will serve a changing selection on small plates that make veg the star of the show. The project is linked with the Sustainable, Ecologically Friendly, Free From, Vegan and Ethically Responsible Restaurant Association and is designed to raise awareness of the environmental and health benefits that come with eating less meat and more vegetables.

'The idea is to give diners an experience of the products. Instead of them sitting down at a table and having a waiter come to take their order, they will come into the kitchen and make the meal that they want. They'll do the peeling, the chopping, the frying, all the stuff a chef usually does. And they'll serve their own meal. Obviously we'll have chefs to supervise them. We want people to connect with food. The aim is to provide a completely new restaurant experience,' said Johnny John.

At just thirty-four, the one-Michelin-star chef seems unstoppable at the moment. Earlier in the year, he opened Johnny's Brassiere in Kensington, along with restaurants in Singapore and Hong Kong, bringing his number of sites to fifteen. He also has a new TV series, Johnny's Meat and Two Veg, which he co-presents with reality TV star Kelly Peepers, and a new recipe book, Johnny Seasons.

DIY has been made possible thanks to a £1.1 million investment from Russian company Global Crimea ...

Frank laughed out loud. He was going to go one better than that.

4

Maurice Padwick, the head of Tish TV, had approached Frank a few weeks before and offered him a deal that paid much more than he had been receiving from the BBC. It had been the BBC that had turned him into a household name. The producer who had eaten at the Burning Bush had arranged for Frank to have a meeting at Broadcasting House with the commissioning editor for food and drink. Frank was offered a contract to present a four-part TV series about regional food in France. His series was called *A British Chef Tastes the Food of France*. The viewers loved his irreverent style, his straight talking, and the way he made them feel that they too were experiencing what he experienced, that they could almost taste those langoustines he cooked on the quayside in the small fishing port in Normandy or that duck he tucked into in a bistro in Lyon. In short, Frank was a natural in front of the camera and a natural when it came to coaxing the best out of the chefs, restaurants owners, and fishermen he met on his travels. Such was his meteoric rise in the public imagination that when the BBC commissioned a series in Spain it was called simply *Frank Goes to Spain*.

Yet any doubts Frank had about leaving the BBC didn't last long when he realised just how much money he could make with Tish. Annalisa had said, yes, the money was fantastic, but shouldn't he think about the kind of programmes Tish made? 'I mean, look at some of the stuff they turn out.' Frank replied breezily that he needed to move on to fresh challenges.

Tish TV was based in a functional two-storey building in a narrow street off City Road that was also home to a vehicle repair workshop, a bottled water company, a dental laboratory, and a timber yard. Frank had expected a more upmarket location for such a downmarket TV company.

He parked the Bentley and strode confidently through the entrance. In reception, he hovered impatiently as the young woman behind the desk briskly signed a pad for a motorcycle courier. With his helmet, black leathers and boots that rose up to his knees, the courier looked like he had stepped off the set of a science fiction movie.

Frank looked the part. What you see is what you get. He was wearing a £10,000 burgundy woollen suit, a white cotton shirt, and a £2,000 pair of handmade brown leather pointy shoes. His tie had been specially made. Luigi Amoretti. It was sky blue and decorated with small yellow Fs. F for Frank. F for food. F for fun. F for first. F for famous. His aftershave was Henri Courau. Limited edition. Only available in Paris.

He studied the woman. The badge on her white blouse said Cherry Smith. She had strawberry red lipstick and hazelnut hair scraped back. But what Frank really noticed was her large breasts. He summed her up. East End. Father a mechanic, mother a shop assistant. GCSEs. Shares a flat in Willesden. Boyfriend, but nothing serious. Gym once a week. Next and Pizza Hut at weekends. Ready meals, healthy options. Clubbing when she could afford it. Sex on the beach cocktails. Credit cards near the limit. Four hundred friends on Facebook.

Realising that he was staring at her breasts intently, he casually glanced around. An expressionless black security guard with cheap shoes stood to attention by a tall Japanese pot plant. Frank felt sorry for him. What a boring job that must be, just standing there all day and not actually doing anything. Armed robbers tended to favour banks or shops, not TV studios. Perched on large orange cushions in the far corner, a woman with short green-streaked hair and a ring through her nose and a bearded guy in a T-shirt and tattoos down both arms were both laughing hysterically at something. The man mimed an action in an exaggerated way and the woman rocked backwards and forwards, shrieking every now and again. Frank looked up at the wall behind the reception desk, where framed posters of some of Tish TV's hit shows were displayed: *Celebrity Pet Secrets*, *What Would You Do For a Million?*,

Every Man Can Be a Woman, *My Dog's Getting Married in the Morning*, *Your Dream Funeral* and *Naked Neighbours – Caught on Camera*.

When the courier slunk away, his boots squeaking on the floor, Frank stepped forward and gave the receptionist his best 'It's-so-nice-to-meet-you-It-really-is' look, his eyes wandering to the V of inviting flesh at the top of her semi-transparent blouse. Was that a nipple? He lingered and then said in the manner of someone announcing the winner at the Oscars, 'Frank.' He never used his surname. Everyone knew he was Frank. The only Frank. The girl smiled at him – mischievously, thought Frank.

She tapped away at a keyboard and a printer whirred. As she printed off a label to slot inside a plastic wallet, Frank leaned on the desk, his eyes sweeping her up and down like a searchlight. And those legs. Nice.

'There you are ... Frank.'

'Cheers, darling.'

She gestured brightly to the lift and said, 'Someone will meet you downstairs.'

'Cherry. Lovely name,' said Frank, letting his eyes wander some more.

'Thank you,' she replied sweetly, while adjusting the collar of her blouse at the same time, making it tighter across her breasts.

'Want a selfie?' he asked, flashing her a smile.

'Cor, can I?'

'Yeah, of course.'

Frank leaned back, grinning and placing his head next to her, as she held out her phone at arm's length. He could smell her perfume. His position gave him an aerial view of her wonderful breasts, and he couldn't resist taking a quick peek.

'I loved those photos in *Real Life*,' said Cherry.

'You did?'

'Yeah, you and Annalisa looked so cool. Like royalty.'

Frank smiled to himself and headed towards the staircase.

There was not one person but five waiting when he stepped into a dimly lit corridor. One stepped forward and introduced herself as the producer, followed by the others, who turned out to be the director, the executive producer, the PR person and the photographer. Breakfast cereal smiles. They were thrilled he was coming on board with Tish. It was going to be super duper fab. The viewers would love it. God, the ratings were going to be phenomenal! Everyone loved Frank.

Frank soaked it all up. He was delighted to be invited to make the show. Of course, he was very busy. Just come back from Dubai. Yeah, great tan, Frank! Off early next year to the States. Guest speaker at a fundraising dinner in New York. Can't remember what it's for, but Coca-Cola are sponsoring it. But he'd always wanted to do a TV show like this. His aim was to encourage more people to cook at home. Get into the kitchen. That's the name of the game. That's all he cared about. The money wasn't important. No, no, no. It was about cooking.

The producer, director, executive producer, PR person, and photographer all nodded, if unconvincingly. We know how passionate you are, Frank, about wanting to get people cooking. That's what we want as well. We see this programme as partly educational, not just entertainment. Get people away from ready meals.

Everyone stood there, jammed in the corridor, looking at each other and waiting for someone to make the first move. Finally, the producer turned around. This way, Frank. Just down here. She opened the door to the green room, which wasn't green at all but beige and brown. Maurice Padwick, a plump, oily-looking man in a tartan check suit, sprang up from the settee with the speed of someone who has just sat on a sharp object. Frank! We're so happy you're doing the show. Take a seat. It's going to be a monster hit. Massive. Frank installed himself on a small two-seater leather settee and sat back, legs crossed. Sorry! A drink? Something to eat? Not up to your standard, of course. But the hummus is pretty good. The show's going to go global.

And – Frank – I mean global! There's a lot of noise about it in the US and the Chinese are sending the right signals. But here's the best bit. North Korea. North Korea wants you, Frank! What about that? It's not done and dusted yet, but our guy in Hong Kong is pretty confident. Frank! Imagine. You in North Korea! We're going to blow the Johnny John show out of the water. We're talking big time. And I mean big time!

By the way, yes, this is my wife. She loves you. More than me. Ha ha. She's got all of your books. When I told her you were coming today, she said, I've got to be there. I have to meet Frank.

Oh, Frank, I absolutely love *You Can Be Frank*! Those photos make everything look so super delicious! You know, I could almost eat them. Frank, quick photo? Do you mind?

So, Frank, that's terrific news about the bridge. When are you going to open it?

Early next year, if things go to plan. Yeah, I was surprised when they came to me with the idea. They said, Frank, what you do is connect people with food. You're about education. You inspire a lot of our students. I said, yeah, that's it. Frank, they said, we're building a bridge from our old campus to our new campus across the river. And we want to call it Frank's Bridge.

Wonderful, Frank! Yeah, really cool, Frank! So cool!

'Frank, about the format of the show?' said the producer, a hard-faced woman with buck teeth, who had been waiting patiently for Padwick and his wife to finish.

'Yeah?'

'It's changed a bit since we last spoke.'

'Okay,' said Frank.

'It's called *Will They Cuck?* No o's. A u and a c instead. It works like this. You demonstrate how to cook a simple dish with few ingredients for two contestants.'

'Sounds straightforward,' said Frank, thinking it didn't sound very imaginative.

'They might be women, men, trans, post-op trans, or whatever.'

'Right,' said Frank in a low voice, trying to take on board this unexpected information.

'Then comes the fun bit. A voiceover says, "So did they?" and we see each of them cooking the dish at home for the other — we film all this the week after.'

'Okay, yeah.'

The producer gushed on. 'The viewers then have to vote for the meal they think is best. The winner gets to either have sex with the other contestant or opt to answer three questions.'

'Come on! You're kidding! What, they have sex?'

The producer nodded. 'Yeah, all the contestants have to agree to hidden cameras in their bedroom.'

'Bloody hell!'

Padwick cut in. 'It had to happen, Frank. And Tish is the one to do it.'

The producer continued. 'If they opt for the questions and they get the answers right, they win £10,000. You see, it's about sex or money. What's more important? They can choose to donate all or part of this to charity. You have to get a charity in somewhere nowadays to make it seem acceptable to the regulator.'

Frank wasn't sure he really liked this new format, but he didn't want to say so, so he said, 'Yeah, great idea.'

'We think so. And we've found some unbelievable contestants,' said the producer.

'Yeah?' ventured Frank, still taken aback by the show's format. He was conservative when it came to public nudity. But he consoled himself with the thought of the £40,000 per show he would receive. What was the harm? It was just a bit of fun.

'We had over six thousand people apply. That's even more than *Naked Neighbours*. You wouldn't believe some of them! Totally off the wall. There's this guy in Leeds who believes – I mean, really believes – he's a donkey. I mean, how cool is that?'

Padwick couldn't hold himself back any longer. 'Guess what, there's a woman – was a man – in Plymouth or Portsmouth or somewhere who has three breasts! Can you believe it? What a world we live in, eh, Frank. Makes you glad to be alive.'

'That's one way of putting it,' Frank said.

Padwick ploughed on. 'You see, it's not your traditional show with men and women. We're including everyone. Gays, bisexuals, men who were women, women who were men, men who are both men and women – not sure what you call them. You name it, we've got it. Pushing the boundaries, Frank. That's what it's all about in telly nowadays. This what the great public want. They want to see ... what should I say? ... okay ... oddities, so they feel normal. But, hey, what's normal nowadays?' He paused. 'You know, Frank, the longer I work in this business, the more I'm amazed at people. You think you've seen it all, and then you hear about a guy who thinks he's a donkey.'

'Yeah.' Frank hadn't looked at the show like that. He couldn't think of any other chefs who had made a show like it. Not even Johnny John. Yes, he was doing something none of them had done before. It was about equality, and didn't the producer say some money went to charity? That had to be a good thing.

'Now, if we can get the church on board, boy, that would be the icing on the cake,' said Padwick.

Frank shot him a puzzled look. He couldn't see how the church fitted in with a show like this. 'I'm not with you.'

'We just need a bishop or someone with a beard or a funny hat – can never remember what you call that thing Jews wear on their heads – to come out and condemn it. It always works wonders for the ratings. Beats paying for advertising.'

'I hadn't thought of that,' said Frank, thinking how little he still understood about the workings of the media world. An image of the Jesus poster on the back of the bus flashed before him.

Padwick gave a throaty laugh. 'When I first started, if we did anything a bit sexual, we could always rely on the Archbishop of Canterbury or the cardinal to say something. Worked a treat. Nowadays we have to go lower down the chain. Probably because of all those scandals. Pot calling the kettle black and all that. But we can usually find a vicar in Norfolk or somewhere who will sound off. And the papers still love it.'

Frank glanced up at the CCTV monitor high in the corner. A studio with a workbench, a cooker, and an oven. Two cameras pointing at it. A guy in jeans arranged some ingredients, while another guy dragged a thick cable across the floor. Waiting for Frank. Preparing for Frank.

How long do you think it will take? An hour? Two? Studio lights don't bother me. They remind me of kitchens. So how's the TV world? A lot of competition nowadays. Not like when I was growing up and we all watched the same programmes. Got to go with the flow.

Was it really a nipple? It had to be.

The crowded room became even more crowded when a young guy came in, awkwardly carrying a life-size cardboard cutout of Frank, grinning and dressed in his chef's whites, giving his trademark thumbs up with one hand and holding a dish of smoked salmon carpaccio in the other. Across it was written, 'You too can cook like me! Thursdays. ITV. 9pm.' Frank looked at Frank and everyone looked at Frank looking at Frank. What do you think, Frank? We're planning to have 200 made – 200! – and place them at railway stations and in shopping centres. You'll be everywhere. And we're working on getting you on the fourth plinth in Trafalgar Square to tie in with National Healthy Eating Day.

Frank liked it. Very much. Could he have one sent to his home. He'd like to put it in the hall.

Of course, Frank. We'll arrange that.

Actually, could he have three, so he can put one in each of the guest rooms?

So glad you like it, Frank. We think it's a fantastic marketing idea.

The phone on the wall beeped. Make-up's ready for you, Frank. Follow me.

Frank heaved himself off the settee and everyone parted, like courtiers before an emperor. See you later, folks.

Frank was led further down the corridor to a brightly lit, compact room, not much bigger than a cupboard, with a black leather chair in front of a mirror. The make-up artist – around forty, sexy mouth, nice pair of peepers, not bad, bet she has a tattoo, bet she goes like an express train, he'd give her a portion, no two ways about it – stood to one side as Frank got into the chair and admired himself. Looking good. It's lovely to meet you, Frank. My husband bought me your latest book for Christmas. The photos were amazing! Really stunning. This will just take a tick. You make the food look so enticing.

It was a nipple! I'm sure of it.

She picked up a small brush, dipped it in a jar, and dabbed his cheeks, his forehead and his nose with fixing powder so he wouldn't look shiny under the studio lights. Nearly done. Just a little bit there! That's it. Can I get you water? Okay. I'll take you to the dressing room. I can't wait to see the programme, Frank. All the team are so excited.

Frank walked onto the studio floor in a pair of chef's whites, looking confident and sporting his well-practised smile. He stood in front of the work bench on which were laid onions, carrots, tomatoes, potatoes, pork tenderloin, and other ingredients along with various cooking equipment. In front of him was the autocue, a mounted TV camera with a screen that would display his script. The sound recordist carefully threaded a thin wire with a small microphone attached to it under his jacket.

'You all set, Frank?' asked the floor manager, coming up to him.

'Ready to rock and roll?' said Frank. He looked around, feeling the heat from the studio lights. To his left he could see a stocky man with a shaved head and bulging biceps, and a blonde woman in her early twenties wearing a very short skirt and lots of eyeshadow, standing anxiously, waiting to walk on to the set. He wondered why they had decided to come on a show like this. Why would you be prepared to have sex in front of millions of people? It had to be the money. Or that old five minutes of fame. It seemed like everyone wanted to be famous nowadays, not for being good at something, but just to have their photo plastered over all the papers.

The floor manager backed away to the edge of the set. 'Okay, everyone! Stand by.'

Frank stared at the camera and waited for the first words to roll up.

Welcome to Cook Off! With Frank. A brand new show where you can learn to cook to impress. You, the viewers, will get to decide who cooks best. Be warned, though, things might just get a little steamy later on. This is a cookery show with a difference.

Our contestants tonight! Lelia, a mum from Wolverhampton who says angels speak to her. Well, I think you'll agree, she looks like heaven. And Darren from Skegness. Darren's a bodybuilder – with a very unusual party trick. I bet Lelia can't wait to see that. So a big hand ... for ... Lelia and Darren.

5

The two young cooks crouching at the bottom of the steps by the wheelie bins, chatting and smoking, looked up with startled expressions as a figure in a bulky white rubber Michelin Man outfit, carrying a bottle of champagne, descended unsteadily towards them.

'Afternoon, gents,' said Frank casually, enjoying their reaction.

The two cooks both murmured something and watched closely as the figure wobbled past them, placed the bottle of champagne on the floor, and fumbled with the handle to the kitchen door.

'Hey, can you help me out, guys?' said Frank, turning around.

They stared at him and then one of them stood up, came over, and yanked the handle.

'Cheers,' said Frank, and he entered the kitchen.

Ambience, situated in Marylebone Lane, had become one of the hottest restaurants in London, thanks to its head chef Nick Nasr. And now it had won a second Michelin star.

Frank counted Nick as his closest friend. They had first met when they were working as commis chefs at the Majestic Hotel in Belgravia. Nick had moved to London from Lebanon with his mother when he was six, after his father had been killed by a car bomb in Beirut. Frank and Nick were both ambitious and keen to learn everything they could. After four years, Frank left to become head chef at the Burning Bush, a restaurant in a back street of Kilburn, then a shabby backwater of north-west London, full of Irish pubs, secondhand shops, and grubby bedsits with mattresses in the front gardens. When his sous-chef quit, Frank invited Nick to join him. Because the two of them shared a passion for quality cooking, they turned the restaurant into one of the most talked-about in London.

One night in 2004, a TV producer and a friend wandered into the Burning Bush. He maintained he'd eaten the best meal of his life, and asked a waiter if he could meet the head chef. A few minutes later, a cocky guy in his early twenties wearing a red and white bandana and striped apron over his whites came through the kitchen doors, beads of sweat on his forehead, and plonked himself down at the table, helping himself to a glass of the producer's wine. Conversation and wine flowed in equal measures over the next hour, culminating in the young chef clambering on the table and calling out to two elderly women sitting nearby, who were delicately spooning pears poached in vermouth and topped with banana ice cream and walnuts into their dainty mouths: 'Hey, ladies! Ladies!' Surprised at the unexpected interruption, they both turned their heads at the same time and smiled politely. As they did, the chef lifted his apron, unzipped his fly in a single movement, thrust himself forward, and shouted, 'I bet you wish this had been on the menu!'

At the end of the evening, the producer staggered out of the restaurant and into his cab, convinced he had an idea for a new programme. He had a new star in the making. What a character! What a cook! This guy was going to be big. Really big.

When Frank had first begun cooking, he had set out to win three Michelin stars, but each year Michelin had ignored him. So, frustrated and angry, he had jumped at the chance to make TV cookery programmes.

The kitchen at Ambience looked like a command centre for a military operation. On the white-tiled wall was a list of menu items, with some crossed out or annotated. On another wall were sketches of dishes. As he entered, Frank could immediately feel the heat hit him. Steam and smoke filled the air and the brigade was in full swing, with line cooks moving expertly around their stations, the roar of the air extractor, hissing, splashing, chopping, and pans clattering. As Frank waddled through the narrow aisles of stainless steel, he waved at the cooks. Some grinned, others looked baffled. Nick stood at the pass and had his back to him. 'Order! Two fish soup. One lamb, one hake!' he called out.

Frank crept up behind Nick, removed the pencil from behind Nick's ear, placed his hands over his eyes, and said in a deep voice, 'Mr Nasr. I'm a Michelin inspector. You're under arrest.'

Nick spun around. 'What the …' He burst into laughter. 'Darley, what the fuck are you up to, man?'

Frank removed the headpiece of his costume and wiped his forehead with the back of his hand. 'I've come to celebrate with you.'

The kitchen staff cheered and whooped.

Nick shook his head. 'Trust you to come up with something like this. Mind you, it looks better on you than those flashy suits.'

Frank waved the bottle of champagne in the air. 'Come on, get some glasses.'

Nick shouted to his sous-chef to take over at the pass.

'Hey, when are we going to see you on the telly, Nick?' the man called back.

'I leave all that to this bugger!' said Nick, nodding at Frank.

He led Frank to his office. A laptop, a pile of invoices with a spike through them, a football magazine, three stained mugs, a jar of mustard seeds, and a can of deodorant littered the desk. The walls were decorated with yellow Post-its, a staff rota, and a map of the wine regions of Spain.

Nick took two glasses down from a shelf and pushed some papers on the desk to one side, as Frank held out the champagne bottle and unfurled the wire around the cork.

'To the real Michelin man,' said Frank, as he poured the frothing champagne. They picked up the glasses and clinked them.

'Nice of you to do this, man,' said Nick, taking a sip. 'Listen, don't you think you should get out of that gear?'

Frank turned his back towards Nick. 'Can you unzip me?'

Nick rolled his eyes. 'Ooh! Who's a cheeky boy!'

Frank climbed out of the costume. 'Were you surprised, then?'

Nick sat down. 'Was I surprised? Fuck me! I was only thinking about keeping the one star. Never imagined I'd get a second.'

'Yeah, but, come on, you're at the top of your game.'

Nick gestured towards the window looking into the kitchen. 'It's not just me. I've got a bloody good brigade in there. They've worked their bollocks off this last year. And it's not been easy with the fire and all that.'

'Yeah, I know, mate.'

'They're all so proud. They've got a real spring in their step now. The only thing now is that we've got to make sure we keep it. The Michelin thing puts a lot of pressure on you. The more stars you have, the more people expect.'

'Yeah, but you've always been able to handle pressure.'

'You reckon?'

'Remember at the Burning Bush when you'd work eighty hours a week and still be out on the razz till all hours.'

Nick smiled. 'Yeah, they were the good old days, weren't they?'

Frank sipped his glass and said nostalgically, 'It was hard work, but we had a lot of bloody fun.'

'You heard what happened last week?'

'Yeah, the vegan activists.'

Nick sighed and shook his head. 'A right fucking carry on. Standing in front of the windows chanting at the customers. I had to call the police in the end. Anyway, what's this I hear about a new TV show?'

'It's all going ahead, but it's a bit different from before. It's got sex in it.'

Nick leaned forward. 'Shit! You having me on? What, you're going porno?'

Frank explained the format. 'They're paying a shedload of money and reckon it'll go global.' He grinned smugly. 'You can't argue with that, can you?'

Nick frowned. 'Yeah, but what about your reputation and all that?'

Frank became serious. 'What you on about?'

'All I'm saying is it just that it sounds tacky.'

Frank was stung by Nick's remark. 'It's not tacky. It's reality TV.'

'I think all that's a pile of crap! It's not reality is, it? What's real about having a fucking TV camera watching your every move? I call it unreality TV.'

Frank snorted. Just because he had two Michelin stars didn't make him the bloody Pope. 'You might not like it, but lots of people do.'

'Come on, Frank! What kind of people do you think watch *Naked Neighbours*?'

'Bet you have,' challenged Frank.

'I looked at it, yeah.'

'Told you.'

'Only to see what all the fuss was about. And it was fucking awful. Twenty years ago you'd have had to go to a sex cinema in Soho to see something like that.'

Frank decided it was wise not to tell Nick that his new programme was going to be made by the same TV company. 'That's just your opinion.'

'Listen, all I'm saying is that you've established a good reputation on TV. Don't ruin it.'

'Don't you worry; I know what I'm doing.' He wondered if he should tell Nick about his idea for a new restaurant, but Nick's attitude to the TV programme told him it was best not to. He might ridicule it.

Nick looked pointedly at his watch and stood up. 'Anyway, man, so long as you know what you're doing.'

Frank hastily picked up his costume and moved towards the door. 'Remember, TV's my world, Nick. Michelin's yours.' As Frank made his way out of the kitchen, he paused by a young cook standing in front of the deep fat fryer. He stood there for a moment, studying him and listening to the angry sizzling. The cook turned around and gave him a look of recognition.

Frank nodded back and said, 'Just be careful with that oil.'

6

1997, Barcelona

Apart from José, who had just started his shift and was mopping the tiled floor at the far end, the kitchen was empty. Frank glanced quickly around again, listening out above the sound of the Latin pop on the radio for any of the restaurant staff who were still out front. It was clear.

He went to his locker near the back door and took out his black rucksack. After peering around the corner to make sure José was still busy mopping, he gingerly entered the walk-in fridge. Looking at all the shelves containing cheeses, cold meats, rolls of bread, fruit, vegetables, and bottles of white wine and beer, he couldn't make up his mind what to take. He felt ravenous after working fourteen hours in the kitchen and having eaten only some two-day-old chicken with a few vegetables.

When he had started working in the kitchen three months previously, he had assumed that the staff would be fed well. Salvador, however, seemed to give little thought to staff meals. Service was all about the customers.

Running his eyes around the walk-in, Frank realised he couldn't take anything that would be immediately missed by Salvador when he arrived in the morning. So that ruled out the bottles of wine. But there were dozens of bottles of beer in blue plastic crates on the floor. He hurriedly grabbed two of them and then a pack of Ibérico jamón, a goat's cheese, a loaf of bread, and a tub of quince, and guiltily stuffed them into his rucksack. As he was about to leave, he couldn't resist picking up two large tomatoes.

He stuck his head around the corner and called out, 'See you, José!'

José looked up and smiled back. 'See you in the morning, Frank.'

Frank had arrived in Barcelona, believing that he would find a restaurant somewhere in the city that would give him a job in the kitchen. He was keen and prepared to do anything.

Two months before, he had quit his studies at the South East London Catering College, feeling he wanted to see Europe and work in kitchens there. He was fed up with grey London and wanted to really learn how to cook.

His father argued with him, telling him that he was throwing away a great opportunity at the college. Frank had refused to listen. He withdrew the little money he had saved from helping out in his father's bistro on Walworth Road and doing occasional shifts in a greasy spoon café run by a Turkish family in Tooting, packed his rucksack, and took the train to Dover, where he caught the ferry to Calais and then a train down to Paris.

After spending the night in a park near the banks of the River Seine, he took a train to Barcelona, where he caught a local train down the coast to Alicante. His father had reluctantly given him the name of a friend who ran a restaurant there and said he might offer him work. The restaurant turned out to be a place with plastic tables and chairs, and it served mainly British tourists, who seemed to care little what went into their mouths so long as not much came out of their pockets. Frank spent several weeks working in the kitchen, living in a room at the back of the restaurant. Most of what he did involved washing pots, cleaning, or heating up dishes such as frozen shepherd's pies or paella in the microwave.

He spent nine weeks there, during which time he managed to learn some basic Spanish from the other kitchen staff and from a local girl he struck up a relationship with after meeting her on the beach late one evening.

Eventually, feeling restless and with a desire to work in a restaurant where he would learn more about proper cooking, he hitched a ride in a truck to Barcelona. He wandered around the centre of the city, asking at restaurants if anyone needed a kitchen porter. Eventually, he was taken on as a kitchen porter at El Molino, a traditional restaurant in the old part of the city. The head chef, Salvador, a hot-tempered and surly man with a thick moustache who had once worked in a hotel in Bloomsbury, took a liking to this enthusiastic young Englishman. He even found him a room a short distance away.

Frank shared duties with José, who was the same age as him and who was originally from San Sebastián.

Frank worked hard in the kitchen, wanting to prove himself to Salvador and prove to himself that he had what it took to be a chef. And he wanted to prove that he was better than José, the other kitchen porter, who also aspired to be a chef. Frank was always the first to arrive and always the last to leave.

Impressed by Frank's dedication, after a few weeks, Salvador taught him knife skills and how to make stocks and sauces. He then promoted him to commis chef and gave him special responsibility for fish and seafood. Salvador taught him how to scale, gut, clean and fillet flat and round fish and to cook clams, mussels, lobsters, and langoustines. For the first time, Frank felt he was learning some of the secrets of a restaurant kitchen, and he grew in confidence. And he could see himself running his own kitchen one day.

Yet as much as he loved his work, he found life a struggle in Barcelona. After he had paid the rent for his room, he had little money left to buy food or anything else. That was when he began stealing items from the walk-in fridge.

Then one morning, Salvador, looking angry, assembled all the kitchen staff and demanded to know who had been taking food from the walk-in. Bottles of beer, ham, and cheese had disappeared, he said. Everyone denied it. Frank stood there trying to look innocent while feeling guilty. Salvador said the guilty person had one hour to come forward. So, when no one was looking, Frank sneaked into the walk-in and took a cheese and ham, and placed them inside José's locker.

An hour later, Salvador called all the staff together again and asked the guilty person to step forward. No one did. Salvador told the staff to remain where they were while he searched the lockers. Frank's heart was pounding. He looked at José, who shrugged. Salvador returned from his search, triumphantly holding aloft a piece of cheese and a packet of ham. Frank watched as he stood there, shaking his head, his eyes blazing. Salvador seemed as if he was about to explode. He then stepped towards José, shouting at the top of his voice, and grabbed him violently around the neck and began dragging him towards the back door. José protested and tried to struggle free. Frank looked on, feeling alarmed at the scene, but helpless to do anything about it. Shrieking his innocence, José attempted to hold on to the handle of an oven door. As he did this, he slipped and one of his hands plunged into the deep fat fryer. He let out a piercing scream and then collapsed on the floor. Frank watched in horror, with guilt and shame surging through him, as José writhed in agony, crying out for help. Salvador shouted for someone to get the first aid box.

Early the next morning, Frank packed his bag, and set off to return to London.

7

2015, Bermondsey

Frank manoeuvred his Bentley into the space with FRANK painted in white letters on the tarmac. He picked up his tan leather briefcase satchel off the passenger seat and got out, slamming the door hard behind him, as a way of announcing his arrival. A smile came to his face at the memory of his mother telling his father off for slamming the car door and his father replying, 'That's what men do.' He straightened himself up, stole a quick glance at himself in the wing mirror, and then strode purposefully towards the entrance.

A brass plaque on the brick wall announced that this was the home of Frank's Restaurants Ltd, Frank in the Kitchen Ltd, Ask Frank Consulting Ltd, Frankly Speaking Ltd, and To Be Frank Cookery School Ltd. He bent down to examine the potted plants that stood in boxes either side of the door. They needed watering. Appearances matter.

When Frank had opened his first restaurant, he had done all the paperwork at home with the help of an accountant he had met at his cricket club. Once his business started growing rapidly, he realised he needed proper offices. So he took out a lease on the first floor of the tower of a converted Victorian church in Bermondsey. Later, he leased part of the second floor, sharing it with an advertising agency, a software development company, and a carbon capture and storage company.

Frank's visits to head office reminded him of how far he had come in life, what he had achieved, and, yes, the empire he had created from nothing. He didn't understand those people who had made money and wanted to keep the fact a secret. If you had made money – real money – then you should let everyone else know. Wasn't that part of the point of making it in the first place? Nothing talked louder than money. Money was the true global language. Everyone knew that, even if some people wouldn't admit it. Of course you had to make it in order to possess it. Frank had certainly done that with his books, TV shows, and businesses.

Frank operated four restaurants, at London Bridge, Shoreditch, Bayswater, and South Kensington, all areas that attracted the well-heeled. The restaurants occupied what had become known in the hospitality business as the casual dining market. Fish and seafood were the speciality, although the menu also offered dishes such as steaks, burgers, and pasta.

To keep ahead in the restaurant game, you had to keep an eye on the trends and future developments. It was such a competitive and fast-changing industry, especially in London, which had become one of the most dynamic cities in the world where eating out was concerned.

There was a time in London when, for many people, dining out meant going to a trattoria, an Indian, or somewhere like his father's bistro. Now, there were restaurants offering cuisines from across the world, including some of the most unlikely countries, such as Afghanistan, Somalia, and Iceland. And it wasn't just the streets of the West End and Kensington that had witnessed this revolution. Go to virtually any high street in London and you would often find at least a dozen restaurants providing dishes from different countries. In fact, Frank often thought, you could travel around the world in London without ever going anywhere near the check-in desks at Heathrow Airport.

Restaurants no longer waited for customers to go to them. Social media had changed all that. They were now jostling each other online, making exaggerated and unconvincing claims about their menus, bombarding customers with special offers, urging them to book now, informing them that their weekend will only properly get started once they've visited this establishment (from Wednesday onwards), tweeting saccharine messages, retweeting good reviews, and uploading photos of their dishes. So desperate were so many restaurants to lure people through the doors that they never stopped to think that some might find this frenzied and incessant online activity irritating.

Frank was aware that customers nowadays wanted not just good food, but new types of food, and eating out had to be an experience. In fact, eating out was entertainment, the restaurant a theatre, and the staff part of a show. Cheap flights to Europe, and backpacking holidays through the Far East and South America, had introduced people to exciting new cuisines, and when they returned home they eagerly sought out that particular food in an attempt to recreate that holiday.

Though he'd never admit it, Frank found it hard to keep up with the restaurant trends in London. It felt as if cooking had become a competition, with pretentious chefs trying to outdo each other in producing the most outrageous dishes. Frank would read about some dish or other and then have to google some of the ingredients to find out what they were.

This food revolution wasn't confined to restaurants. Across London, so-called farmers' markets had sprung up in side streets, small public spaces, and car parks. And Borough Market, where it seemed you could buy just about any produce imaginable, had become a temple of gastronomy where tourists came not to buy, but to wander among the stalls taking photos.

Elsewhere, chefs wanting to do their own thing and aspiring chefs seeking a way out of an unfulfilling desk job were doing pop-ups in pubs, empty shops, even small art galleries and nightclubs – or turning up at festivals in muddy fields in food trucks to sell organic burgers, sourdough pizzas, souvlaki, or doughnuts.

The critics and bloggers tried to outdo each other in displaying their knowledge of this ever-changing scene and, breathlessly, be the first to predict a new development. There was never any shortage of those. One week they would announce the next big thing was huitlacoche or rotisserie chicken; the next week it would be soup dumplings or purple yam. London seemed to have become one huge food laboratory. But Frank suspected that many of these trends, after an initial burst of excited publicity, would melt away to be replaced by a new one. And he knew that many of the new restaurants would close their doors within a couple of years. One of the lessons he had learned about restaurants was that the public were fickle.

Frank entered his office building and gave a cheery 'Hi, darling!' to the receptionist, then took the stairs to the main operations office, where six staff were tapping away at their PCs, or talking on the phone. On the wall were framed colour photos of some of the dishes on the menu at Frank's restaurants – roast pork belly, herb-encrusted lamb with new potatoes, crispy squid, pan-fried sea bass with ratatouille and basil, raspberry sorbet with fresh cream and pistachio nuts. They all looked mouthwatering. At the far end of the office, a stained glass window depicted Jesus holding a loaf of bread and a fish with a crowd of people gathered around him. But the face wasn't actually Jesus's. Not any more.

Frank stood by the coffee machine, took a deep breath, and then broke into Bon Jovi's 'Livin' on a Prayer.' All heads turned towards him, startled. Frank climbed up on to a desk, and, with his arms outstretched and his eyes closed, continued his performance. Oh no, was he going to sing the whole song? All of it? Surely not. Frank jumped down off the desk, ran his hand through his hair and tossed a wide grin to everyone. 'You all happy?'

Everyone shouted back as one, 'Yeah!'

'All together. F is for?'

'Frank!'

'F is for?'

'Food!'

'F is for?'

'Fun!'

'F is for?'

'First!'

'F is for?'

'Famous!'

'Brilliant! Okay, crack on.' Frank sauntered out, waving over his shoulder.

When he arrived in the boardroom, Adewale, the operations manager, Tim, the brand and marketing manager, Carmen, the personnel manager, and Liz, his PA, were all seated around the circular glass table, their faces impassive and expectant. Framed black and white photos of Frank decorated the walls: Frank as a young chef in a busy kitchen, Frank in a dinner jacket clutching an award, Frank shaking hands with the prime minister, Frank with a shotgun under his arms walking through a field, Frank dressed as James Bond, holding a blender across his chest.

Each of his team had the agenda in front of them, along with the obligatory plastic bottle of water. Frank sprayed a smile around the room and took his seat at one end of the table. He didn't like lengthy meetings. Half an hour ought to be plenty.

'Okay, let's kick off,' he said as he sat down. 'Oh and before we start, can someone water those bloody plants at the entrance? They look appalling.'

Everyone murmured and nodded and looked at everyone else. So whose job was it? Somebody's.

Frank opened his briefcase satchel and pulled out a blue folder. 'Right, we've got the draft of the new menu. Have a peek and tell me if you've any comments.' He passed a copy to each of the team. 'As you can see, we're adding a few more classic British dishes.'

The week before, the celebrated restaurant critic Malcolm Malden had written an article in *The Fork* in which he dismissed Frank and his restaurants as being stuck in the 1990s, with the fish and seafood tasting 'more of an industrial canal than the sea'. He wrote, 'Being a decent bloke, I wouldn't like to see any restaurant catch fire – but at least if we had been evacuated by a false alarm I wouldn't have had to eat the food.'

Frank had been livid, even though he knew Malden had a personal vendetta against him ever since they'd both attended a dinner at the Savoy following the Menu of the Year awards. Afterwards, the two of them had got into an argument in the bar over whether an authentic cassoulet should be topped with breadcrumbs. They were like two theologians in fourth-century Greece arguing over the doctrine of the Trinity. Frank insisted a cassoulet had to have breadcrumbs and called Malden an arsehole for claiming otherwise. Malden swung at Frank and the two of them ended up rolling around on the carpet before being ejected by security.

At one time, most restaurant menus were easy to read. Nowadays, though, many appeared to have been written by someone with frustrated literary ambitions. Everything was delicious or succulent, as if the food should be otherwise, and cod and chips was now posh beer-battered cod and hand-cut or rustic chips. And some menus seemed more about the kind of food a restaurant would like to serve than the food it was actually capable of serving.

Frank changed his menu twice a year, once in the winter, and once in the summer. When he used to help his father in the bistro and he had suggested changing the menu, his father had shook his head dismissively and said sternly that the customers wanted the same thing, not something new.

Frank was proud that his restaurants served quality food. None of it was produced offsite, as it was with some restaurants, and it was all made with fresh ingredients. At one time, he used to drive over to Billingsgate Market early in the morning to select the fish and seafood for his restaurants. It had been some time, though, since he had done that.

His menus weren't long. A restaurant shouldn't have forty or fifty dishes on a menu, as there was no way the chefs could cook them well. Instead, have a short menu and make sure each dish is cooked to perfection. And if everything in your kitchen had been prepared by you and your colleagues, then you wouldn't be saying to customers, this product may contain nuts. You would know whether nor not there were nuts in it.

It wasn't just nuts that some people claimed to be allergic to. Menus now came with coloured icons representing the ever-expanding number of ingredients that might trigger allergies people claimed to have. Frank wasn't convinced by all this, suspecting that in most cases people just didn't like a particular product; they weren't allergic to it. He couldn't remember so many allergies when he was at school, or when his father ran the bistro. So how come everyone's now got allergies of all of a sudden?

His theory was that some people made out they were allergic to a particular product in an attempt to try and edge themselves into the coveted victim category. If you were a victim, you were beyond criticism, and others were duty bound to give you sympathy. God almighty, you couldn't move for victims nowadays. At one time, only people who had suffered terrible injuries – say in a war or a car crash, or some act of violence, like being beaten up or raped – were victims. Now, if you felt a joke was racist or sexist, you were a victim of it. If someone accused you of talking bollocks on social media, you were a victim.

A few days before on breakfast TV, a well-known actress had broken down in tears after describing how she had been traumatised by a road sweeper winking at her in the street as she walked by. As a consequence of this traumatic experience, she told the presenter, she was now 'in therapy'.

Nevertheless, Frank had to keep up-to-date in the game, so he had included nine allergy icons on his new menu: gluten, peanuts, lupin, celery, milk, eggs, fish, shellfish, and crustaceans. He knew of some places that had as many as twenty.

After a discussion about the menu, Frank brought up the topic of portion sizes. Because a number of recent reviewers had complained that his restaurants were stingy with the amount of chips they served, he was going to increase the portions. The last thing he wanted was to suffer the same fate as Tom Kettle, another celebrity chef with a group of restaurants, who had earned the nickname 'Six Chips' because of the small portions he served.

Frank then gave an update on the site in Marylebone he had leased. 'As you know, my plan is to open a different type of restaurant. The problem's still finding an investor. It's taking a bit longer than I'd imagined, but I'll get someone. Okay, then, Adewale, over to you.'

Adewale, the operations manager, was a British-educated Nigerian with a shiny bald head, big eyes and a liking for jazzy ties and flat tweed caps. He cleared his throat and said, 'Not that much to report, Frank. Sales figures are pretty stable with the restaurants.'

'What about the new café at the Elephant and Castle?'

'Down eight percent on the first six months since we opened. But I don't think we should worry about that.'

'The Elephant's an up-and-coming place. We can take a few hits in the early months. There's a lot of students moving into the area. We're going to do special deals for them. So what about the cookery school and the kitchenware?'

'Bookings at the cookery school have dipped a little.'

Frank was particularly proud of his cookery school in Clerkenwell. Seeing that the well-established cookery schools were coining it, he had figured that he should have a slice of the action. People were happy to hand over two hundred quid just to watch a chef show them how to make a spring roll or how to chop, slice and dice vegetables. And if the school bore the name of a TV chef, then you could charge much more, of course. It was easy money.

He turned to Tim with an accusing look. 'Tim, I thought you did a big social media push with it.'

Tim, a twenty-nine-year-old who wore T-shirts with ironic slogans and the names of bands Frank had never heard of, said, 'Yeah, I did. And we ran a campaign on Thames Radio.'

Carmen, a feisty Spaniard who, Frank thought, had more make-up on her face than you'd find at Debenhams' cosmetics counter, said, 'The prices are too high! I –'

'Listen, you've got to pay for quality,' interrupted Frank.

Carmen wrinkled her nose. 'Two hundred and twenty pounds for a two-hour course is a lot of money.'

Frank looked thoughtful. 'So maybe we need to have another look at them. And we might have to do a new brochure.'

'There's another matter,' said Carmen.

'Go on,' said Frank.

'A woman who signed up for a pastry course claims that she was bullied by the chef and now she has no confidence.'

Frank rolled his eyes heavenwards. 'You're kidding!'

'She claims he shouted at her and criticised the way she made a Victoria sponge. And she says some of the other students stole things from her ...'

'Stole things? What things?'

'Some vanilla extract and raspberry jam.'

'That's bloody ridiculous!'

'She's now demanding her eight thousand pounds back and wants compensation.'

'I can't believe what I'm hearing. Are these people real?'

Adewale shook his head. 'Afraid so, Frank. It's getting like America now. Everyone is looking for an excuse to sue someone.'

Frank sat there in silence. What should he do? Just give in to this woman, who was clearly chancing her arm? Or refuse to pay out? If she went to the press, it could set back the cookery school.

'Okay,' he said, sighing heavily. He looked at Adewale. 'What you reckon, then?'

'I think she's trying to get one over on us. There's no doubt about it. But the problem is, the school has only just opened and if this got into the media it would look bad.'

'So we pay up?'

'I've spoken to our lawyer and he says if we don't, it might cost us more.'

'This is crazy! Bloody crazy! What's to stop other people doing the same?'

'Nothing. It's an occupational hazard in business nowadays.'

'There's some other issues,' said Carmen, and then went on to say that a waitress at the Bayswater restaurant was threatening to sue the company for sexual harassment. She claimed to have been offended by a sous-chef drinking tea from a mug with an image of a woman in a bikini on it.

Frank flung his pen down on the table. 'A bloody mug, for Christ's sake!'

'She said it was inappropriate behaviour.'

Finding offence where none existed seemed to have become a new national pastime, mused Frank glumly. Each day the media was full of stories of lives and careers being wrecked by these crazy witch-hunts. And who decided what was appropriate and what wasn't?

'What else?' asked Frank, unable to conceal his exasperation.

'Another waitress – at Kensington – claims that a waiter posted naked photos of her on the internet. She said they'd had a relationship and he was angry because she ended it. She also says he's racist towards her.'

'Why did she let him take photos of her? Maybe I'm a bit old-fashioned, but what is this thing nowadays with all these women wanting to be photographed naked? I don't get it. You know, when I was growing up it was only Page Three or top shelf magazines. It's as if everyone nowadays wants to be a porn star. What country's she from?'

'Switzerland.'

'Switzerland? And the waiter?'

'Bulgaria.'

'Hang on. I don't get the racial discrimination bit. Aren't they both white? So how the bloody hell can she say she's being discriminated against?'

'In her letter she says he made fun of her country. He said he couldn't trust anyone who came from a country that made cuckoo clocks.'

'Cuckoo clocks. Jesus! That's called having a laugh.'

'Nowadays you can never tell how a tribunal might see it.'

'The world's gone bonkers. Racial discrimination, because he made fun of Switzerland. I mean, come on. That's nuts.'

Reluctantly, Frank agreed that Carmen and one of the legal team should meet with the young woman to see if they could resolve the issue and keep it out of court. Reluctantly he went along with her suggestion that if the young woman didn't back down, she should be offered a better-paid position in a different restaurant. If that didn't work, then they would have to review the situation, which Frank knew could mean doing an out-of-court settlement with a confidentiality clause. He'd done that once before, when a waiter had slipped on a tomato on the kitchen floor and made out he had been badly injured. He had hired a solicitor and demanded compensation while threatening to go public about what he claimed were poor health and safety standards in the kitchen. Frank had taken the advice from his solicitor to reach a settlement so as to avoid damaging publicity. He hated doing it. It felt like he was being had over. So now he was going to have to cave in once again to someone on the make. What he couldn't have was bad publicity, especially this close to the Golden Pan award.

8

Later that afternoon, Frank drove across London to Kensal Green for a meeting at the offices of Sticky Lettuce, his PR company. As usual, he had ended up stuck in traffic for ages, due to an accident at the Euston Road underpass. He was getting so fed up with congestion on the roads in central London that he found himself wondering if he should start taking the Tube. It would certainly be quicker. But he wasn't sure he could sacrifice the feeling of luxury and power he felt sitting behind the wheel of his Bentley.

Sticky Lettuce was based on the second floor of a former technical college. An American-style bar and an Iranian restaurant flanked the building's entrance. Sticky Lettuce handled footballers, their wives or girlfriends (sometimes both), models, pop stars, reality TV stars, TV presenters, installationists, artists, bloggers, vloggers – anyone, in fact, who possessed the currency called celebrity. Some people hired Sticky Lettuce to get them into the media; some people hired Sticky Lettuce to keep them out of the media.

Frank sat at a large stripped-wood table in an office with exposed brickwork walls and a scuffed wooden floor. The office was open plan. There were no desks. Instead, several stacks of wooden pallets were dotted around. Frank wasn't sure if this was some ecological statement or a sign that Sticky Lettuce couldn't afford desks. But given the retainer he paid them, he figured it couldn't be the latter. A life-size statue of a serene-looking Virgin Mary dressed in a red tank top and white miniskirt stood in one corner and a popcorn machine in the other. A battered settee was suspended from the ceiling by chains. All the furniture was mix-and-match retro, purchased from a company in a railway arch in Bethnal Green who bought it from a factory in Lancashire.

He was surprised that there were so many people sitting around the table. It was just answering a few questions for a magazine, he had been told. He looked at the faces around him. There was Zoot, the director, originally from LA and who had worked in publicity for Disney Studios at Burbank, and Jake, the creative director, in his purple-framed glasses. Jake was the man behind the famous series of TV adverts for shampoo that featured fashion cats, and who also was responsible for the memorable *Chic* opening ceremony show, when the models fell down on the catwalk only to get straight back up and break into a dance. Then there was Nisha, the account director, a quietly spoken Asian woman who walked around the office in her bare feet, and two of the account execs. This being PR, they were called Sarah, Sara, Sarah, Hannah, Anna, Ana, Laura or Lauren. Frank could never remember who was who whenever he came to the office. They were all in their twenties and looked so much alike – all that long blonde hair, those lips, those Estuary English meets Home Counties accents. It was impossible to distinguish between them. The only way he could do so was by resorting to that tried and trusted method of noting the size of their breasts, a skill that he had got down to a fine art over the years. But even a man with Frank's appreciation of and close attention to the female form had to admit that his breast technique still left him struggling.

Frank was going to appear in *Out and About* magazine, which promoted itself as London's leading lifestyle magazine. You could pick up a copy of it every Friday at most of the capital's 408 railway and Tube stations. Within its glossy pages you could read about beauty, fashion, travel, food, the latest trends, nightlife, the power players, the talents of the future, the disruptors, the taste-makers, and the influencers. It presented an image of London that bore little resemblance to the city that most of its inhabitants knew. And that was the point. It was aspirational. This was the London – the opulent city of the rich and attractive – you would really like to be a part of, went the thinking of the magazine, even though to the vast majority of its inhabitants, that London would remain unattainable.

Frank had never read *Out and About*, but he was going to be included in the regular feature 'Why I Love London', regarded as the most popular page in *Out and About* because readers felt they got a real insight into the life of a celebrity and into that other London, that world of big houses, expensive cars, exclusive restaurants, glittering gala dinners, and exotic holiday locations. But, of course, in the world of PR and journalism, things were not always what they seemed.

Zoot, with his greying preacher beard, his hair brushed at an angle across his forehead and dressed in a white T-shirt ('See. No slogan'), black distressed skinny jeans and trainers with no laces, started the meeting. 'Right, guys, we need to work some magic with Frank for this interview and we need to make him fireproof.'

'Fireproof?' said Frank.

'That's right, Frank. Fireproof,' repeated Zoot. 'In this game you've got to cover all the entrances and exits. So Ana's going to walk us through the questions.'

The account exec, who was nibbling a carrot, flicked back her hair and looked down at her tablet. 'Okay. The first question is heroes. Who is Frank's hero?'

'My hero?' said Frank. 'That's got to be Pierre Limogne.'

Blank expressions around the table. 'Who's he, Frank?' asked Ana.

'You don't know Pierre Limogne? He was the greatest chef in France. An absolute genius.'

'Was?' said Ana.

'Yeah, he died about ten years ago.'

'I get you, Frank, but daisy-pushers are no good,' said Zoot. 'We need someone alive.'

'I mean, that's the truth. He *is* my hero.'

'That's cool, but sometimes the truth needs a little help, right? Can you think of someone else?'

Frank was deep in thought. 'Er … Let me see … No one springs to mind … er … I know!'

'Who?'

'Clint Eastwood!' said Frank with a rush of excitement. 'Brilliant actor. And a bloody good director.'

'Mmmmm. I know he's a great actor, Frank,' said Zoot. 'You know, though, he's sort of a bit too misogynous for the readers. Around seventy per cent are women.'

'What are you talking about? He's not misogynous. He's a man's man.'

'Zoot's right,' said Ana, screwing up her face. 'And there's all those spaghetti westerns and stuff.'

'Absolutely, and he's quite old now,' said Lauren, another account exec, who, Frank noticed, had some small Chinese letters tattooed on her upper arm. He doubted that she knew what they meant. 'I mean, he's, like … a bit yesterday.'

'Frank, the thing is, we need someone more … cuddly and who's on the same platform as the readers,' said Ana.

Frank wasn't sure what she meant and he felt miffed that Pierre Limogne and Clint Eastwood had received such negative reactions. Wasn't it supposed to be who *his* hero was? What, they'd never heard of Pierre Limogne? Pierre Limogne! He thought everybody liked Clint Eastwood. 'Yesterday?' He was getting on, true. But what about all that he'd achieved? All those fantastic films. What was wrong with spaghetti westerns? When Frank had done his first interviews for newspapers, he had said whatever he wanted. He couldn't do that now, it seemed.

'Well, I can't think of anyone else,' he said with a sigh, leaning back in the chair and cupping his hands behind his head.

'Don't worry, Frank, we'll come up with someone,' said Zoot, sucking on his pen. 'Ideas?'

'How about music? What about Broken Toaster or the Cleaners?' suggested Lauren.

'Never heard of either of them,' said Frank dismissively.

Lauren raised her eyebrows. 'Don't you know Cocktail Killer or Stick It Up Cinderella?'

'No,' said Frank. 'I'm more classic rock, like Bon Jovi.'

'I think I know where you're coming from, Frank,' said Zoot soothingly. 'Tell you what, how about U2?'

'Some of their early stuff's okay. Not keen on their last two albums.'

'Everyone cool with U2. Right, we've got petrol in the tank, right? Okay, Ana, next question.'

'This should be a bit easier. Favourite restaurant?'

Frank thought for a moment. 'There's a few, but if I had to choose one then it would probably be Luigi's.'

'Oh, where's that?' asked Ana.

'Beckenham. It's an Italian place. Family run. No fuss, just bloody good food.'

Zoot nodded. 'The only problem, Frank, is that's a bit, you know, far out.'

'How do you mean?'

'Well, *Out and About* likes to focus on the West End. Kensington, Knightsbridge. Those sorts of areas. Or the South Bank or the City.'

'But Luigi's is where I'd choose to go.'

'I hear what you're saying, but we need somewhere more central, right? You know, not way out of town.'

Frank frowned and then said, 'Okay, how about the Barn in Islington?'

'That's a fantastic place!' jumped in Jake. 'I took my girlfriend there last year. Incredible duck.'

'Bump in the road, guys,' said Zoot, absent-mindedly stroking his beard.

'Unh,' said Frank.

'There was some bullshit recently about it not using sustainable fish.'

'News to me. Who by?' asked Frank.

'Some kind of marine eco-activist group. They did a sit-down in it and took down the website. No, Frank, you'll have to choose another.'

'Okay, Ambience,' said Frank.

The team loved the choice, because they loved Nick. Nick was edgy and moved in the right circles, if not necessarily always in the right places.

Frank now had to decide what he would do if he was mayor of London for the day. That was easy: get rid of the cycle lanes. They clogged up traffic and half the cyclists never even used them. Waste of space and money.

'We're going to need something else, Frank,' said Zoot, glancing at Jake.

'But that's what I'd do. Bloody half-baked idea.'

'Sure, sure, but, Frank, we can't risk upsetting the cycling community. A lot of the readers cycle to work – as do some of us around this table. Cycling's good for the environment and all that jazz.'

'Absolutely,' said Jake. 'Cuts down on pollution.'

Lots of vigorous nodding around the table accompanied by approving *mmm* sounds, but not from Frank.

'I've got an idea,' piped up Lauren. 'What about banning lorries? From the congestion zone area, between certain hours. That would go down really, really well with the readers.'

'Home run, Lauren! Awesome!' said Zoot.

'Thank you.' Lauren smiled.

'Hang on a minute,' said Frank sternly. 'I've got restaurants. Lorries have to make deliveries to them. What a ridiculous idea!'

'But, Frank, this is an opportunity to paint yourself green,' said Zoot.

'I don't want to paint myself bloody green!'

'Totally understand, Frank. That's cool. Okay, how about painting Nelson's Column pink?'

'What are you on about?'

'It would score you brownie points with the gay readers.'

'Listen, I'm not painting myself green and I'm not painting Nelson's Column pink. I'm not painting bloody anything.' Frank banged his fist on the table.

'Sure, Frank,' said Zoot, glancing anxiously around.

Jake had an idea. 'I know: what about something like people complimenting each other? So instead of people sitting on the Tube or standing at the supermarket checkout and not saying anything to anyone, people say, "I like your hair," or "That's a nice coat you're wearing." People could say to someone at work, "Thank you for producing that report" or "You're very professional." That kind of thing.'

'Frank could say he would introduce a London Compliment Day, with badges given out,' said Ana brightly.

'Terrific idea!' said Zoot. 'What do you think, Frank?'

Frank thought it was a bonkers idea, but he was keen to get this meeting over with. He didn't know how much more he could take. His mind drifted to the art exhibition he was going to in Kent that evening. The thought made him feel glum. He couldn't stand the stuff that B.O. Gussmann produced. How could people call it art? Then another thought. How much am I paying Sticky Lettuce?

'Yeah, terrific. How many more?'

'Nearly done,' said Ana, through a mouth full of carrot. 'Favourite building?'

'Probably the Monument.'

'I'm not really sure about that,' said Ana.

'What's wrong with the Monument, for God's sake?'

'Any disabled readers won't feel comfortable with that.'

'It commemorates the Great Fire of London. What's it got to do with the disabled?'

'The problem is – I once worked for Wheelchair Raiders – there's no lift and the steps only have a handrail on one side, and they don't have colour-contrasting nosings.'

'Guess, it's a no-no,' said Zoot. 'Ana's right, we can't upset the disabled community. We'll have to park it. What about … Tate Modern … or City Hall? Or that new one, the Beanstalk?'

'Tower Bridge, then,' said Frank, trying to hide his exasperation.

Everyone looked at everyone else. Is Tower Bridge okay? Yes? Okay. Let's go with that.

'Next one. Least favourite part of London?' said Ana.

Frank thought for a moment. 'I don't know … er … Probably Whitechapel. It's scruffy and the traffic's always horrendous.'

'That sounds totally fine to me,' said Zoot, anxious not to annoy Frank even more. 'Everyone cool with that?'

Nisha spoke up for the first time. 'The only thing is, it might sound a bit racist.'

'Tell me more,' said Zoot, surprised. 'I don't know Whitechapel very well.'

'It's got a big Muslim population. That's where the East London Mosque is. If Frank says he doesn't like Whitechapel it's like he's sort of saying he doesn't like Muslims or Asians.'

'Well spotted, Nisha. Hell, we can't risk Frank been seen as a racist.'

'I'm not a racist,' protested Frank, a wave of indignation rolling over him. 'Come and see my restaurants. I've got people from Poland, Russia, Brazil, Africa, and God knows where working in them. I've got more foreign staff than British staff. How could I be accused of being racist?'

Zoot nodded in a conciliatory manner. 'What Nisha means is that if you single out Whitechapel as the worst part of London, you'll be seen to be sending out a racist message. Hell, I can see the headlines: "Does Frank hate Muslims?" "Frank enters race debate." "Frank says too many Muslims in London." And then we have a serious oil spillage. We can all remember Currygate. That was one hell of a story.'

Currygate referred to an incident when the England football manager was secretly filmed by a fellow diner at an Indian restaurant in Tooting and was heard to make remarks about how terrible the food was. At one point he said to his wife, 'Is this supposed to be chicken? ... I don't believe it ... Uugh ... It's bloody disgusting ... You know what, it's probably dog or something.'

The film went viral and quickly became known as Currygate. Kill Racism and Root Out Racists led the vilification of the manager, each attempting to outdo the other in issuing condemnations. When the man came out of his house the following morning, he found cameras and microphones being shoved into his face.

Celebrities across the world quickly came out in support of the restaurant, even though none of them had actually eaten there, but this was regarded as inconsequential when weighed against the opportunity to signal their anti-racist credentials. Many were photographed smiling and wearing a T-shirt – 'Nice with Spice' – and holding a plate of curry. On a TV chat show one Hollywood actress, her eyes welling up with tears, said that when she had heard the manager's remarks – her cleaners were all Asian – she had been unable to sleep for two days and felt so distressed, she had to see her therapist.

At the Bafta awards, the British actress Emily Miller, who won best supporting actor for her role in *Love You, Too 5*, said in an emotional acceptance speech, 'We live in a world that right now I'm finding hard to recognise, a world where people of colour are not valued.'

Justice 4 Dogs, K9 Power and other animal charities attacked the manager for having eaten dogs. 'Dogs are for life, not dinner' was their slogan. A columnist in *The Daily Dirt* suggested that the only dog in the restaurant was sitting at the table with the manager.

Protesters marched on Downing Street, where they gathered at the gates and burnt an effigy of the manager, demanding that he be sacked. The matter was even raised during Prime Minister's Questions in Parliament. The president of India and the prime minister of Bangladesh summoned their respective UK ambassadors for an urgent meeting. The Indian cricket team threatened to pull out of their English tour that summer, and there was talk of Bangladesh cancelling a deal with a British company to supply the country's army with 250 armoured vehicles. A casual comment made in private over a curry in a restaurant had become an incident and the incident had become an issue and the issue had become a crisis.

Several sports writers did stick their heads briefly above the parapet, pointing out that under the manager, England had won eighteen of their nineteen games and had qualified for the next World Cup. All he had done was make a remark about the quality of the food he was eating. He was just stating an opinion. But the mob rounded on the columnists, claiming that they were just as racist as the manager. Football was a hotbed of racism! The manager needed to be made an example of. The FA did what any esteemed body would do after a thorough examination of the allegations and the facts of the matter: it sacked the manager.

Having attained the lofty status of victim, the curry house won Restaurant of the Year at the British Curry awards and a Lifetime Achievement Award at the UK Hospitality awards – to the great surprise of the owner, who had been awarded a zero rating for food hygiene only weeks before. He brought out a recipe book, *Curry in a Hurry,* was the subject of a BBC TV drama *Let's Go for an Indian,* and fronted a campaign to eliminate racism from sport. For good measure, he also found himself being invited to Buckingham Palace, where the queen awarded him the CBE.

Frank hadn't forgotten Currygate. He had done several TV and radio interviews about it, saying how Indian food had helped change the cuisine of Britain and how he loved nothing more than a good curry. What he hadn't said, as Sticky Lettuce had set up and overseen the interviews, was that his sympathies were more with the England football manager than the restaurant owner.

At the end of the meeting, Zoot looked pleased with himself. 'Terrific, Frank! Hell, the readers of *Out and About* are going to love this.'

Frank did hid best to smile, but a thought kept nagging away at him. None of the answers people would read were true.

9

The critics hailed it as one of the shows of the year – *the* show of the year, according to some. And Annalisa had tickets for Frank and herself. That's why Frank was behind the wheel of his Signal Red 1967 E-Type Jaguar 4.2, speeding along the outside line of the M2 under a brooding grey sky towards the Kent coast.

'Oh, I'm so looking forward to the exhibition,' said Annalisa with excitement in her voice.

Frank grunted, staring ahead at the road. 'I'm interested to see what this B.O. Gussmann character you're always on about is like.'

Frank hadn't wanted to go to the exhibition, but he had agreed to please Annalisa. He could think of far better things to do, such as trying to find someone to invest in the new restaurant he was planning.

'I can't believe I'm going to meet him! We're so lucky to receive invitations, you know. Everyone's talking about it. They mentioned it on the radio this morning.'

Frank laughed sarcastically. 'James could do what he does.'

'That's not the point.'

'Ah, so you agree, do you?' said Frank victoriously, taking his eyes off the road momentarily.

'Yes ... No ... B.O.'s creating something. It might look like anyone could do it, but it all has meaning.'

'How much did you pay for that bloody thing in the hall?' Frank said sneeringly, referring to the twisted paste of toothpaste mounted on a piece of rock.

'Oh, I can't remember,' she said curtly. 'But I bet it's worth double that now.'

'What do you reckon?'

'How should I know. Anyway, why are you so interested in it?'

'Just curious, that's all.'

Annalisa sat there in silence, sulking.

'Take the next turning left,' instructed the sat nav. On cue, a sign for Dombey-on-Sea appeared by the roadside and Frank slowed down. It had been several months since he had driven the Jaguar, and he had forgotten just how much he loved the feel of it and, since it had been reupholstered, the smell of the leather seats. Most of all, though, he loved the envious glances he would attract from other drivers as he flew past them.

Dombey-on-Sea, like many small ports along the south coast of England, had fallen into decline. With its narrow cobbled streets running down to its harbour, it had once been a popular holiday destination, for both day trippers and those wanting a week by the sea. But now tourism had dwindled to the occasional coachload of pensioners spending a few hours walking around on Sunday afternoons in the summer. Cheap flights to Europe had only added to its woes, as had EU fishing policy. Dombey's fishing fleet, made up of tiny boats, had shrunk to less than half of what it had once been; many of the shops in its small high street had *to let* signs above them; restaurants and cafés had folded; and several once elegant and imposing hotels along the promenade had closed their doors and been leased by London boroughs whose housing waiting lists far exceeded the empty properties available in the crowded capital.

B.O. Gussmann had grown up in Dombey and still had an affection for the town. That was why he had decided to build an art gallery there. The gallery – called BOG – stood overlooking the harbour on the site of the former fish hall and had been designed by the Danish architect Hans Fabricus, whose work included the Museum of Gold in Riyadh, the Invisible Theatre in Amsterdam, and Harvard University's Centre for Al Capone Studies. At the gallery's opening, Fabricus gave a speech and explained the ideas behind his creation: 'My design embodies the idea that architecture can eclipse the personality of its occupants, where the character and style of the architecture dictate the mood of the inhabitants. Landscapes have always inspired me to put something weird, unreal and out of human scale into them. A building is about telling a story. It should be part of our personal narrative. We short-circuit our collective memory. We don't need the Greeks to tell us what architecture is. We can tell each other what it is.'

Fabricus's gallery was described by some as resembling a teapot. Others said it looked like a duck. Others weren't quite sure what it looked like. Given Dombey's maritime history, locals had expected that the design of the new gallery would reflect this in some way. If it did, they couldn't see it.

The gallery, with its large, angled, star-shaped windows to let in natural light, was made of micro-reinforced concrete using 3D printing. The entrance was not at the front but at the back, reached by a glass walkway that led up from the promenade, jutting out above the water.

There was much interest among the art critics in B.O. Gussmann's radical move in bringing modern art to a depressed Kent fishing port. B.O. Gussmann said he hoped that crowds would come to the gallery, and he was not disappointed. However, the local shopkeepers and owners of cafés and restaurants were, because once people had been to the gallery they went straight back home. The café and restaurant owners were particularly vexed, as the gallery's café – smoothies, maple roasted soup, crispy salt and pepper squid, roast lemon and thyme chicken, line-caught tuna and apple on granary bread – did a roaring trade.

Frank and Annalisa had been invited to a private party to launch B.O. Gussmann's retrospective, officially called 'B.O. Gussmann 1997–2017. No Title'. Annalisa, who had purchased not just the tube of toothpaste stuck to a rock but several other pieces of the artist's work, had persuaded Frank to do a cookery demonstration at an auction Gussmann had put his name to, staged to raise money for his charity Safe Haven for Indo-Chinese Tigers. Frank knew nothing about Indo-Chinese tigers and had no particular inclination to find out about them, but he had agreed to Annalisa's request out of guilt for having neglected her.

This particular launch party boasted an even more eclectic line-up of celebrities than the auction had been able to muster. Specially flown in for the occasion were a Chicago rapper named 3499, a ten-piece disabled transvestite orchestra from Berlin, and a choir made up of members of what had been a lost tribe in the Amazon until they were discovered by a TV crew and turned into reality TV stars.

Frank and Annalisa arrived at the entrance to the gallery, where they were met by a young woman dressed in a flowing white robe and holding a small silver dish. Beyond her was a dimly lit room where Frank could just make out ghostly faces. Gregorian chant played faintly in the background. The young woman stepped forward, bowed, and, without saying anything, dipped a finger into the dish and then carefully drew a circle around Annalisa's forehead and then did the same to Frank's. Frank stood there, shifting from foot to foot, feeling awkward and unsure of what to do next.

'You have been anointed with the oil of life,' said the young woman in a solemn voice, as she bowed again and backed away.

'Thank you,' said Annalisa brightly, quite touched by the gesture.

Frank was slightly puzzled by it and could only murmur, 'Yeah, thanks.'

'Wasn't that lovely, Frank,' said Annalisa as they moved past the young woman.

'I didn't really understand what it's all about.'

'It's symbolic, Frank. I read that B.O. Gussmann's big into symbols.'

'Symbolic of what?' said Frank grumpily.

'Well, I don't know. But it doesn't matter. She said we've been anointed with the oil of life. I think that's sweet.'

They took off their coats and handed them over a counter to another young woman in a white robe, who smiled benignly at them, then gave them each a pebble with a number written on it. Frank stuffed the pebble into his trouser pocket. Annalisa secreted hers in her Marini Martini dark teal python box bag with red leather lining.

The two of them walked on to the main room, where they could only just make out the shapes of the other guests. The only light was from candles attached to holders on the walls. At the far end was the stage.

'Why's it so bloody dark?' complained Frank.

'I don't know,' said Annalisa. 'But it's nice … It's different.'

'It's different, I'll give you that. You can't bloody see anyone.'

Another young woman in white appeared out of the dimness in front of them, like a spectre. She was holding a tray with small glasses.

'What's this?' asked Frank.

'It's tum,' she replied.

'Tum? What's that?'

'It's made from the urine of Indo-Chinese tigers, mixed with mango.'

Frank turned up his nose. 'Have you got anything else?'

'Other drinks will be served later, sir. This is just to welcome you.'

'I think I'll pass,' said Frank, waving the drinks away.

'I'll try one,' said Annalisa, reaching for a glass. 'I'm all for new things.'

Frank shook his head and muttered under his breath. 'Tiger's urine! What sort of a bloody drink is that?'

Annalisa took a sip. 'It's ... not bad actually ... sort of tangy.'

Frank ignored her and looked impatiently around the room, which was rapidly filling up with guests. Even though there was so little light, he thought he could make out an actor who appeared on one of the soaps and advertised DIY funerals on TV. And there was that silly woman who campaigned for school exams to be abolished because they hurt the feelings of those children who didn't pass them. What nonsense. And was that thingummybob, the bloke who was married to whatsername, the politician who covered his car in manure after she discovered he was having an affair? God, I must be getting old. Ah, that's that comedian who was in rehab. The one who put naked photos of his girlfriend on Facebook.

Just then, a portly man in his sixties with a jowly, burgundy face topped by short silver hair, almost military in style, sidled up to Frank. He was wearing a charcoal pinstripe suit and pink shirt.

'Frank, I've always wanted to meet you. Casper Bullion,' he said, extending a hand.

'Pleased to meet you,' said Frank, glad to make contact with someone, and he shook Casper's hand.

'You know, I'm a big fan of yours.'

'Yeah?'

'You taught me how to cook. I mean, I'm still learning. Good Lord, yes. There's so much to learn. But you have given me some basics.'

'That's always nice to hear,' said Frank, hoping he was not going to have to listen to the guy recounting in minute detail how he had cooked one of his recipes.

'Yes. I must say the way you demonstrate how to cook a dish is absolutely brilliant. You make it so easy for home cooks like me.'

'That's what I try and do. Oh, this is my wife,' said Frank, suddenly remembering that Annalisa was standing next to him.

'Delighted to meet you,' said Casper. 'You're a very lucky lady having a chef like Frank for a husband.'

Annalisa feigned a smile. 'Yes, he's a great cook.'

'I have to make a confession.' He lowered his voice. 'I often watch Frank on YouTube in my office. I have to say, it's far more interesting than dealing with property and investors.'

'Do you know this B.O. Gussmann, then?' asked Frank, unable to think of anything else to say.

'A little. I helped him finance the gallery.'

'Ah, you in the City, then?'

'You could say that, but my office is in Canary Wharf.'

'What you in, then, banking?'

'I'm in the property game. For my sins. I'm a middle man for foreign investors wanting what you might call a slice of the London property cake.'

Frank examined him with more interest. 'Yeah?'

'It's not that exciting. I have to say, it's what you do, Frank, that I really admire. What you can do with a few ingredients. Like B.O., you're an artist.'

'Oh, I wouldn't say that,' said Frank, quite liking the idea that he was creating art.

'You are. It's not just about cooking ingredients. It's about choosing the right combinations, like with paints, knowing how to use them and creating something that is visually exciting. I like to say, art lasts, and food is art that disappears.'

'Sounds like you should be a chef,' said Frank.

'Actually I would have liked to be, looking back. But my father had other ideas.'

'That's the way it is sometimes, isn't it?'

'It is. Well, I always say it's not what cards you are dealt, but how you play them. So do you mind me asking if you're a B.O. fan, Frank?'

'It's Annalisa. I'm not into modern art that much.'

'I see. I love B.O. He's so original, isn't he?'

'I agree,' said Annalisa. 'He sees things in a different way.'

'Absolutely,' nodded Casper, and then added with a grin, 'That's probably why we're all standing here in the dark.'

'Oh. You know, I hadn't thought of that,' said Annalisa. 'That's very true.'

'Well, I don't get it,' said Frank in a combative voice. 'I mean, I don't know a lot about art, but you can't tell me that sticking a tube of toothpaste on a bit of rock or welding a load of dustbins together is art.'

'It's how he expresses himself,' said Annalisa.

'Bullshit! Look. Rembrandt, Turner, Canaletto. That's art. That takes real skill. I could put a tube of toothpaste on a rock. But I couldn't do what Rembrandt did.'

'Well, Frank, whatever you think of it, it's going for a fortune,' said Casper. 'On average his work is going up 22 per cent a year in value.'

'See! I told you,' said Annalisa.

Casper smiled. 'If you buy one, you've made a pretty good investment.'

'That's the only reason people buy the stuff,' said Frank, suddenly wishing he hadn't agreed to go to the bloody launch.

'Don't you think it's a splendid idea building a gallery here,' enthused Casper. 'Dombey could do with a new injection of life. It's a bit run down from what I've seen. Shame with the lovely harbour and everything. B.O. might turn out to be its saviour, as it were. The locals must be delighted.'

'It reminds me of a teapot,' said Frank in a derisive voice.

'I do agree. Some people have said that. I think it's very playful, actually. The architect likes to do that, I gather.'

Just then the sound of a voice could be heard coming through the speakers. Its tone was solemn and each word was pronounced slowly. The chatter of the guests dissolved, like a balloon being deflated. Everyone started looking around, wondering where the voice was coming from. But they couldn't see anyone. *This is fun! I've never been to an exhibition like this before. It's quite mysterious.*

'Thank you for coming to my retrospective,' said the voice. 'It's wonderful to see so many here for this celebration of art, this celebration of exploring the meaning to human existence. The mystery of life.' The voice paused. Everyone stood there in silence.

'What's going on? Who's speaking?' hissed Frank to Annalisa.

Annalisa elbowed him. 'Ssshh. It's B.O.'

The voice continued, as if reading a prayer. 'Art is not about answers … Art is about questions … Art is not about certainty … Art is about uncertainty … Art is where we can meet who we are … Art asks us to question who we are. Art accepts us … Art nourishes us … Art is life.' The voice paused again, this time for longer. Everyone was wondering if they could speak now. No one was sure. Wait and see if someone else speaks. 'Repeat after me, "Art is not about answers."'

Art is not about answers.

Frank didn't know what to make of it all. The whole thing seemed ridiculous. But Annalisa, and Casper, and all the other guests were enthusiastically taking up the responses.

'Art is about questions.'

Art is about questions.

'Art is not about certainty.'

Art is not about certainty.

Frank stood there, listening to the responses and wondering how long all this was going to go on for. He began feeling the pebble in his trouser pocket. The whole experience was like being in a theatre – or a church. It was thingummybob, the bloke who was married to whatsername. He was talking to a blonde in one of those short shimmering dresses. Nice legs.

Then the room suddenly exploded into light and the Chicago rapper launched into his first number. The guests all gave a little start and began looking around at each other. The young women in white appeared at the far end of the room, each carrying a silver tray of small pastries with fillings, and fanned out into the throng. Voices began to murmur and then quickly rose into chatter, and soon the room was bubbling excitedly away.

On the walls of the room were large white canvases. Most seemed to consist of nothing more than a few splashes of paint in different colours. Some of the guests began pointing at a large flat object draped in a bright green cloth hanging above. Two cameras on the ceiling were trained on it. A second wave of young women appeared, each one carrying a tray with a wine bottle and glasses on it. Frank needed a proper drink. Then he remembered he was driving. Damn. He knew he shouldn't have come. He'd been right. But Annalisa had complained that he never took her anywhere she wanted to go.

He decided he needed a pee and excused himself, leaving Annalisa and Casper chatting. He threaded his way through the crowded room, searching for the toilets sign. Several of the guests nodded and smiled at him and he mouthed a greeting back. This recognition briefly lifted his glum mood. When he eventually found the toilets, down a corridor, he frowned and stood there, moving his head from side to side, wondering what to do. There were six doors, all with symbols of circles, crosses or arrows on them. What the bloody hell did all this mean? thought Frank. It looked like some kind of mathematics formula. Which was the gents? He looked round, hoping to see someone he could ask.

Just then, one of the doors opened and a very tall black woman with close-cropped green hair came out. She was decked in long earrings made from bullets and wore a short red dress, fishnet stockings and red platform shoes with straps that went up to her knees.

'Any idea which of these is the gents?' Frank asked, gesturing to the doors. He felt foolish.

'You bi, honey?' asked the woman casually in a husky voice.

Frank did a double take. He didn't know what to say. The woman was actually a man. No shadow of a doubt. That deep voice was a man's. 'Er ... No.'

'Gender fluid maybe,' said the man playfully, running his eyes up and down Frank in a provocative manner.

Frank felt himself squirming. 'What?'

'Gender fluid – like B.O.'

He didn't have a clue what this meant. 'I'm a bloke ... Straight,' he announced firmly, not wanting to leave any room for doubt in the mind of this strange figure standing in front of him.

'Shame. Well, honey, then that's yours,' said the man, indicating a door marked by a circle with an arrow on top pointing to the right. As he tottered off, he called back, 'Have fun, big boy.'

When Frank returned to the room, Annalisa and Casper were still deep in conversation.

'You okay?' asked Annalisa.

'Bloody weird loos.'

'How do you mean?'

'They've no proper signs. Just symbols. I didn't have a clue what they meant.'

'B.O.'s big on what I believe they call nowadays gender identity,' said Casper helpfully.

Frank shook his head. 'What kind of world are we living in? It's crazy! Since time began we've had men and women. Opposites. Ying and yang. Or whatever the Chinese call it ... Adam and Eve ... Romeo and Juliet ... Now you've got some people wanting to choose who they are. Can you believe it? Like choosing a bloody pizza off a menu.'

'Don't understand it all myself, Frank, but there you go. We live in strange times, you could say.'

Frank muttered something under his breath and glanced impatiently around him. 'So, then, where exactly is this Gussmann bloke?'

'Actually I don't think you'll get to see him,' ventured Casper.

'Oh. Why's that?' said Annalisa, looking disappointed.

'He never appears in person at his shows. Or very rarely.'

'But he's just been speaking,' protested Frank.

Casper smiled knowingly. 'That was a recording.'

Frank screwed up his face. 'How can you invite people to an exhibition and not turn up?'

'I was really looking forward to meeting him,' said Annalisa.

'That's very unlikely, as he's at his house in Mexico, I believe,' said Casper.

Frank was still processing the information. 'So let me get this right. We've all driven down to this two-bit town in Kent to attend his exhibition and he's sunning himself thousands of miles away on a beach in Mexico.'

Casper nodded sympathetically. 'I don't claim to understand the thinking, Frank. But it's no doubt got something to do with the difference between the artist and the art, as it were.'

Frank snorted. 'Does it?'

'B.O. is a very profound thinker. A very impressive man, I have to say.'

Frank puffed out his cheeks and scanned the room, wishing he was at home. Then he looked up. 'What's that thing hanging from the ceiling?'

'That's a new piece of art by B.O.,' explained Casper.

'Why's it covered in that cloth?'

'He hasn't unveiled it yet.'

'Oh, what are those cameras?' asked Annalisa.

'They're streaming across the internet. I gather that people all over the world are watching, hoping to catch the moment it's revealed.'

'So when's it going to happen, then?' grumbled Frank, curious to see what all the fuss was about.

'That I can't tell you,' said Casper and then, breaking into a chuckle, he added, 'Knowing B.O., it might not happen at all.'

Frank had heard enough. 'It's all bloody nonsense if you ask me,' he blurted out.

'Frank!' chided Annalisa, worried that other guests might hear.

'Well, it is. He's having a laugh.'

'Frank,' said Casper in a conciliatory tone, 'you might well be right. So what's your next big project? You're a man who always seems to have something on the go. And your restaurants must be doing well.'

'People always want to eat.'

'But it's a tricky business, isn't it? So many factors to get right. I used to go to this fabulous Vietnamese place in Chelsea. Some of the best food I've ever eaten. The most amazing pork dishes! Most nights it was packed. But the owner – I forget his name – had overreached himself. Massive debts. And he went bust. Just shows you.'

'Yeah, there's always winners and losers.'

'Like in life,' said Casper. 'Well, Frank, I think we can both safely say we're winners.'

'I'm looking to open a new restaurant. A different kind of place to the ones I have.'

'I see.'

'Well, that's the idea. But I need to find an investor.'

'Mm,' said Casper, looking interested.

'It's going to need substantial capital, but it's going to be an amazing place that everyone will be talking about.'

Casper leaned in to Frank and said, 'This might be something I can help you with.'

Frank brightened. 'You reckon?'

'I've actually been thinking about dipping my toes in a restaurant. I'd find that far more interesting than luxury flats. I love everything about restaurants.' Casper pulled out his wallet and took out a business card. 'Tell you what, let's meet next week for lunch if you're free, and you can tell me all about it and what you're looking for.'

'Brilliant!' said Frank, barely able to believe his good fortune.

10

1994, Walworth

'Two steaks and a coq,' called Frank through the serving hatch to the kitchen, hoping his mother didn't hear. She didn't like him referring to the dish as a coq, as it sounded vulgar, she said.

His father looked up from the stove. 'You been to the cellar?'

'I'm going now,' murmured Frank.

'When I ask you something it's because I need it straight away, not next week. Now. Go on, get down there!'

It was Saturday night and La Bistro on Walworth Road was packed as usual. It only had fifteen tables, which meant Frank's parents only had to pay for one member of staff, Trevor, to help with prep, cleaning, and washing up. Trevor, an unshaven Glaswegian with a bald head and a pot belly, was often late for work, and sometimes didn't turn up at all. Terry had threatened to sack him on several occasions, but never did.

The walls were lined with black and white photos of Brigitte Bardot, Maurice Chevalier, and Charles Aznavour, and posters of French films. A framed, yellowing newspaper cutting – 'Famous French chef visits Walworth' showed his father, with a wide grin, and Pierre Limogne standing in front of the restaurant. There was a map of France with wine corks identifying the major cities and towns, and a copy of the first menu, which had hardly changed over the years. The Formica tables were covered in red and white check linen tablecloths, with candles stuck in the tops of wine bottles and scallop shells as ashtrays.

While Terry ran the kitchen, his wife, a quiet woman with a warm smile, took care of front of house. Sue knew not only the names of many of the customers, but also the dates of their birthdays and the names of their children. Nothing was too much trouble for her.

Terry had opened the bistro after receiving a generous redundancy package from the printing company he had worked for. He loved France, even though he'd only been there once, on his honeymoon, and decided to bring a French-style bistro to Walworth Road, an area in those days known more for greasy spoon cafés.

At the beginning, Terry had known nothing about running a restaurant – had never even done much cooking, although he'd always had an interest in food. So he took several short catering courses at a local college, along with a wine and spirits course run by a pub company. Through trial and error – and there were a lot of errors – he gradually learned all the nuts and bolts of running a restaurant and how to organise a kitchen.

Frank had first begun helping out in the evenings and at weekends when he was eleven, setting tables, mopping the kitchen, and cleaning out the walk-in fridge, which he hated the most. At first, he was resentful, mainly because his brother Michael never helped out. Michael was six years older and studying for his A levels; he could do no wrong. Frank felt it was unfair that his father made him do all the work.

However, the bistro soon cast a spell over Frank and he grew to love the smells of garlic, onions, and fish, the sounds of frying and sizzling, the exotic names of the wines – Bordeaux, Beaujolais, Côtes du Rhône, Chianti, Lambrusco – and the artistic pictures on the labels. He found the restaurant far more interesting than school. The only subjects he really enjoyed were French and PE.

And more than anything he loved seeing all those smiling faces sitting at the tables in the dim light, with the small candles flickering, and hearing the laughter ricochet around the walls. Most of the customers were couples and lived on one of the local council estates. Some of the men looked tough and the women always smelt of strong perfume and wore lots of jewellery, and would start laughing loudly after a couple of glasses of wine. At the end of the evening the glasses would have lipstick stains around the rims.

He had discovered there was a magic about restaurants, and that you could bring happiness to people.

Eventually, his father allowed to him to chop and peel vegetables and even help in making sauces. And he began to think that when he was older he would become a chef.

After the kitchen had closed, Terry would perch on a stool at the bar, puffing away at a Cuban cigar and holding court, telling the same stories over and over again and finding out all the local gossip. He often allowed his favourite customers to stay behind after closing for a lock-in, when drinks would be on the house. The police never bothered him, as several senior officers at the nearby police station were regular customers. So were a number of villains who specialised in robbing cash from Transit vans and post offices. Terry loved the fact that the good guys and the bad guys came to his bistro. It was like being in the movies, he always said.

Frank was now fourteen and taking dishes to the tables and doing anything else his father asked. He had read his father's battered copy of Pierre Limogne several times. The famous chef's account of growing up in a tough Paris neighbourhood, training to become a cook after leaving school, and then, after many struggles, going on to win three Michelin stars captured Frank's imagination. But he couldn't understand how someone so celebrated had visited his father's bistro, of all places.

As usual on Saturday night, a crooner called Charlie Spencer, a small man with a limp who wore a gold chain around his neck and a toupee, was singing Frank Sinatra and Tony Bennett songs accompanied by an elderly pianist with a cigarette hanging out of the corner of his mouth. Frank couldn't understand why his father liked Spencer so much. He was a terrible singer and the suit he wore was frayed and too tight for him. Worst of all, he always spoke in a fake American accent, often beckoning Frank over after he had finished a set and saying, 'Hey, kid, gimme a bourbon – on the rocks.'

Frank returned from the cellar carrying a bottle of Cognac and a bottle of Cointreau. He placed them behind the bar and then went into the kitchen.

'I've been to the cellar, Dad,' he said, looking for approval.

'Do some plating up,' ordered Terry as he flipped a steak in the pan.

'Don't bother saying please,' muttered Frank under his breath.

'What was that?'

'Nothing.'

Sue came in.

'And get that coq out,' ordered Terry.

'Terry, you know I don't like you saying that.'

'What's up with it?'

'It sounds so vulgar,' she said. 'Imagine if the customers heard you.'

'You're making a fuss about nothing.'

'And don't be so bossy with Frank. He tries his best. He's still a child, you know.'

Frank picked up a white plate and began spooning ladles of coq au vin on to it. It looked much darker than usual, he thought, and not as appetising, so he took a small handful of parsley from a plastic storage container and sprinkled it on top. He stood back, admiring his artistic touch.

'What the bloody hell do you think you're doing?' shouted his father.

'I'm just trying to make it look nicer,' said Frank meekly.

Terry wiped his hands on his apron and came over to him. 'Listen, have any of the customers ever asked for parsley?'

'No, Dad.'

'And you know why? Because they like their food the way I cook it.'

'Yes, Dad.'

'So you just do as you're told. Now take that bloody parsley off! If I wanted parsley on it, I'd have done it myself.'

'Sorry, Dad,' murmured Frank.

'If you ever run a restaurant, then you can put as much parsley on a dish as you want. Until then you do as I say.'

'Yes, Dad.'

'You need to get rid of these fancy ideas in your head. People just want decent food.'

Stung by his father's words, Frank obediently removed the parsley. One day, he thought to himself, I'm going to run my own restaurant and I'll do things my way.

11

2015, Canary Wharf

Frank had arrived at Canary Wharf for his meeting with Casper forty minutes early, so, to kill time, he went for a stroll around the old docks, where smart bars and restaurants lined the waterfront and short red and blue DLR trains passed overhead every few minutes. Canary Wharf seemed more American than English, like a mini Manhattan. The grey, harsh-looking office blocks with their smoked glass windows rising into the sky reminded him of that *Batman* movie he had watched with James. The City, all higgledy-piggledy streets with quaint names, old churches, and livery companies, had once been the financial heart of London. Now Canary Wharf had taken that role.

When Frank entered the Beanstalk, the tallest building in Europe, he paused to take in the scene before him. Six receptionists dressed in grey suits sat behind a long desk. Above them electronic signs gave the current time in Hong Kong, Dubai, Shanghai, and New York. One entire wall was decorated with hundreds of banknotes from different countries. A young woman tinkled at a grand piano beside leather couchettes and a table with an oversized book containing samples of fabric overseen by a tailor who flew in from Milan every two weeks to take orders for handmade suits.

After swiping the ID card he had been given and passing through the glass security turnstiles, where two security guards in peaked caps stood, hands behind their backs, he entered one of the forty-two lifts that rose and fell, in a constant reminder perhaps of how precarious the world of business is. As the lift silently ascended, Frank kept his eyes fixed on the floor, as did the other occupants who got out or in as the lift made its way to the ninety-second floor. He couldn't tell Casper that the only reason he wanted to open this new restaurant was to impress the judges of the Golden Pan award. That would look too opportunistic and Casper might back out. He needed to talk about the restaurant as a place that would have a future.

Frank stepped out of the lift and walked along a corridor with a grey carpet, grey walls, and sensor lighting on the ceiling. He pressed a buzzer at a set of doors with a sign saying Capital Opportunities. An immaculately dressed woman, he guessed in her forties, gave him a professional welcome and led him past dozens of desk workers into an office containing a series of small pods with seats facing each other. Around the edges of the room were coffee and fruit-juice machines, a red telephone box, and a sand pit. The woman opened a door to one side and ushered Frank in.

'Mr Bullion won't be long. Can I get you anything?'

'No, thanks,' said Frank. He had never seen an office as big as this. At the far end was an enormous curved desk, possibly of oak. He felt like a little boy about to meet his headmaster. He wandered over to the huge glass window that ran along one side of the room and stared out at the enormous sprawl of London. It seemed to go on forever. It took him a few seconds to work out that he was looking west. He tried to locate Beckenham, but soon gave up. From this perspective, he could only identify well-known landmarks. All the other buildings seemed to merge into a single mass, occasionally broken up by patches of green. Immediately below he saw a skeleton of steel girders, cranes, and Portakabins built one on top of the other.

He turned away from the window and scanned the office. On a table in the corner were two flat screens that looked like the open pages of a book. On closer examination, he saw that the keyboard had blue, red, green, and yellow keys. LAW. GOVT. CORP. MTSE. M-MKT. MUNI. PFD. EQUITY. CMDTY. INDEX. CRNCY. ALPHA. None of this made any sense to him.

On a large interactive map of London on one of the walls, certain areas were lit up in green – projects underway, he guessed – and others in orange, possibly projects about to be underway. By far, most of the areas illuminated were green or orange. Many of them were in outer East London and along the south shore of the Thames between Woolwich and Erith. These areas were once cheap to buy a house in, he reflected, because of the number of council estates around and all the crime and drug dealing. Nowadays, of course, any area of London was desirable, such was the scramble to buy properties.

How fast and how radically London was changing from the city he had grown up in. Everywhere you went, cranes marked the skyline. It felt like perfectly good buildings were being torn down overnight and replaced by featureless blocks of flats with tiny balconies and glass offices. It was as if a group of drunken architects had been let loose on the city for a bet. Corner pubs, police stations, and hospitals had closed and been converted into apartments or offices, and once-shabby high streets were now lined with chic coffee shops, sushi bars and estate agents. You might not be able to visit a police station or hospital in your area any longer, mused Frank, but you could take comfort from the fact that you could visit the showroom of a new luxury block of flats seven days a week.

Frank wandered over to another wall and studied a long, framed certificate made of parchment. The words, written by the court calligrapher, announced that Casper Winston Bullion, a financier of London, had been awarded the Freedom of the City of London.

A wooden stick in a glass case hung next to it. Frank didn't have a clue what this was. Nearby was another glass case, this one containing ... a grey sock ... with holes in it, nothing more, and a large painting with three red question marks on black. Both were by B.O. Gussmann. Frank snorted.

A shelf unit stood at one side of the office. It contained a photo of Casper with a woman and two teenage children, with the peaks of mountains behind them. Another photo was of an older man in a three-piece suit, standing on top of a skyscraper, looking down on a city, his arms outstretched – like the statue of Christ that embraces Rio. On a shelf were differently shaped bottles of aftershave laid out in a line; various knick-knacks, presumably from Casper's travels in the Far East; and a pile of *Home Cook* and *Yacht Owner* magazines. And what was this on the shelf below? His own books. All twelve of them, arranged in chronological order. Next to them, again in chronological order, were the DVDs of all his TV programmes. He smiled inwardly and no longer felt intimidated.

The door opened and Casper bounced in and barrelled towards him, his hand extended. 'Frank! So sorry to keep you waiting. The Chinese always want so much information.'

'No worries,' said Frank, making sure to give Casper his best firm handshake.

'I'm trying to buy a farm at the moment. Prime piece of land. Ideal for luxury flats. But these Chinese don't understand our planning laws and all the hoops one has to go through. Anyway, it's great to see you. I hope you don't mind but I've taken the liberty of booking a table at a marvellous fish and seafood place that's just opened up here.'

'Sounds great.'

'Yes, I do hope you'll like it.'

'You know, I was just looking around your office. What's that stick?'

'Oh that. It's called a tally stick. It dates back to King Henry I, I believe.'

'A tally stick?'

'Yes, they were a way of recording debts. The stick's made of willow. You split it in half down its length from one end to the other. The debtor would retain one half and the creditor the other half, called the stock. Because of the willow's distinctive grain, the two halves would match only each other. If someone owed you £5, say, then the stick became worth £5, so you could use it as a form of money. I do like a little bit of history.'

'I see,'

'Are you a history man, Frank?'

'Yeah, history's important.' In truth, Frank gave little thought to history.

'I think so. We should never forget where we have come from, should we? I sometimes feel that in our busy world we're always looking forward. Sometimes you need to look backwards to see where you're going.'

'Yeah, I agree.'

'Anyway. Now, shall we go to lunch?'

The two of them left the Beanstalk and made their way across Reuters plaza, where smartly dressed young workers queued at stands selling noodles, salads, and protein drinks. What resembled a toy truck dispensed cups of roasted coffee from the rear. The faces of six clocks mounted on steel poles closely watched over the scene, like vigilant teachers standing in a school playground at break time.

Casper seemed delighted when several people stopped to stare at Frank, or came up and asked for a selfie. As they walked on, he explained how his company helped clients navigate the often murky legal and political waters surrounding the purchase of UK property.

'So who's buying all this land or flats?'

'Rich overseas investors – Chinese, Malaysians, Russians, Arabs, Indians, Americans. You name it. They see London as a safe haven to stash their money and see it grow at, frankly, what is a staggering rate.'

'Yeah, London's certainly changing.'

'And, to be honest with you, I'm not entirely sure it's for the best.'

'How do you mean?' asked Frank, surprised at Casper's candour.

Casper became reflective. 'You know, when I was a boy, I played Monopoly with my father – he always won; he couldn't stand losing – buying and selling bits of London. That was just a game. Now I do it for real. But I sometimes think that it still feels like a game. Of course, it's not. All of this foreign investment is changing the very nature of London. Ordinary people who just want a home can't afford to buy one. I have to say, I don't think this is a good thing. London is becoming a giant casino. And I have to admit that I'm one of those responsible for it.'

'I suppose it's all about supply and demand, isn't it?'

'It is, of course ... but ... Frank, I've been in the business all my life. My father set it up – he used to joke that the first words he ever spoke were profit and loss. When I was a small boy, I didn't play with those colourful bricks, like most children. Do you know what I played with?'

'No,' said Frank.

'Piles of pennies. I had to stack them as high as I could. Needless to say, they soon toppled over.' Casper smiled at the memory. 'And do you know where my father took me for my seventh birthday?'

'Go on.'

'The Bank of England Museum. I can remember being fascinated by all those old banknotes, all those documents, brass inkwells, typewriters. That was probably when I got hooked on making money. I wanted to go to university after leaving school, but my father said to me, "My boy, don't waste time on more education when there are much more important things to do. It's money that makes the world go around." I can still see him now.'

'Yeah, money's what keeps us all going.'

'I suppose so, but as I think I told you at the Gussmann exhibition, it's cooking that I really love. That's why I'm interested in this restaurant idea of yours.'

The Fillet of Fish was situated alongside North Dock. It was a bright, spacious restaurant with fishing nets and lobster baskets hanging above the open kitchen in the centre. Watercolours of marine life and fishing scenes decorated the white walls. At the far end was a bar shaped like a boat.

The manager greeted them at the door, clearly startled at the sight of Frank, and, backing away obsequiously, led them over to a table by one of the large windows.

'I come here whenever I can. You've got to taste the fish! It's superb,' said Casper. 'And it's all line-caught or farmed, and most of the shellfish are hand-gathered.'

Frank glanced down at the menu. Its range of fish and seafood was extensive, everything from Scottish langoustines and whelks to wild halibut and swordfish.

'Looks good,' he said approvingly.

A dreamy-looking waitress appeared and took their drinks order. A red wine for Casper; a beer for Frank.

Like an enthusiastic schoolboy, Casper bombarded Frank with questions. How do you prevent yourself from crying when you chop an onion? How do you stop pasta sticking to the bottom of a saucepan? Was it true the stalks of coriander contained the most flavour? What do you do if you're making mayonnaise and it splits? How do you prevent breadcrumbs from coming off? How do you make sure your garlic doesn't burn? Wooden spatula or stainless steel? Should you pod or not pod broad beans? Frank answered the questions patiently, but what he really wanted to talk about was his plans for the restaurant and whether Casper would finance it.

The same waitress reappeared and asked them if they were ready to order. 'Mm ... It's always so hard to know what to go for,' said Casper, speaking more to himself than to the waitress. She stood there, forcing a smile as he ran a finger up and down the menu. In the end, he opted for the grilled skate wing with veg of the day and a tartare sauce. Frank chose smoked haddock with a poached egg and anchovy sauce.

At last Frank seized his chance and explained his big idea. Casper listened intently. From time to time he arched his eyebrows, let out an exclamation, or gave a look of astonishment. 'Goodness me!' When Frank had finished, he let out a chuckle and said, 'I have to say, Frank, if someone else had put this idea to me, quite frankly, I'd have thought they were bonkers. But when you are the man behind the menu, then it's a different matter.'

Frank smiled. 'Nothing like it has ever been done before.'

'It's such an original idea. Amazing! You know, it reminds me a bit of Ferran Adrià. Did you ever eat at his place?'

Frank shook his head with regret.

'Frank, it was an extraordinary experience. All those unusual ingredients and all that science behind it. You know, spherification and foam and things.'

'Yeah, they called it Spanish nouvelle cuisine.'

'You know, a thought struck me recently. It's as if restaurants have become the new churches. When I went to El Bulli, it felt like I was on a pilgrimage.'

Frank looked at him with curiosity. 'Don't get you.'

Casper leaned back in his chair and spread his hands.

'No? Well, let me explain. Both use the word "service" to describe what happens. Both have a table, candles, wine, water, and bread, with waiters hovering around tables like altar servers do around an altar. Just as religion has its rituals, so do restaurants. And both follow a script: a menu in a restaurant; the order of service in a church. If you're Catholic, you believe the priest turns bread and wine into the body and blood of Christ, as it were. Or you're supposed to believe. In a restaurant, a chef turns some ingredients into a meal. One is supposed to nourish the soul, the other the body. Fascinating, isn't it?'

Frank laughed. 'Yeah. I'd never looked at it like that. I mean, I'm not really religious.'

'Nor me any more. I was an altar boy when I was a child. Typical Catholic upbringing. Priests and nuns and all that kind of thing. But I stopped going to church in my teens. Couldn't see the point of it, I suppose. But you know a lot of it stays with you. Did you know that the word restaurant comes from the French verb meaning to restore?'

'No.'

'Makes sense, doesn't it. I like to think restaurants – good ones anyway – restore the soul as well as the body. At one time, this was supposed to be the job of churches. Not now. Most of the churches are half empty on a Sunday.' There was a hint of regret in this last sentence. 'But go to many restaurants or gastropubs and they're full. The world has changed.'

'Yeah,' said Frank, thinking that his places too were usually full, but his company was still losing money.

'What you're planning to do sounds like something similar to Adrià.'

'I mean, you've got to be innovative now as a chef,' said Frank, absent-mindedly fiddling with his watch strap.

'Would you plan to replicate the model elsewhere?'

Frank nodded. 'I could see it working in Bristol, Manchester, places like that.'

'So it's got scalability is what you're saying?'

'People want novelty when it comes to food. They want an experience. Restaurants are like theatres now. That's why the chef's tables at my places are nearly always booked up.' He gestured over his shoulder. 'It's why they put the kitchen at the centre here.'

'Mm. Tell me, have you found a site?'

Frank took a long sip of his beer. 'A former pub in Marylebone.'

'Marylebone's a hot area right now, isn't it? Lots of big names have opened up restaurants there. Johnny John, Nick Nasr, the Candy brothers, you name it. Tell me, what's the lease?'

'Ten years. The site's perfect. I'm planning on a 90-seater.'

'And what average spend are you looking at?'

'Between a hundred and a hundred and eighty.'

Casper rubbed his chin thoughtfully and smiled. 'Mm. I can already hear the tills ringing and the card machines whirring. Shall we talk numbers, then?'

Frank took out a pen from his jacket pocket, picked up a paper napkin, and began scribbling down the costs. He then scribbled some more numbers and gave Casper his sales projections: £110,000 per week.

'Impressive,' said Casper.

'The other thing is, I want it to open in four months,' said Frank, trying not to appear too keen.

Casper looked surprised. 'That soon?'

'Yeah. It's all about seizing the moment. I've never believed in hanging about.'

'What sort of advertising are you planning to do?'

'None.'

'None?'

'No. Bad restaurants advertise. Good restaurants get talked about.'

'Very good. I like that. Well, Frank, with your record, I can see this working.'

'You reckon?'

'You've built up successful restaurants and you have a strong brand. You're as safe a bet as they come.'

When Casper said this, Frank could feel himself churning inside, but he managed to put on a confident look. 'Everyone knows Frank,' he said with a smile.

'Indeed. I like your idea, Frank, and importantly I like you. And I trust you.'

'I'm a hundred per cent,' said Frank, shame washing over him.

'I've read all your books and I think I've seen every TV programme you've made – most of them several times ... This is terrible, isn't it? I'm beginning to sound like a fan.'

Frank waved his hands. 'Oh, don't worry.'

'Your idea excites me. And that's important. It's exactly the kind of thing I could invest in.'

'Yeah?'

Casper drummed his fingers on the table. 'So here's the proposal. Tell me how this sounds? We set up a separate limited company. I'll provide the investment, but with monthly repayments with interest. How about 4.5 per cent?'

'I'm happy with that,' said Frank, relief flooding through him.

'But I want a 15 per cent stake in the business.'

Frank paused to make it appear that he was giving this condition serious consideration. 'Okay. I can live with that.'

'Excellent! Have you thought about a designer?'

'Er, not really, but, you know, I've a couple of people in mind.'

'Can I suggest that we invite B.O. to design it?'

'Gussmann?'

'Now, Frank, I know that you're not that keen on his kind of thing, but, trust me, he will come up with something that will get people talking.'

Frank was thrown by Casper's idea. B.O. Gussmann! What a load of crap. There was no way he was going to have anything to do with that arsehole. With an effort, he replied, 'Okay, I was a bit negative about him, but he's obviously talented. Yeah, it would be good to get him on board.'

'That's agreed, then. I'll get in touch with him.'

Casper pushed his plate to one side and ran his tongue around his lips. 'That was good, I have to say. Do you think so?'

'Yeah, not bad,' said Frank.

Casper raised his eyebrows. 'Oh. Only not bad?'

'My haddock was slightly overcooked.'

'Was it?' said Casper, wiping his mouth with his napkin. 'That's a shame.'

'Yeah, and the sauce was so-so.' In fact, Frank thought the fish was excellent, but he wasn't going to say that. That would put him on the same level as Casper. He needed to demonstrate his superior knowledge, the knowledge you can only gain working in a professional kitchen.

'I see. I can't argue with you. Making food is your game. Making money is mine.'

They shook hands outside the restaurant and agreed to meet again the following week with their respective lawyers to sign the lease and complete all the other legal documentation.

Frank walked back to the underground car park, still thinking about Casper deciding B.O. Gussmann should design the restaurant. That slightly dampened his upbeat mood. Yet Gussmann had a big following, so there would be loads of publicity. The restaurant might even become a destination for art lovers. Actually, he reflected, it was a masterstroke by Casper. Bloody brilliant.

12

'Oh! Good effort, Little Man!' yelled Frank, rocking backwards on his heels and clapping his hands as the ball smacked into the wall.

He was standing with Annalisa and the other parents on the side of a sports hall hired for James' football birthday party, watching fourteen small boys in an assortment of kits – Barcelona, Manchester City, Chelsea – tearing about excitedly, their shrieks echoing around the hall.

Frank was still thinking about his visit the previous day to the site of his new restaurant. The opening night was only a week away. As he had stood there in his hard hat and high-vis jacket, surrounded by dust, rubble, and the sounds of hammering and drilling, for the first time he could see his idea really taking shape. There had been occasions over the previous weeks when he had been frustrated at not being able to talk to Gussmann face to face. Each time Frank had asked for a meeting with the artist, he had been informed by his PA that he was either in another country or on a retreat. Yet Gussmann and his team were doing a fantastic job and, what's more, they were on schedule.

After an hour, Annalisa brought the game to an end and all the children trooped into the dining hall for the party meal.

Annalisa had decorated one end of the dining room with coloured balloons and a banner with James's name written on it. Still excited from playing football, the children sat down to slices of pizza, salad, and cups of fresh orange juice.

'I thought you were going to order chicken and fries, what James asked for,' said Frank.

Annalisa pulled a face. 'I know, but I thought vegetarian would be healthier. So I ordered pizzas – they're gluten free.'

'Why, are they all allergic to gluten, then?' said Frank sarcastically.

'It's better for them.'

'Who said?'

'Well, it is.'

Conscious of other parents standing nearby, Frank lowered his voice. 'But he said he wanted chicken.'

'He likes pizza.'

'That's not the point. We told him he was having chicken.'

'Oh, Frank, stop making such a big deal.'

'I'm not making a big deal. And they won't eat bloody salad,' said Frank, trying to stay calm.

'How do you know?'

Katarina and her partner Fawad came over. Frank didn't particularly like either of them. He found Katarina irritating because she was one of those people who always seemed to have a smile on her face, even if she was talking about something serious. This meant it was impossible to tell if she was being sincere or not. And everything was always 'amazing', 'incredible' or 'super super'. And she always wore these ridiculous coloured ribbons in her hair, like a bloody schoolgirl. Her only saving grace was that she had a great pair of tits. Christ! They were like bloody nuclear warheads.

Fawad was one of those arrogant and condescending former public school boys. He came from a wealthy Pakistani family who ran a chain of pharmacies in North London. Frank had never understood what Fawad did for a living. All he knew was that it was something to do with communication technology and involved him flying off to some country or other all the time for meetings with politicians. Frank found him a shifty character and wondered, as Nick had suggested, if indeed he was involved in those shady deals in the Middle East or somewhere that sometimes got exposed in newspapers.

'It's all super super amazing!' gushed Katarina, glancing around.

'They seem to be enjoying it, don't they?' said Annalisa.

'And it's so great that it's all vegetarian.'

'It's better for them, isn't it?'

'By the way, I brought some vegan biscuits. I put them on the table with the drinks.'

'That's sweet of you. You shouldn't have done.'

'If they don't eat them, can I have them back?'

'Er, of course.'

Katarina edged closer to Annalisa. 'Listen, did I tell you about my new job?'

'What?'

'She's going to be a pet therapist,' cut in Fawad.

'Wow! You mean you use pets to help people who are ill and things?' said Annalisa.

'No. I'm going to provide therapy to pets. You know, most people don't have any idea about depression and pets. They see a cat or a dog and they think it's okay. What they don't realise is that pets have feelings, just like us.'

Frank struggled not to laugh.

'That never occurred to me,' said Annalisa thoughtfully, 'but it makes sense.'

'So, Frank, any new projects on the cards?' asked Fawad.

'He's opening a new restaurant,' said Annalisa.

'That's right,' said Frank.

'Another one? Good man.'

Frank hated the patronising way Fawad always spoke to him.

'It's top secret, though,' mocked Annalisa.

'Maybe it's going to be vegan,' said Katarina.

'You must be kidding,' retorted Frank.

'Don't say that,' said Fawad. 'What you should understand is that veganism's growing fast. People are realising they don't have to cause suffering to innocent animals to survive.'

'Haven't you heard of the Vegan Mary?' said Katarina. 'She's so, so amazing.'

'Yes, you were telling me about her,' said Annalisa. 'Didn't she get vegan-only loos and vegan-friendly zones introduced in Florida?'

Katarina nodded vigorously. 'California. She's an incredible visionary – in fact, I'd call her a revolutionary. Did you know that she only eats plants and nuts and lives in a shed in the woods? Isn't that so cool?'

'And I heard she sleeps on a wooden board,' said Annalisa.

'Yes, it's absolutely true. In years to come people will be talking about her like they talk about Gandhi or Martin Luther King.'

Frank gave a snort.

'Just you see,' insisted Katarina.

'Yeah, well, I'm not into veganism,' said Frank with irritation.

'You know what they say, Frank?' said Fawad.

'What?'

'You are what you eat.'

Frank laughed sarcastically. 'So if you eat a cucumber, does that mean you're a cucumber? Course not. What a load of rubbish!'

'I didn't mean –'

'Listen, I get being a vegetarian, but I don't get the whole vegan thing. I think it's all bullshit.'

'It's about the rights of animals and our responsibility towards the planet,' said Katarina in a self-righteous voice.

'Look, the fact is most people like meat,' said Frank, feeling his anger rising. 'And that's the way it's always been. You don't know what you're missing, Katarina.'

'I know exactly what I'm missing. You forget that I used to eat meat.'

Frank couldn't resist waving his hands in the air. 'So you've seen the light. Alleluia!'

'Animals have a right to life,' said Katarina, her eyes narrowing.

'So do babies.'

'What do you mean?'

'Well, if you're so concerned about life, why aren't you protesting about abortion? Don't babies in the womb have a right to life?'

'Frank! You can't say that,' said Annalisa.

'That's not the point,' snapped Katarina.

'You see, I think this whole vegan thing's all about trying to be morally superior.'

Katarina screwed up her face as if in pain. 'Your problem, Frank, is that you don't believe animals have rights.'

'And your problem, Katarina, is you're more concerned about a bloody cow being killed than a baby being killed.'

Katarina scowled at him. 'I'm concerned about saving the lives of innocent animals. Our planet's not just for humans.'

Just then, James appeared. 'You said I could have chicken and fries.'

Annalisa crouched down and stroked his hair. 'Yes, but I thought you might like pizza.'

'I want chicken,' he complained.

'Well, you've got pizza,' said Annalisa sharply.

'That's not fair!'

Annalisa gently pushed him in the direction of his friends. 'James, listen, just go and enjoy your lovely pizza.'

Frank looked on, feeling vindicated. Well done, Little Man, he thought. There's nothing wrong with chicken and fries. He resisted the temptation to say to Annalisa, I told you so.

13

2006, Covent Garden

It was a balmy summer evening and the Fox and Rabbit in Covent Garden was packed with the usual boisterous Friday crowd, mostly office and shop workers. It was so noisy that everyone was talking at the tops of their voices, and so dark that the rows of bottles behind the bar glinted like fairground lights. The lyrics of U2's 'I Still Haven't Found What I'm Looking For' reverberated around the pub. Frank, wearing black jeans, a white T-shirt, and a leather jacket, his eyes closed as if in ecstasy, waved the microphone in the air and did a little jig, his head furiously bobbing up and down to the rawness of the pumping music. He could feel the sweat on his forehead. His heart was racing. He didn't need to look at the words on the screen of the karaoke machine. He knew them by heart.

Frank had gone to the pub with Nick Nasr, who had been working with him in the cramped kitchen of a pleasure cruiser sailing up and down the Thames. He had been asked to cook a five-course meal for seventy people attending a birthday party for an airline executive. After spending ten hours cooped up in a hot kitchen, Frank wanted some fun. 'When you've spent hours in the steam, you need to let off steam,' he often told his brigade. So after the boat docked at Charing Cross Pier, Frank and Nick, both carrying holdalls containing their chef's whites, headed straight up Villiers Street and on to Covent Garden.

When Frank had finished the song, he stood there triumphantly, grinning and punching the air, as applause and whoops rang out from around the pub.

'Fucking brilliant, man,' said Nick as Frank came back to the bar. 'You should have been a rock star.'

Frank picked up his pint. 'You know what, I'm going to be a rock star – of the kitchen.'

Nick laughed as he lit a cigarette. 'So cooking's the new rock'n'roll, is it?'

'Didn't you know?'

The two of them stood there sipping their drinks, while sneaking glances over the tops of their glasses at the women around them and wondering who they might be in with a chance with. Frank gently elbowed Nick in the ribs. 'Target, target! Those two standing by the pillar?'

'You mean the dark-haired one in the tight jeans and the blonde with big tits?'

'Worth a shot?'

Nick drew deeply on his cigarette, squeezing his eyes half-shut. 'Reckon so. Mine's the blonde.'

'What a surprise.'

'Hey, you know me, man.'

'Listen, no cheesy chat-up lines.'

'What, you mean like, is there an airport nearby or is that my heart taking off?'

'That's one of your milder ones.'

'So I can't say I'm afraid of the dark, will you sleep with me tonight?'

Frank rolled his eyes. 'I don't know how you come up with them.'

The two of them picked up their holdalls and edged through the crowd, holding their drinks in the air, and casually stood a couple of feet away from the two women, who were deep in conversation in between sipping cocktails with small umbrellas on top. Frank liked the auburn-haired woman even more now he had a better view of her. She had a good figure, alert eyes, and not too much make-up. He nodded to Nick. When they were out on the pull, Nick was always the one who made the first move. Frank likened him to an opening batsman and himself to a number three.

Nick leaned towards the women and said something, looking back over his shoulder at Frank. The pub was too noisy for Frank to hear what it was.

The women both looked at Frank with curious expressions and then back at Nick. Nick motioned to Frank to come over.

'Hi, I'm Frank,' he said.

'I'm Caroline,' said the blonde.

The auburn-haired woman smiled at him. 'Annalisa.'

The four of them exchanged the usual biographical information the dating game required, each doing their best to make themselves sound more interesting and likeable than they perhaps really were. Caroline and Annalisa worked for the same recruitment company in Holborn and were both looking to find a new job. Caroline shared a flat in Harrow and Annalisa shared a flat in Shepherd's Bush. Caroline had grown up in Oxfordshire and Annalisa in Hertfordshire.

The two women giggled as Nick launched into his war stories from the kitchen, occasionally miming actions. Because he told the same stories to every woman he met for the first time, he was as polished as a stand-up comedian. A man's job is to entertain and a woman's job is to look good, Nick often told Frank. With Nick on top form, Frank was happy to take a back seat and let him do all the foundation work, but occasionally, so as not to appear dull, he chipped in with a one-liner, all the while trying to lock eyes with Annalisa.

Nick hit it off with Caroline and at the end of the evening he announced they were going to a jazz club in Stoke Newington. Frank and Annalisa hadn't wanted to go, so when they came out of the pub they found themselves heading in the direction of Covent Garden Tube station.

'Fancy a walk?' ventured Frank, doing his best to appear casual. He had no intention of trying to get Annalisa into bed. There was something about her that would make this seem wrong. He knew that would be where Nick was planning his evening with Caroline to end up. This thought made him feel virtuous, not something he was used to feeling.

'Why not,' said Annalisa. 'It's a lovely evening.'

Frank led her towards the Strand and then down past St Mary-le-Strand church into Fleet Street, which was empty apart from occasional purring black cabs or squeaking night buses. They passed the Royal Courts of Justice and then wandered through the dark, narrow lanes of the Inns of Court in the

Temple area, with Frank making fun of some of the posh-sounding names of the barristers on the brass plaques, and down to the bank of the Thames. They stood in silence for a while looking at the coloured reflections of the buildings twinkling on the water, as late-night trains rumbled out of Charing Cross station and across the bridge.

'Tell me something,' said Frank.

'What?'

'What did Nick say to you and your mate when he came over in the pub?'

'He said you were a vicar who was pretending to be a chef.'

Frank roared with laughter. 'A vicar! Me? Typical Nick.'

'I did wonder if it was true. I mean, you don't usually see a vicar in jeans and a leather jacket trying to sing a U2 song.'

'Hey, what do you mean trying?' said Frank, playfully.

Annalisa grinned. 'All I'd say is, don't give up your day job.'

'Thanks very much.'

They walked on to St Paul's Cathedral, where they stood on the steps gazing up at it and marvelling at its size, and then continued through silent streets lined with imposing but cheerless buildings containing banks, insurance companies, and other financial institutions. Eventually they ended up in the Barbican, where they got briefly lost along the concrete walkways. Neither of them noticed how late it was.

Along Farringdon Road, they came across an elderly woman sitting in the doorway of an electrical shop. She had a blanket draped over her and her toes were peeping through the holes in her shoes. Next to her stood a supermarket shopping trolley piled with different-coloured plastic bags and a teddy bear attached to the handle. Frank stopped and bent down, pressing a five-pound note into her hand. 'Go and get yourself something to eat,' he said. The woman looked up with surprise and mumbled a thank you.

'That was kind of you,' said Annalisa as they walked off. 'See, Reverend Frank.'

Frank smiled. 'Yeah, well, you've got to help others, haven't you,' he said, pleased that his act of generosity had impressed Annalisa.

'It's a scary thought, isn't it? I mean, living on the streets. I can't imagine it. She must have had a home at some point.'

'Yeah, guess so. There's no way I'll ever end up in that situation.'

'You sound very certain.'

'I am. I know what I want.'

'And what's that?'

'To run my own restaurant and become the best chef in the country. No. The world.'

'You're ambitious, aren't you?'

'Life's about aiming high. You know what they say. Two men looked out of the prison bars; one saw mud, one saw stars.'

'So you want to be rich? Is that it?'

'Doesn't everyone? If you're rich, you'll never end up like that woman.'

'But money's not everything.'

'Yeah, but it determines the kind of life you'll have. You have choices when you have money. If you're poor, what choices do you have? Bugger all. The people who tell you money doesn't matter are always the people who have lots of it.'

'I've never wanted to be rich. Not like a millionaire or anything. I just want a nice life. You know, a house, a garden, the usual. Not to have to worry about bills and all that. Maybe I'd like to live on a farm one day.' She let out a little sigh. 'A simple life for a simple girl.'

'Life's never simple,' said Frank, sagely.

'I know.'

As dawn broke, London started to wake up. Delivery vans dropped bundles of newspapers tied with string outside shops, empty buses and articulated lorries passed by, and dustcarts groaned as they angrily digested the rubbish of the previous day.

Frank took Annalisa to a pub he knew near Smithfield Market, where, surrounded by loud market porters in blood-streaked white coats, they tucked into plates of bacon, eggs, sausage, tomatoes, and mushrooms.

'I can't remember when I last had a proper English breakfast,' said Annalisa, slicing into the bacon.

'Good, isn't it,' said Frank.

'Mm ... It's delicious.'

'I wondered if you might be vegetarian or something.'

'Me? God, no.'

'Guess what?' said Frank, buttering a slice of toast.

'What?'

'I'm going to be on TV. My own show.'

Annalisa leaned across the table, her mouth wide open. 'Wow! Really?'

'Yeah. I met this producer at the BBC and I'm going to film some programmes in France. You know, look at French food and talk to chefs and other people. It's sort of part travel and part cookery.'

'So you're going to be famous.'

Frank shook his head firmly. 'I'm just a chef. I've always fancied doing some TV, though.'

Annalisa threw her head back and laughed. 'I can say to people, you know, that chef on TV ... I knew him before he was a star.'

Frank smiled broadly. 'What about you, then? I mean, career.'

'Oh, I thought about becoming an interior designer when I was at school. I've always loved textiles and things. Anyway, in the end I didn't think it was for me.'

'Still could be, you know. Don't give up on your dreams – they're all you've got.'

Annalisa giggled. 'I've heard that one before. Anyway, have you always wanted to be a chef?'

Frank pushed his plate away and dabbed his lips with a paper napkin. 'Yeah, although when I was young I liked the idea of being a racing driver. My dad bought me a Scalextric set and I'd play with it for hours. But I loved cooking – I helped my dad in the bistro he ran. I reckon some people are destined for certain things and I was destined to be a chef. You know what they say: if you have a passion, you'll never work a day in your life.'

'I haven't heard that one before. You'll have to give me some cookery lessons.'

'You like cooking?'

'Well, I'm not very good, but I enjoy it – my mum could cook anything.'

'You can't beat home cooking.'

'The problem is, in the flat there's three of us and the kitchen's quite small. But if I'm in and the other two are out, I'll sometimes cook something. You know, a Bolognese or a chicken curry, that kind of thing. Nothing fancy. It's more fun cooking when you have someone coming around.'

'Tell you what, you cook me a meal one evening and then you come to my place and I'll show you some of the basics.'

Annalisa studied him for a moment and then said, 'Okay, you're on.'

'What about sometime next week?' asked Frank, trying not to appear too keen.

'I'm busy then. Alan will be staying with me.'

'Alan?' What, she already had a boyfriend! Bloody hell. This had never occurred to him. He felt deflated and a fool.

'My brother.'

'Oh, I see.' Relief. 'The following week. Monday?'

'I'm meeting a friend to go to the cinema.'

'Tuesday?'

'I've a Portuguese class then.'

'Portuguese?'

'My dad's from Portugal. I can speak it a little, but I want to be more fluent.'

'Wednesday, then?' Now he was beginning to sound desperate. He was supposed to be working that evening at the Burning Bush, but he figured Nick would be able to cope without him. Wednesdays weren't usually that busy.

'Sounds as if it might be okay. Let me check my diary when I get home.'

Frank shot her a mischievous look. 'That means you'll have to give me your phone number.'

Annalisa grinned back at him. 'I think I can trust you.'

'Course you can. I'm Reverend Frank.'

14

2015, Marylebone

Frank, wearing a white linen suit with a red handkerchief in the breast pocket, stood in the quiet Marylebone street in sparkling June sunshine and admired the frontage of his new restaurant. The white walls, the smoked glass windows, the hanging sign above the entrance with Concept F written in small white letters on a black background, the heavy wooden door and the shrubs either side of it. It looked unassuming, contemporary and intriguing. It was perfect.

He had to admit that B.O. Gussmann and his team had done a fantastic job in transforming the former pub, and in only a little over four months. Frank had emailed him a sketch of the restaurant and detailed notes. Gussmann had brought in a software development company, a sensory experience consultant, a costume designer, an interior designer, a lighting specialist, a video wall company, a photographer, and a horticulturist.

As he stood outside the restaurant – his restaurant – Frank felt a warm glow inside. Life was good. He had not only created a unique restaurant, but he had the new TV show in the pipeline and, after a meeting yesterday with his publisher, Butler & Sutton, his editor had offered him a very generous deal for three more cookery books, which would form a mini-series called *Frank Knows*. The first would be about meat, the second fish and the third vegetables. The editor admitted that, true, the books might recycle some of Frank's earlier material, but probably no one would notice. Frank wasn't going to argue about that. What's more, he wouldn't have to do much writing, as he would be assigned a ghostwriter.

It felt like he had the golden touch. He found it hard to remember those days when, as a young chef, he'd struggled to pay his rent some months. A local paper had even included his name in a long list of people the council intended to prosecute for council tax arrears. He laughed to himself at the memory, remembering how he had proudly taken the paper to the pub and waved it around in front of some mates. It was his first taste of fame.

He went back inside, and, as he gazed admiringly around the interior of Concept F, he congratulated himself. The specially invited guests – food critics and bloggers, friends, celebrities, key people in the hospitality business – would be coming through the doors in the next hour. Zoot and his team at Sticky Lettuce had been busy creating a buzz on social media through what were known as influencers and disrupters. The restaurant was fully booked for the first five weeks. Everyone would surely agree that they had never been to a restaurant like it before, and they would all leave at the end of the evening saying how imaginative he was, how brilliant, how groundbreaking.

Eight hundred small green, yellow, orange, and red lights made in the shape of vegetables were suspended from the ceiling. From speakers positioned in each corner came the sound of the sea roaring and seagulls squawking, which then became birds chirping, and then sheep bleating. Around the walls, video screens showed cows grazing in fields; a wild ocean; close-ups of crabs on a beach and onions, carrots and herbs growing on a farm; mountains; a forest; an orchard; and a vineyard. Several olive trees had been planted inside the restaurant.

The tables were old wooden school desks with inkwells, and the seats were those small plastic chairs used by nurseries and schools. Between them drifted the front of house team, all drama students or out-of-work actors, all young and attractive, all dressed as either fishers, farmers, shepherds, or bakers.

Nodding to one or two of the prettiest, Frank passed through to the kitchen, which was painted in immaculate white. There, under bright striplights, a chef and three cooks were working in silence. But there was no sizzling, boiling, banging, or clattering. That was because were no stoves, fryers, grills, vats, pots or pans. And there was no food to be seen anywhere.

It was perfect.

Satisfied, Frank strolled over to where the chef and his cooks – all, like Frank, dressed in white suits – were standing at the long stainless steel work surface filling small silver canisters with aromas. The canisters were attached by Perspex tubes to large glass containers. At one end of the kitchen, a large flat screen hung from the ceiling, showing the layout of the restaurant with an icon identifying each table. Below it on a table was an iPad, which the chefs would tap when a dish was ready to go out.

"All right, lads," said Frank, and picked up one of the silver canisters. It wouldn't hurt to do one last run-through with the front of house staff before Zero Hour.

Back amongst the tables, he clapped his hands repeatedly. 'Okay, everyone! This is it. Rock'n'roll time,' he announced, like a football manager giving a pep talk at half time. 'Gather round.'

His young staff looked up from their study of the computer screens that were built into each place setting. The screens, which came with headphones attached, showed a menu of fifteen items, which included stewed jellyfish with samphire puree, roasted pumpkin topped with corn and kimchi, deep-fried duck with beetroot and rocket, egg and goats' cheese candyfloss, poached Jerusalem artichoke with three-way oranges. An icon illustrated each dish, with prices starting at £25. At the top of the menu was a quote from Professor Bumgarner: 'If you have the four senses of sight, touch, smell and sound present, then, as if by magic, you also have taste.'

The drinks menu operated the same way. When a diner tapped the icon for the drink of their choice, a photo of it would appear, but, of course, no drink would materialise.

There were also icons that listed any allergens in dishes – the list ran to twenty-one – and how many calories each dish contained. At the end of the meal, diners could write a review on the computer screen and post it on the internet.

'Remember who the most important person is tonight,' Frank announced to his team. 'The customer. And we're going to do something tonight no one in the history of cooking has ever done. You're going to remember this evening for the rest of your lives. So you all know what you're doing?'

Yes, each of them said, if a little unconvincingly.

'Once a diner has placed an order, your job is to deliver the visualiser,' he said, picking up a small circular computer from a nearby table. The visualiser would show a high-definition image of the dish of the diner's choice. 'And don't forget the canister, which will contain the aromas. The cap of the canister needs to be carefully unscrewed and placed on the table.' He demonstrated. 'Then you give the diner their headset. They put it on, and you need to make sure the right set of sounds are piped in from the kitchen. Tell them to stare at the image on the visualiser, which will get smaller and smaller until it disappears.

'Now, I want you to watch this film,' said Frank, signalling to one of the team to press a remote.

On one of the wall screens, an image of Canada geese flying gracefully through the sky appeared. Frank let it run for a minute and then nodded to the team member with the remote to pause it.

'So, who wants to tell me what the geese are doing?' he asked, scanning their faces.

The team stood there, fidgeting, everyone waiting for someone else to speak up. Finally, a guy dressed as a shepherd said, 'Flying?'

'Flying. Yeah. But what else? What kind of noise are they making?'

'Er, honking, I suppose,' ventured a young woman dressed as a baker.

'Honking. I like that. Yeah, the geese are honking. Now what I want you all to do is honk and flap your arms at the same time.'

No one moved.

Frank repeated his instructions, this time more sharply. So each member of the team began to half-heartedly honk and flap their arms.

'I can hear you honking, but it doesn't sound quite right,' said Frank, frowning. 'Do it again and flap your arms more. Do it faster! Go on, imagine you're one of those geese!'

The team did more honking and flapping, and a couple of them began to giggle.

'Okay, that will do. I can see that you all found this embarrassing. This was the purpose of the exercise. I want to get you to experience what it's like to be out of your comfort zone. Because this is what will happen tonight. So

I want you all to honk – to signal to each other when you need to – and I want you all to flap, to move around the tables with energy. Got that?'

Yes, they all murmured.

'And remember your service needs to be attentive but not be noticeable,' said Frank, studying the face of each one of them closely.

'Er, I've got a question,' said a woman dressed as a farmer.

'Go on,' said Frank.

'I mean, what if some of the customers complain?'

'What about?'

'You know, not having food and all that.'

'Yeah, I was thinking the same,' said a guy in a fisher's costume.

'Look, the kind of people who are coming here tonight are expecting an experience, not Kentucky Fried Chicken. They don't go to a restaurant to fill up; they go for … the theatre of it. You got that?'

Lots of nods and murmurs.

Happy that they had understood his big idea, Frank dismissed them with the wave of a hand. As they scattered, he pursed his lips and glanced anxiously at his watch and then at the doors.

Frank struggled to contain his excitement. He couldn't wait to see the faces of the guests when they discovered this unique dining experience he had created. What an amazing idea, to open a restaurant that didn't serve actual food but still allowed you to experience it. You could eat as much as you wanted and never put on even an extra ounce. This was healthy eating and gourmet dining combined. Sheer genius. How on earth did he think of that?

He had wanted Terry to come, offering to provide a taxi to pick him and Jill up and take them back to the care home. But Terry had complained that the journey to central London would be too long. Frank had struggled to hide his disappointment, wondering yet again why his father showed little enthusiasm for his career.

But it was no use dwelling on his father; better to focus on what mattered. If Concept F was going to be a success, and Frank was going to be in with a chance of winning the Golden Pan award, then he had to win over London's food critics and bloggers, who acted as judge and jury with restaurants. They were never satisfied with existing restaurants, no matter how good they already were. They always wanted something new, something different, and the more adventurous or outrageous it was the better. Frank disliked the critics for their self-importance, and he thought most of the bloggers had little talent and were just out to try and make a name – and money – for themselves on the foodie gravy train. The ones he disliked the most were those that Instagrammed their meals. He still couldn't understand why they thought anyone would be interested in looking at photos of every dish someone else had eaten in a restaurant. Some of the bloggers published so many photos of a meal that they must have spent more time fiddling around with their phone than actually eating.

As Frank inspected each table to make sure it was set up properly, Casper arrived with his wife, a distinguished-looking woman in a rose pink suit who was several inches taller than him. He introduced her as Dolores.

'So, Frank, are we all set?' asked Casper, his eyes sweeping around the restaurant.

'Yeah, ready for take-off,' said Frank.

'Well, I have to say it looks absolutely fantastic,' purred Casper. 'I told you B.O. would do a great job.'

'Yeah, but the funny thing is, though, I never once met him. I had to deal with his PA or someone in his team.'

'It's the same with me. I've never met him either.'

'No?' Frank was surprised, given the way Casper had spoken about him at the art exhibition in Dombey-on-Sea.

'I'm afraid not. As I often say, he's a mystery man is our B.O.'

Dolores chuckled. 'I've said to Casper: does he even exist?'

Half an hour later, excitable chatter and shrieks of laughter reverberated around the restaurant. One famous food critic seemed to be particularly enjoying herself, Frank noticed. From her infectious high-pitched shrieks, she seemed to find the canisters a great source of amusement. Frank took all this as a good sign. A food blogger, a loud young woman with reptilian eyes and brown lipstick, who was known for taking photos even of the loos when she visited a restaurant, seemed equally delighted by the novel experience Frank had dreamed up. What must they all be thinking of him? If any of them had doubted his ingenuity, they wouldn't ever again.

He glided from table to table, distributing smiles, saying hello, and enjoying the astonished expressions on the faces of his guests as they tapped their computers and waiting staff arrived with their orders.

'Frank, I'll tell you what, mate,' said an actor famous for playing one-dimensional gangsters. 'I've eaten in some places in my time, but this one takes the biscuit – pardon my pun.'

'You like it, then?' said Frank, fishing for a compliment.

'Mate, it's bloody amazing! Computers. Bleedin' computers! How did you come up with that?'

'It's called staying ahead of the game,' said Frank, pleased with himself.

He stopped at the table where Annalisa was sitting with her friend Sarah and her husband Alex, a train driver, who Frank occasionally played squash with.

'So what do you reckon?' Frank asked.

'Oh, Frank, I don't know how you came up with this,' said Annalisa with a nervous laugh.

'It's amazing! Absolutely amazing!' said Sarah.

'That's the idea,' said Frank.

'Thing is, though, I'll be stopping off for a takeaway after,' said Alex, breaking into laughter.

'Alex!' reprimanded Sarah. 'It's super cool, like being in a theatre. And the school chairs are great. I feel like a kid again.'

Frank grinned. 'It's all about stirring childhood memories.'

'You're an entertainer, Frank,' said Alex with a flourish. 'And restaurants nowadays are about entertainment, aren't they? It's showbiz.'

'Yeah, maybe,' said Frank.

Nick Nasr had turned up with a woman Frank hadn't seen before. She was wearing an extremely short black dress. He guessed she was Italian or Spanish. It was hard to keep up with Nick's turbulent love life. Only a few weeks before, he had been dating a New Zealand woman he had met at an STD clinic where he had gone for a check-up.

Nick had also grown a thick beard and he sported a ponytail, which made him look even more roguish than he was. Frank wandered over to the table. 'You're looking at the future, Nick,' he said with a flourish.

'Yeah, man, it's something else,' said Nick, trying to sound enthusiastic.

'You like it?'

'Yeah, yeah. Very clever.'

'B.O. Gussmann designed it.'

'What, the bloke who does all that stuff with socks and that?'

Frank bridled at the dismissive way Nick spoke about Gussmann. 'I used to think he was a load of rubbish, but he's done a fantastic job. The guy's a genius!'

'It is very creative,' said the woman with Nick in a thick accent.

'Thanks,' said Frank, wondering if she was Nick's new regular or just another casual.

'Anyway, Frank, congratulations,' said Nick.

'Cheers, Nick.'

Frank carried on moving from table to table, drinking in the praise and astonishment from his guests, and beaming back. The front of house team was operating brilliantly. His talk about honking had paid off. He hadn't felt so alive and excited in ages.

Later on in the evening, when he was in the kitchen checking with the cooks that everything was running smoothly (there had been a computer problem and Frank had had to call a 24-hour emergency IT company), he looked up to see Casper standing in the doorway.

Casper stood there for a moment, as if searching for the right words, and then said, 'Frank, I really don't know what to say ... Words fail me.'

'You reckon it's gone well,' asked Frank, thinking Casper had a very intense expression on his face.

Casper came towards him and said with emotion in his voice, 'It's been an extraordinary experience! Absolutely extraordinary. I really can't ... For me it's almost been – and I know how this must sound – a sort of spiritual moment.'

'Really?' Frank was delighted by Casper's praise, although he didn't understand what he meant by spiritual. Then he remembered him talking about the parallel he saw between restaurants and church services. Was that what he was on about?

Casper nodded vigorously. 'Without a doubt. It's been incredibly powerful!' He stared dreamily into the distance. 'I could feel … I don't know what I could feel – but something. I'm almost speechless.'

'I hope everyone else feels the same way.'

Then Casper opened his arms and pulled Frank towards him. Embarrassed by this sudden display of affection, Frank found his body stiffening. He could smell Casper's fruity aftershave. He hoped Casper wasn't gay. You never knew with people nowadays.

Casper gripped his shoulder blades tightly and whispered in his ear, 'Frank?'

'Yes?' said Frank, warily.

'You have no idea what you've done. Absolutely no idea.'

15

During the following week, Frank spent more time than usual googling himself. The reaction of the food critics and bloggers to Concept F had been better than he could have dreamed of, praising him for his inventiveness and for taking food to a new level. Several hinted that a restaurant that didn't serve food might find it hard to reach a mainstream market, as, generally, diners usually liked to go to a restaurant to eat. Nevertheless, they all concluded that those who really understood food and appreciated the skills of modern chefs would be in for a fantastic/unforgettable/incredible experience, one that demonstrated London's restaurant scene was 'leading the world in creativity' and 'pushing boundaries'. Frank had done something truly astonishing by combining the sensory experience of food with science and theatre. There had even been a discussion on the BBC Radio 4 arts programme *Hidden Meanings* with an agreement among the panel members that Frank was the world's first artist-chef. He loved that. Casper had said something similar to him.

But, crucially, it wasn't just the media in the UK who had picked up the story. It had made it into magazines and newspapers in the USA, France, Spain, Italy, and many other countries. All this international coverage would impress the judges of the Golden Pan award.

Maybe a knighthood would be on the cards. Frank saw an image of himself arriving at Buckingham Palace. Tops and tails. The queen saying that she loves his books. The garden party. Annalisa would love it. She would be in her element. Arise, Sir Frank. Did the queen actually say those words? Did she hold a real sword or a pretend one? It didn't matter. Sir Frank. He loved the sound of it. Thank you, Sir Frank. Come this way, Sir Frank. And now I'd like to introduce Sir Frank. 'Cooking with Sir.' What a great title for a TV programme or book! Would that mean Annalisa would become Lady Annalisa? Or was that when you became a Lord. The House of Lords! He could end up getting a seat there. Lord Frank. Oh, that would be even better. He chuckled out loud at the thought. That would be unbelievable!

Frank usually visited each of his restaurants once a week. To keep the staff on their toes, he never announced his visits in advance. Today he was at his Shoreditch site, hunched at the desk in the back office, taking his manager, a young Romanian guy with close-cropped hair, through the new menu.

'You need to make sure that if the staff are asked about anything, they're clued up about it,' said Frank.

'Yes, Frank,' replied the manager sheepishly.

'They need to know as much about the menu as they do their boyfriend or girlfriend's bad habits. If a customer asks where the hake was caught, they don't just say, oh, in the sea.'

The manager nodded and murmured yes.

'And we need to do some more upselling on the wine. The best time to ask someone if they want another drink is just before they finish their glass or bottle. Don't wait until they ask. Don't ask what they want to drink as soon as they sit down. Give them time to look at the menu and bring them some water.'

The manager nodded again.

The restaurant in Shoreditch, like Frank's other three, was decorated in a contemporary minimalist style with lots of grey and black, large glass windows and a wooden floor. The ceiling was made of unvarnished wood from which stools hung upside down, and the walls were decorated with black and white photos of rock stars, actors, and historic newspaper front pages. The pastel chairs and tables were made from polypropylene and had Eiffel metal legs. Small pots of basil and parsley and tins of olive oil stood on top of the horseshoe bar, while rows of green, red, and blue empty wine bottles that lit up in the evening lined the wall behind.

New dishes on the menu included Cumberland pie, oysters fried in tempura batter, Italian-style grilled octopus, chicken wrapped in Parma ham, and honeycomb cheesecake topped with a scoop of dairy ice cream. More vegetarian and vegan dishes had also been added. New options for children included mini Batman burgers and 'broccoli trees with cheese snow'. To try and lure more customers through the door, Frank was introducing two-for-one deals on mains Monday to Thursday, fifty per cent off mains Friday to Sunday, and a 'squid for a quid' night on Tuesdays.

Frank continued. 'When people come to a restaurant, they expect good service – I expect excellent service. So what happened last week with that couple?'

The manager rubbed the back of his neck. 'The guy was new. He didn't know.'

'Listen, if a customer says they expected eggs benedict to be served on a muffin, not sourdough bread, you don't shrug your shoulders and tell them if they don't like it they can go to the place across the road. Christ! We might as well put a sign outside saying, if you don't like our menu, then piss off. Your job's to win customers, not bloody lose them.'

'I've spoken to him.'

'It's no wonder that couple was pissed off. I would have been. You read the review?'

'Yes, Frank.'

'Make sure all the team does. This is the hospitality business, not the in-hospitable business. Everyone who walks through that door wants to feel special. You got that?'

The manager was staring with a transfixed expression at the CCTV screen above Frank.

'You listening?'

'Er ...' He nodded at the screen.

Frank swivelled his head around and looked up. 'Christ almighty! What the ...'

He watched in astonishment that quickly turned to alarm as a group of people dressed in some sort of costumes and waving placards entered the restaurant. And behind them were, what was this? Two bloody sheep! He leapt up and stormed out of the office.

He pushed open the door to the restaurant to be greeted by the sight of a dozen people dressed as chickens, cows, and fish stomping around the petrified diners and bemused staff. 'Meat is murder! Fish have feelings!' they chanted, blowing whistles. The sheep wandered aimlessly around the tables.

'Oi!' screamed Frank at the top of his voice. 'Get the fuck out!'

The protesters ignored him and only chanted all the louder. He advanced towards them, waving his arms furiously in the air. He was pumping with rage. 'Get out of my restaurant! Get the fuck out!' he screamed again.

The protesters continued chanting. Frank lunged at a man dressed as a chicken. The man tried to grab the collar of Frank's jacket. Frank shoved him hard in the chest and sent him keeling over onto the floor. Someone dressed as a fish attempted to hit Frank with a placard, but Frank blocked him with his elbow and kicked him in the shin. The man let out a yelp and hopped back.

Frank stood there in the middle of the restaurant, panting, his eyes blazing.

A white woman with dreadlocks and a ring through her nose stepped towards Frank, jabbing her finger and shouting hysterically, 'We're the Vegan Liberation Front and we accuse you of murder!'

Cheers from the other protesters. Several had their phones out and were filming.

'I couldn't give a fuck who you are! I want you out of my restaurant!'

The woman with dreadlocks ignored Frank and moved to the middle of the restaurant. With emotion in her voice, she addressed the diners. 'Let me tell you about my little girl ... She was hurt ... Abused ... She cried ... because she was so scared ... just a little girl. She knew she was going to be killed ... to be murdered.' The woman paused dramatically.

'Piss off out!' shouted Frank, standing there helplessly.

The woman carried on, her voice becoming more and more hysterical. 'But I and some other humans rescued her ... And her name is Sophie ... You're going to remember that name ... She's a beautiful little girl ... But she misses her sisters, her friends.' The woman gave another dramatic pause, ignoring Frank's order to leave. 'Don't laugh, because their bodies are on your plates in this restaurant ... Innocent children ... who just wanted to ... live.' The woman then shouted, 'Meat is not food! Meat is violence!'

The other protesters began to chant, 'Meat is not food! Meat is violence!'

Frank stood in front of the woman and exploded again. 'Hey, don't give me all that bollocks! You fucking vegans make me sick. You think you're so bloody virtuous, don't you?'

A protester with a face that suggested he'd been shucking oysters all day clambered up onto a table and began yelling, 'Animals have feelings, too!'

'Listen, if you don't want to eat meat, don't fucking eat it. But don't try and push your fucking views down everyone else's throat. If you ask me, you should all be locked up. Fucking vegans! Coming in here upsetting my diners. Get the fucking hell out!'

'He hit me!' cried another protester.

'You're veganphobic!' shrieked the woman with dreadlocks.

Frank spotted a burger on the plate of a man with his wife and children. He grabbed it, pulled the meat out and waved it inches from the face of the woman. 'See this. It's a piece of fucking meat! And people come here to eat it. And you know what? They like it!'

The woman recoiled, letting out a gasp, and then fled towards the door. The other protesters shouted angrily and shook their fists at Frank. He laughed at them. He was enjoying himself now.

Still shouting, the protesters then rounded up the two sheep and began to file out of the restaurant, chanting as they went 'Veganphobic! Veganphobic!'

Frank gave them the two fingers, and then suddenly realised all the customers were staring at him. He switched on a smile. 'Sorry about the interruption, folks – we don't normally have entertainment. Please continue enjoying your meal. And I'll be knocking twenty-five per cent off the bill for any inconvenience.'

16

Two days later, Frank sat disconsolately at a table in the plush bar at the Gilkin Hotel in Piccadilly, waiting for Zoot. Piped piano music from a speaker tinkled optimistically in the background. It was in the middle of the afternoon and the only other customers were three Arab businessmen, all thick moustaches, dark suits and gold rings, huddled conspiratorially around a laptop in the corner. Frank glanced restlessly at his watch for the second time in a minute and took another sip of beer. He was conscious that the young barman, neatly turned out in his waistcoat, white shirt and black tie, kept sneaking glances at him while wiping glasses with a tea towel. *You'll never guess who came in today. Frank!*

A YouTube clip of Frank shouting at the vegan protesters had gone viral. It had made the TV news headlines, newspaper columnists wrote about it, and radio phone-in presenters discussed it with listeners. Everyone had an opinion on the matter, it seemed, even if they didn't know the facts. A few wisely held back from making a judgment, but most rushed in gleefully to convict Frank. One newspaper called for readers to boycott his restaurants, another his books, while a vegan MP urged Tish TV to drop him. At one time, if someone accused you of something serious, a court would decide the verdict. Nowadays, reflected Frank grimly, it felt like the media was the judge, jury, and executioner.

Frank had wondered if Katarina had had something to do with the protest. He wouldn't have put it past her. When he suggested this to Annalisa, she dismissed it, saying he had no proof and anyway he was only saying that because he didn't like Katarina. She'd shown an annoying lack of sympathy over the protest. In fact, he had a sneaking suspicion that she actually supported the action of the vegans.

A few minutes later, Zoot arrived, with Jake tagging along behind him like a lapdog. They were both talking on their mobile phones. After they had ordered a drink at the bar, they sat down with Frank.

'What a bloody mess,' said Frank with a shake of the head.

'Sure, sure, Frank, but, hey, don't worry, it's all going to be cool,' said Zoot soothingly.

'Someone sticks something on YouTube and all of a sudden I'm supposed to be veganphobic! Christ almighty!'

'The thing is, it's all about perception, not reality, right?' said Zoot.

'Don't I bloody know it.'

'Let me tell you something,' said Zoot softly. 'The internet's like the wild west. It's lawless out there. Totally. You see, everyone's pretty much a reporter or broadcaster right now. Everyone wants to be famous. They think they'll become a YouTube star and make big bucks.'

'Well, they're deluded,' said Frank bitterly.

'One hundred per cent. It's just like when the printing press came along. Or the big scientific discoveries. The industrial revolution. Hell, Hollywood even. At the moment, the internet's still just a kid.'

'Yeah, but my reputation's at risk. You need to do something, Zoot. This could become another Currygate.'

Zoot put on a well-practised empathetic expression. 'And so we've put out a statement saying you respect those who don't eat meat, fish and dairy products, and we've flagged up that your restaurants cater for everyone, including vegans. Hey, so how can Frank be veganphobic, folks?'

'Yeah, but what else you going to do?' said Frank with irritation.

Zoot nodded. 'We need to repackage the story. So we've figured out a plan.'

'The bloody story is that a bunch of nutters tried to scare the shit out of my customers! That's the story, Zoot.'

'Sure, I get you. Frank, listen, you've gotta trust me.' Zoot leaned forward across the table. 'Remember Carly Diamond, right?'

'Who's she?'

'You don't remember?'

'No.'

'Not even the Africa photos?'

'No,' repeated Frank, searching his mind for any reference to Carly Diamond.

Zoot seemed surprised. 'Let Jake fill you in. It's a hell of a story.'

So Jake recounted the story. 'Carly appeared on the TV show *Show Me Yours, Show You Mine*. Up until then, she'd been a sales assistant in a bathroom and kitchen shop. You know, just another single mum in a shithole Essex town full of takeaways. She applied to go on the show – she'd already had a boob job – and took out a loan from one of those internet companies. She saw it as an investment in her career, like money for a small business. She stormed the show. In the first episode she stripped off and joined Steve Black – the footballer – in a hot tub, and in the next one she was on all fours with Ross Diklik.'

'Ross Diklik?' Frank couldn't believe anyone could be called Ross Diklik.

'Yeah, you know, the actor who was in *Slasher* and *Bone Crusher 2*,' continued Jake. 'Anyway, the two of them got it on. The show's ratings went through the roof after that and everyone was talking about Carly. Who was this Carly? In the following episode, Steve Black's girlfriend – Danielle Tanning – came on. The viewers thought there was going to be some big showdown. It looked like it, with all that shouting and screaming. But then the four of them, Carly, Steve, Danielle and Ross, got into bed together and really went for it. I mean, it was full on.' Jake roared with laughter. 'The complete works. Then Carly's ex came on the show – with their three-year-old daughter. And, boy, things went mental. He really laid into her. Said she was a bad mum. Neglected the child. Was always out partying. Drugs. You know, the usual kind of stuff. And the viewers turned and Carly got booted off the show. That's where Sticky Lettuce got involved. We had to reinvent her, show another side to Carly. So what can we do, we thought?'

Frank was finding it hard to keep up with Jake's story. He was wondering how it related to him. What was the connection? He wasn't keen on being bracketed with some bimbo. 'So what did you do?' he asked, wanting Jake to get to the point.

'We took her to Africa,' said Jake.

'Africa?' said Frank.

'Yeah. We needed to tell a different story.'

Zoot jumped in. 'As you know, Frank, we're experts when it comes to creating an illusion, right? It's all about getting the public to see things in a different way. The way our client wants to be seen, or, as in the case of Carly, needs to be seen. Our job is to tell people what they should think. She was totally smart, given her background, but not smart enough to see what an opportunity being slated in the show presented. We figured we needed to create a new Carly.'

Ah, Frank understood now. He could see what they did. 'So you photographed her on a safari, with lions and tigers and things?' he said, feeling pleased that he'd finally got a handle on the story of Carly.

'Lions and tigers? No,' said Jake, breaking into a grin. 'Aids, Frank.'

'What do you mean, aid?'

'No, not aid. Aids. We sent her to an Aids clinic. We created a flightpath for her. That's what we need to do for you, Frank, create a flightpath.'

'Hell, just listen to this. It's sheer genius! Sheer genius!' cut in Zoot, barely able to contain himself.

Jake smiled smugly and continued. 'You see, Carly was being seen as a bad mum. So, I thought – we thought – we need to show that she loves children. So I phoned a mate who does PR for Every Child Matters and I said, how about we take Carly to one of your Aids clinics in Uganda or wherever they are and we get some shots of her with dying children. Like Princess Diana. He thought it was a cracking idea. You see, I knew that Every Child Matters were losing their market share big time ever since Charity Begins at Home and A Pound Makes a Difference started muscling in on the overseas stuff. All those posters on buses and in cinemas, the radio adverts. So I said, he could use Carly for a TV appeal? Mind you, Carly wasn't that keen at first. She was worried about snakes, tribesmen with spears and all that stuff. Typical Essex girl. But I told her she didn't have to worry about that. She'd be staying in a five-star in Kampala with a Jacuzzi, steam room, the lot. And it would only be for a night. So that's what we did. We flew her out with a team. Photographer, art director, stylist, the usual. The charity paid. A limo picked her up at the airport, drove to the clinic in some remote area. The shoot only took three hours. She had to dress down a bit, of course. No short skirts or low-cut tops. And that pink headband that looked like a crown had to go. She understood. A real pro. Anyway, some great pics of her with the kids. Holding them, leaning over them as they lay in bed, stroking their hair. Such concern and compassion on her face. That evening, she was sipping cocktails on the balcony of one of the best hotels in Africa. The photos went out and she was everywhere. Carly's Compassion for Aids Orphans. Caring Carly. The Kindness of Carly – '

Zoot interrupted. 'But the best was The Angel of Africa. Totally brilliant! And you know, she was even on *Newsnight*. Sitting there talking about how the government needed to increase overseas aid, especially for poor African countries. If you didn't know her, you would swear she knew what she was talking about. You've never seen anything like it. Every Child Matters loved it.'

'So what's she doing now?' asked Frank, still unable to picture Carly. He must have heard of her. Ah, yes … No, that was the one who had an affair with that TV presenter. Another image entered his mind. Wait a minute … No, she was the one always photographed with her tits out, the one who had a hit with that song. What was it? 'I'm for life, not for a night.' Or something like that.

'Now?' Jake seemed surprised by the question.

Zoot spoke. 'You see, Frank, that was Carly's moment. And she did very well out of it. A big house, cars, all that jazz. She's expired now. It was two years ago. The last I heard she was doing porno movies – I mean, adult productions. I think she was photographed naked in *Trendy* magazine with a story aimed at young women. Be what you want to be was the gist of it, as far as I can remember. It didn't work, though. But good pics, I have to give her that. I seem to recall talk that she was going on some bullshit shopping channel. What was it? Lingerie? Or was it garden furniture? Hell, I can't remember, but I don't think anything came of it.'

'So what's this got to do with my situation?'

'We have to totally change the narrative,' said Zoot.

'How do you do that?' asked Frank impatiently.

Zoot grinned back at him, as if to say, *You don't really understand the powers we possess in PR. We can change what people see. Reality is what we say it is.* 'Frank, we make up stories. And we can rewrite the endings. What we need to do here is junction it.'

'Unh. Junction?' murmured Frank, even more lost in PR World. And then something strange happened to him. He found himself thinking about a kitchen, a busy restaurant kitchen with bright lights on the ceiling, all that banging, clattering and sizzling, the stainless steel, the shouting, the tickets, the white plates landing on the pass, the military operation everyone is engaged in to get those orders out, the smells, yes, the smells, garlic, basil, coriander, steak, onions, pork, fish stock. He was thinking about a world he understood.

'Like with a railway,' said Zoot. 'You know, something to send the story along another track. Anyway, Jake's got an idea.'

'Okay, let's go for it,' said Frank wearily. Suddenly he remembered Carly being flown to Africa. He didn't fancy Africa, not that bit with Aids, men in bandanas and shades standing in the backs of battered pick-up trucks with machine guns, the insects, the heat, the lack of running water, all those black faces sitting on the ground, scooping rice with their hands from plastic containers. He too would want to stay in a five-star, just like Carly Diamond did. A new Frank. Frank the good Samaritan in Africa. Frank leaving his comfort zone to help the needy. Frank getting back to basics. Frank shaking coconuts from tall trees. Frank hunting wild animals. Frank cooking in a big pot in a village. Frank the adventurer. He liked the sound of all of that. But not in bloody Africa.

'I've got you on *Late Night Confession*,' said Jake excitedly.

'You what? There's no way I'm going on Baz Boggins!' said Frank firmly. He had appeared on *Baz Boggins Live* three years before to plug his book *Frank's Fast Meals*. When he was demonstrating how to cook the perfect omelette, the handle came off the frying pan, sending Baz into fits of laughter. Frank had felt humiliated and had been convinced Baz had set him up.

'He's the biggest chat show in the country,' said Zoot.

'Over 3.6 million,' said Jake.

'Yeah, but I don't want to look a complete tosser.'

Zoot took a sip of his mineral water and said. 'Frank, this is the way it is right now. If you want forgiveness, then you have to go on a TV show.'

'I don't need forgiveness! Those bloody vegans should ask for it. For causing chaos in my restaurant.'

'The truth doesn't matter. It's perception that counts. And right now people perceive you as veganphobic.'

'It's bloody ridiculous.'

'Frank, it's all a game. You just have to play along with it.'

Frank sighed. 'So when is it?'

'Saturday night,' said Jake. 'It's filmed at the London Studios in Waterloo. I'll email you all the details.'

Zoot said in a reassuring voice, 'It'll all be cool. Just remember, most people will soon forget what's happened. That's the way it is now with so much content out there. They say around 300 hours of video are uploaded to YouTube every minute, right? Think about that. The media's a beast and it constantly needs feeding. Okay, you've fallen, but, hey, you'll rise again. And the media loves all that.'

17

Baz Boggins, wearing a mustard-coloured suit and open-neck white shirt, shrieked with laughter as a teenage boy singer with spiky hair recounted a story about a party after one of his gigs. It seemed to revolve around an inflatable doll, a jar of Vaseline, and some musician Frank had never heard of. Every so often the camera panned to the audience, who appeared to be loving it all. The set consisted of a backdrop of a series of stained glass windows, one with a large plasma TV screen built into it, and a tall, polished wooden structure with a partition down the middle and two light bulbs on top, one green, one red. Baz and the singer were seated opposite each other in leather swivel chairs with a low wooden table between them. To one side of them, a group of four musicians dressed as priests or vicars stood around a keyboard and drum kit.

'No one will remember him a year from now,' growled the actor sitting opposite Frank in the green room.

'Yeah,' said Frank in a faraway voice, trying to remember the actor's name.

'Not long out of nappies. He's cashing in on his five minutes. Of course, none of these bands can really sing. It's all packaged. But you don't have to be able to sing nowadays, do you?'

'So what are you here to talk about?' asked Frank.

'My new series,' said the actor, with boredom in his voice.

'Yeah, what's it called?'

'The Zombie Detective,' he said with disdain.

'Sounds interesting,' said Frank, trying to be polite.

'It's a pile of crap,' said the actor. 'But it pays the bills, I suppose. This will be my ninth interview this week. God, how I hate all this! It's all so bogus. It's all a game, isn't it? Don't do what I did.'

'What was that?'

'Oh, I made a casual remark about Sir Charles Bantam and landed in all sorts of shit. It was all over the papers the next day. Caused me no end of grief and put an end to me working at the National.'

'Bit like me,' said Frank.

'Poncey lot anyway. No great loss.'

The door opened and a young woman holding a clipboard peered in. 'Hi there, everybody!' she said in an exaggerated cheery voice. 'Frank, would you like to follow me? You'll be on in three minutes.'

Frank got up and turned to the actor. 'Good luck.'

The actor grunted back.

Frank followed the woman down a long corridor. He could hear whoops of laughter ringing out from the studio audience. He began to feel nervous. This wasn't like him. What would he say? He was used to going on TV chat shows to plug his programmes or books, not to … what? Defend himself? Confess? 'You need to come across as a good guy,' Zoot had said. 'Say you totally sympathise with the way vegans feel about being discriminated against.'

When the young woman reached the end of the corridor, Frank could see Baz and the teenage singer on the set. Baz was rocking backwards and forwards in his chair and hooting with laughter. The lights were so bright, Frank couldn't see the audience. The young woman whispered in his ear, 'Frank, just wait here. When you hear Baz say your name, just walk straight towards him. He'll do the rest.'

'Yeah, sure,' Frank whispered back, rehearsing in his mind what he would say and reminding himself of the golden rule of TV interviews: that you needed to smile and grin a lot.

The young woman disappeared, leaving Frank standing alone watching Baz. He felt even more nervous now. There was no turning back. The audience applauded loudly as the singer stood up and began walking towards him. He nodded as he walked past. When the applause died down, Baz grinned manically and said, 'My next guest is – and I can honestly say this – a true legend. He needs no introduction. He's the king of the kitchen ... The chef with the F ... Ladies and gentlemen ... *pleeease* welcome ... *Fraaank*!'

The audience erupted into applause again. As Fran walked jauntily across the studio floor towards the grinning Baz, the musicians launched into a rendition of Morrissey's 'Our Frank'. He could hear whooping, whistles, and, as he'd anticipated, some boos. It was deafening.

Baz stood up as he approached and then moved towards him, arms outstretched, and the two of them embraced awkwardly. Frank sat down in the black leather chair opposite Baz, and found himself staring out at a sea of faces, but he couldn't see them clearly because of the glare of the bright lights.

Baz, still grinning manically, 'So, Frank, lovely to have you on the show. It's always such a pleasure.'

'Lovely to be here,' said Frank, switching on a smile.

'Now, Frank, you can relax, because I won't be asking you to make a soufflé tonight. Ha, ha, ha.'

'Good, because I wasn't planning to.'

Baz mopped his brow in an exaggerated fashion. 'That's a relief ... No, seriously, though, Frank, tell me, how's the restaurant world?'

'You know, always something happening.'

'I heard about this new restaurant you opened.'

Frank nodded. 'Concept F, yeah.'

'I've got to be honest and say that a restaurant that doesn't actually serve food is certainly ... different.' Baz opened his mouth and shot an incredulous look at the audience.

Frank gave a nervous laugh. 'It's about experiencing food in a new way.'

'I mean, it is serious, isn't it? It's not some sort of joke or something. Ha, ha, ha, ha, ha.'

'I'm always looking to take food to a new level. Give people a new experience.'

'Because I thought it was – I had to check the calendar to make sure it wasn't April. Ha, ha, ha, ha, ha.'

Frank forced a laugh.

'Still, there's one thing, isn't there?' continued Baz.

'What's that?'

'Ha, ha, ha, ha, ha. It saves on the washing up!'

Frank forced another laugh. He could tell these were just the warm-up questions, and readied himself for Baz asking about the vegan story.

'Now, what I always want to know when I meet a celebrity chef is what you cook at home – I can't imagine you popping into the supermarket and picking up a ready meal.'

Frank stared back, momentarily lost. 'I leave most of the cooking to Annalisa.'

'Ooh! And there was me thinking you were going to say a nice Dover sole or a rack of lamb.' Baz faced the audience again. 'Ha, ha. Now, ladies, you see – there you are thinking if you marry a celebrity chef, it lets you off the cooking!'

'You see, Baz, my wife's the boss in the kitchen.'

'So hands up everyone who has bought one of Frank's books!' A sea of hands. 'Look at that. See, they all love Frank. They really do.'

Frank beamed out at the audience. 'Thank you.'

Baz pulled a face. 'Well, nearly all ... A little birdie tells me that you have your eye on winning' – he pulled a card out of his jacket pocket and briefly looked down at it – 'the Golden Pan award.' He turned to the audience. 'If you are not into gastronomy matters, the Golden Pan's a bit like a Nobel prize. Isn't that right, Frank?'

'Yeah, kind of,' said Frank casually.

'You must be in with a chance, then?'

'You know, it's not something I've thought about, Baz.'

'But wouldn't it be great?'

'Listen, I mean, yeah, all awards are nice. We all like to be acknowledged, don't we?'

'Oh, come on! It would look lovely on your mantelpiece. Ha, ha, ha, ha, ha.'

'Honestly, I don't think about it.'

Baz grinned. 'Now, Frank, we all know there was a little ... what shall we say? ... incident that happened recently. Do you want to tell us all about it?'

Frank paused, searching for the right words and trying to appear jocular. 'Yeah, well, I got into a bit of what you might call hot water with ... some vegans.'

Baz arched his eyebrows and slapped his knees, placing his hands over his mouth. 'Oh, you did, didn't you? Ha, ha, ha.'

'It wasn't what it seemed, though.'

The smirk was replaced with a mask of sincerity. 'How do you mean, Frank?'

'It looked as if I don't like vegans.'

Baz leaned forward and said in a confidential voice. 'Some people accused you of being ... veganphobic. Oh, Frank! You're not veganphobic, are you?'

'How can I be veganphobic when I have vegan dishes on the menu?'

'So you do, do you?'

'Of course.'

'So why all this big fuss, then?'

Frank shrugged. 'When you're in the public eye, you can become a target.'

'Yes ... well, I know all about that, don't I? Ha, ha, ha.'

Frank smiled. 'I didn't say anything, Baz.'

'Now, the audience and the viewers have probably seen the footage in the restaurant.'

'Yeah,' said Frank guardedly.

'But in case they haven't, let's have a quick look.'

Frank turned to see a video of himself yelling at the vegan protesters appear on the plasma TV screen. As the film continued, he heard hisses and boos from some in the audience.

'So what on earth was going on? Goodness, it really kicked off, didn't it? It was like a Millwall away game! ...You probably won't be getting a Christmas card from the Vegan Mary this year.'

Frank explained how the incident had occurred, being careful to downplay the anger he'd felt at the time.

Baz gave sympathetic nods every now and again. 'Tell you the bit I loved. When you picked up that poor chap's burger. Did you see his face? I hope you gave him another one!'

'I did.'

'So, what did you think when you saw the sheep? I bet that's never happened to you before?'

'You can say that again.' Frank was switching his smile on and off so many times that he felt like a set of traffic lights.

'Okay, Frank, you've got to admit that the vegans have a point. About the way … well … you know, the way animals are killed. Imagine those poor sheep with their innocent eyes being taken to be slaughtered.'

'That's life, isn't it?'

'Ooh, Frank, I don't think the sheep would say that.'

'Yeah, but they can't speak, can they?' said Frank, trying to keep himself in check.

Baz barked with laughter and clapped his hands in an exaggerated fashion. 'Oh, I couldn't watch a sheep being killed.' He turned to the audience and crinkled his face. 'Uugh!'

'Yeah, but you don't have to.'

'It's interesting, though, isn't it, how many people today are identifying as vegans – not for me, I'm afraid, though.' He paused and shot a mischievous look at the audience. 'I love my meat – and two veg!'

The audience hooted with laughter.

Frank thought veganism for most people was nothing more than a trend, part of a new food puritanism mixed up with animal rights beliefs. What he didn't like was the way extreme vegans were trying to force everyone else to share their ideas. He couldn't say that, of course. Could never say that. Especially not on this stupid show with its idiotic host who deserved a massive kick up the arse.

"The fact is, Baz, veganism for most people is nothing more than a trend, part of a new food puritanism mixed up with animal rights beliefs. And these extreme vegans, they're trying to force everyone else to share their ideas."

Baz put on a look of mock horror. 'Oh, Frank!'

Frank wriggled in his chair. 'Well, it's true. Look, if you don't want to eat meat or whatever, that's fine. Just don't expect everyone else to do the same. The thing is, you can't say that. It's all this political correctness.'

'Ooh! So you don't think much of political correctness.'

'I'll tell you what, you won't find any vegans in Alaska!'

Baz roared with laughter.

Frank carried on. 'I call it as I see it. What I think we should encourage is politeness and respect. And that means you don't go bursting into a restaurant trying to ram your views down the throats of other people.'

'Ooh, Frank! You've got to get with the times!' shrilled Baz, gesturing widely and looking out at the audience.

Frank stared back at Baz, feeling the interview was spinning out of control. He'd never intended to talk about political correctness. Now Baz was making him look old-fashioned. He needed to keep his cool. 'Baz, you need to come to Concept F and you'll see I'm ahead of the times.'

'Anyway, Frank, as you know, this is Late Night Confession ...' Whoops from the audience. '... where our guests have to ask the studio audience for forgiveness.'

'Yeah, yeah.'

'So ... come with me ... into the *confessional*.' Cheers and whistles from the audience. Baz leapt up from his chair, signalling Frank to follow him.

'Now, Frank, in you go,' said Baz, gesturing to the wooden structure. 'You know how it works. The studio audience press a buzzer. If most forgive you, the green light flashes. But if they don't, it's the dreaded *red light*.'

Frank cautiously stepped into the structure.

'Come on, Frank, you have to kneel down.'

Frank knelt down, feeling slightly ridiculous, and then Baz did the same on the other side of the panel. He found himself looking at Baz through a metal grille.

Baz placed the palm of his hand to his face and put on a deep, solemn voice. 'So ... Frank ... you're here to seek forgiveness?'

'Er, yeah.'

'What for, Frank?'

Frank hesitated and then coughed. 'For, you know, maybe offending anyone vegan.'

'Is there anything else you want to say?'

'No.'

'Are you sure? Baz giggled. 'No hanky-panky or anything?'

'No hanky-panky.'

'Because I know what some of you chefs are like.'

Baz stood up and stepped forward. 'Okay, Frank, you've made your late night confession. So let's see what the audience think. Okay, everyone, press the green buzzer if you think Frank should be forgiven and the red one if you think he shouldn't. So *hit* those buzzers!'

Frank continued to kneel in the box. The sound of a church bell rang out from somewhere.

'Ah, Frank! I'm sooo sooo sorry. It's the *red light*!'

Frank eased himself up, smiling thinly, and took several paces towards Baz. Just play the game, Zoot had said. This was a humiliation. Looking at the grinning Baz, he couldn't think what to say. He just wanted to get off the show as soon as possible.

Baz placed his arm on Frank's shoulder. 'Frank, listen, you've been a great sport.'

Frank nodded, doing his best to smile. 'Yeah, it's been fun.'

'Thank you sooo much for coming on the show. I'm sorry you weren't forgiven. But, look, good luck with everything – and let's hope you win the Golden Pan. A big hand everyone for *Fraaank*!'

18

Frank paid the man at the window of the ice cream van and handed a bubblegum ice lolly to James. It was Sunday morning and a burst of sunshine had brought everyone out in Kelsey Park in Beckenham: parents strolling along the path with toddlers in buggies, older children hurtling ahead on scooters or bikes, young women in tight-fitting sportswear jogging, couples walking hand in hand.

Frank had taken James to the park to play football, as Annalisa had gone with Katarina to the Lentil Festival at the South Bank, where the Vegan Mary was scheduled to make an appearance. A few weeks before, Annalisa had attended a Find Your Inner Vegan weekend retreat in Milton Keynes, and when she returned she announced to Frank that she had really been a vegan all her life, but just hadn't realised it. 'I prefer to eat things that don't have a face,' she had said.

Soon after, a photography crew from *Celebrity Vegan* magazine turned up at the house to do a photo shoot. To please Annalisa, Frank agreed to the art director's request that he appear in some of the photos, but insisted it was made clear that he wasn't a vegan.

Frank hung around impatiently as the crew spent over an hour getting set up. Much of this involved preparing Annalisa to look as natural as possible, as the art director put it without any sense of irony. Annalisa sat regally on a chair in the main bedroom as several of the team hovered around her, carefully brushing her long auburn hair, painting her lips, powdering her face, dabbing her eyelashes with mascara, painting her fingernails and toenails red. All of these products, of course, were vegan friendly. Necklaces and bracelets were placed on her and then taken off. She got in and out of the dozen or so dresses hanging on a rail, slipped her vegan shoes on and off, clutched this faux-leather vanity bag and then that one. It reminded Frank of a Formula One racing car being got ready in the pits. Annalisa, however, seemed to love all the attention.

Frank was alarmed at how his wife had embraced veganism with the zeal of a born again Christian. He had returned home one afternoon to find her piling black bin liner bags into the back of her Range Rover Discovery. 'Oh, I can't wear this stuff now, so it's going to the charity shop,' she had told him. She was getting rid of her leather bags, belts and shoes, her woollen jackets and skirts, and her silk negligees and underwear. And she didn't use toothpaste, soap, cosmetics or anything else that might contain animal products. Her cull of things not vegan friendly also extended to furniture polish, cleaning liquids, and some of the porcelain.

Any time she wasn't sure if something was vegan friendly or not, she would pore over her copy of *The New Veganism* by the Vegan Mary, a thick book with a green cover which set out in forensic detail what vegans could eat and use and how they could prevent themselves from being contaminated by the evil committed by humans using animals for their own ends. If that wasn't enough, Annalisa now stored her food in a separate fridge.

Frank was still reeling from the fallout after the vegan incident. Following his appearance on *Late Night Confession*, Maurice Padwick had cancelled his TV show, telling him without any sense of irony that Tish TV had its reputation to think of. His publisher, Butler & Sutton, had pulled out of the book deal. They issued a statement saying they couldn't be associated with anyone who might be guilty of veganphobia. It was this, the collapse of the publishing deal, that especially irked Frank. A few days before, he had spent five exasperating hours hanging around in a photography studio as the art director and food stylist argued over what would be the best shape for the aubergine that was going to feature on the cover of the vegetable recipe book.

As well as that, the university that had planned to name a bridge after him had emailed to say the governing body had changed their minds. Instead, the structure would now be called Vegan Mary Bridge. The mayor of London, never one to miss spotting a bandwagon coming down the road, had appeared outside City Hall with an expression on his face that suggested World War Three had just begun, saying in a saccharine voice to the cameras that he wanted to express his deepest sympathies with the vegan community and he shared the pain they were going through. Pain? This was all bloody ridiculous.

Frank had been furious with Zoot for persuading him that *Late Night Confession* would repair his image. And he was beginning to wonder what, in fact, he was paying Sticky Lettuce for.

'Daddy?' said James, looking up at Frank as they walked alongside the lake.

'Yeah, Little Man?'

'We've been talking about work at school.'

'Very good.'

'What is work? Is it a place? Mummy says you go to work.'

'No, it's not a place.'

'What is *work*?' James repeated slowly.

'Work is what you do ... It's what grown-ups do to earn money.'

James looked puzzled. 'Does everyone work?'

'Well, not everyone. Granddad doesn't work.'

'Is that because he's lazy? That's what Mummy says.'

'No, he's too old.' What on earth was Annalisa telling James that for? 'I mean, you work, don't you? At school.'

'But I don't get money.'

'Yeah, but you see children don't get paid to work.'

'That's not fair.'

'You're right, Little Man,' chuckled Frank, bouncing the ball with one hand.

James paused. 'What's your work, Daddy?'

'My work? Well, I'm a chef. A cook. You know that.'

'Like Mummy.'

'No. Mummy isn't a cook.'

'Mummy is a cook,' James protested.

'Yes, she cooks. But that's not her work.'

James gave him a curious expression and began bouncing the ball. 'So cooking isn't work.'

'Er ... no. Cooking's work. Very hard work, Little Man.'

'But, Daddy, you never cook. Mummy cooks.'

'She does. I'm a cook, though.' Frank couldn't recall the last time he had cooked for him. This thought troubled him.

'Oh.' James did his best to process this information in his tiny mind. *My daddy is a cook. But he doesn't cook. That didn't make sense.* 'I've never seen you cook. Daddy?'

'Because Mummy cooks at home.'

'Mummy said you have a new restaurant.'

A look of pride. 'I do, yeah.'

'But ... Mummy says it has no food.'

'It has food ... but it's ... er ... different.'

'She says it has computers.'

'It does. Very clever ones.'

Looking perplexed. 'Daddy ... how can you have a restaurant with no food? It doesn't make sense.'

'It's for grown-ups, James.'

'But you can't eat computers. Ugh!'

Slightly miffed at his son's mockery. 'You don't eat them.'

'What do you do with them?'

He thought for a moment. 'They give you an ... experience.'

'Is it a game?'

'No, it's not a game,' said Frank, exasperation creeping into his voice.

'Like Fifa?'

'No.'

'Are there prizes?'

He sighed out loud and patted James on the head. 'Listen, when you're older you'll understand.'

James took a final lick of his ice lolly and looked up at him. 'It sounds a silly restaurant. Ugh! I don't want to go there and eat computers.'

Of course, you couldn't expect a six-year-old to understand. How could they? Do you eat computers ... Was it a game? ... Then troubling thoughts rushed in. Was it a game? His attention was caught by a flock of Canadian geese, with their long necks, flying low and gracefully over the water.

'Those birds make a funny noise,' stated James, staring intently at them.

'Yeah,' said Frank in a distant voice, 'it's called honking.'

19

There was a soft ping and the signs above the seats lit up. Frank pressed his face against the round window. Below the wing he could see clouds, looking like the tops of mountains covered in snow. The 747, which had been flying at 35,000 feet, was now beginning its descent. One of the cabin crew made her way down the aisle, her head moving quickly from left to right, checking that all the passengers had fastened their seat belts. As the plane banked sharply, its wing tilting upwards, the sound of its engine becoming louder, he could see through the wisps of cloud fields of different shades of green, trees, white houses with orange roofs and, beyond, the sea, shimmering in the hazy sunshine.

As Frank admired the greenish-blue hues of the water below, his mind drifted back to Concept F. Despite the initial excitement among critics and bloggers about the restaurant, it had failed to capture the public imagination. In the four months since its opening, Frank had watched with alarm as the number of diners fell each week. It had attracted nearly 300 scathing reviews online, with customers complaining that they left the restaurant still feeling hungry and accusing Frank of ripping them off. One even branded him a confidence trickster.

Alarmed by the falling numbers and worried that the situation might blow his chance of winning the Golden Pan, Frank had told Zoot to do something. Zoot's response had been to fill the restaurant with film extras one evening for a photo shoot. The photos had appeared in leading magazines, newspapers and websites with a story headlined, 'The Restaurant Everyone Wants to Go to.' But the problem was, people didn't.

The plane shuddered and began to drop rapidly out of the sky. Frank could see the runway ahead with its white markings, flanked on either side by grass, jutting out into the sparkling water, which was speckled with small boats. Behind stood a range of dark mountains. A thrill ran through him. The wheels bumped as they hit the tarmac, and a deafening noise filled the cabin as the plane shot along the runway. Frank could see the terminal buildings, several planes parked in front of it at angles, and a fire engine. The airport was very small, handling only a few flights each day to Barcelona and Madrid. This regular service to Gatwick had only recently been introduced. There was another ping and a monotone voice spoke rapidly in Spanish and then English, 'Ladies and gentlemen, welcome to San Sebastián. It is now just after eleven o'clock in the morning local time. Please remain seated until the aircraft has reached its final stop. Thank you for flying with Quick Jet. We hope you enjoy your stay.'

'Tell you what,' said Nick, unclicking his seat belt and stretching his arms out.

'What?' said Frank.

'I need a beer.'

Frank smiled at the thought. 'Me, too. Nice and cold.'

'Yeah, man, I think we'll have a lot of cold beers while we're here.'

'And bloody good wine.'

Frank had invited Nick to go to the awards ceremony with him. Annalisa had told him that she couldn't attend, as it would make her appear that she was an accomplice to murder. Frank hadn't been surprised. Since she'd come out as a vegan, and started attending weekly vegan meetings, the two of them had become more and more distant from each other.

The week before, Frank had been awoken one night by the sound of Annalisa screaming. He had sprung up out of bed to see her standing in the middle of the room with a horrified expression on her face. 'Christ! What's the matter?' he exclaimed.

'It's the pillows!' she cried.

'What you talking about?'

'They've feathers in them!'

Nick had been delighted to go with Frank. He'd been saying he wanted to visit a particular vineyard on the border of Spain and France, and, as it was October, it was grape harvesting time. Nick liked to meet as many of his suppliers as possible, so he could learn about the produce he used in Ambience and also verify that the working conditions for the staff were good. Nick's morals might have been flexible when it came to women, thought Frank ruefully, but with regards to food production, he maintained high ethical standards. He usually made two or three visits a year to suppliers. A few months before, he had travelled to a farm in Derbyshire that supplied him with beef and to a cheese manufacturer in Lincolnshire.

Nick was the perfect companion to go with on such a break. There would be no arguing, like when he and Annalisa went on holiday, and Nick could make him laugh. Frank couldn't recall the last time Annalisa had done that. But then, more worryingly, he couldn't recall the last time he had made her laugh. The thought that he might have lost his sense of humour disturbed him. He had always believed humour could light up a person and that it could make up for many other things that might be missing. And increasingly he had been feeling a hollowness in his life.

San Sebastián had become a place of pilgrimage for devoted foodies. It contained more Michelin star restaurants per capita than anywhere else in the world. Some pilgrims even made the 500-mile walk from Paris on what was known as the Sendero, stopping off at designated vineyards and restaurants along the way and sleeping in hostels.

Frank and Nick emerged from the airport terminal building into thin sunshine. Nick immediately lit a cigarette, while Frank searched his wallet for the hotel details he had printed. They sauntered towards a queue of smart white taxis with green signs on the roof. Frank leaned through the window of the one at the front and spoke in Spanish to the driver. The driver got out and shoved their cases and garment bags in the boot.

'I didn't know you could speak Spanish!' said Nick, taking one last drag of his cigarette before hurriedly stubbing it out on the top part of a litter bin.

'Yeah, I picked it up when I worked in Spain years ago,' said Frank as he slid into the back of the taxi. 'But I'd forgotten a lot of it, so because of the awards ceremony I started an online course a few months ago.'

Nick got in beside him. 'I'm impressed.'

'I mean, I'm not fluent and that, but I know enough to hold a basic conversation.'

The hotel Frank had booked turned out be a large, imposing white building topped at one end by a gold dome. It overlooked the sandy beach and the bay.

'A bit classy for you, isn't it?' joked Nick, when they entered the lobby, which had a smoky grey marble floor, chandeliers, reproduction oil paintings on the walls, and an antique writing desk in a corner.

'I'm a classy guy,' grinned back Frank.

After they had dumped their bags in their rooms and had what Nick called a quick wash and brush up, they headed out to find somewhere to eat. Nick was wearing jeans and his trusty leather jacket, while Frank was dressed in cream chinos and a pale blue open-neck shirt and cream jacket. Nick had been to San Sebastián before and said he knew of a little place in the old quarter that did some of the best pintxos in the city. When Frank suggested they check out one of the Michelin restaurants, Nick pulled a face and said he wanted real food.

They strolled in a leisurely manner along the wide promenade, which was lined with trees and benches, where elderly men and women sat watching the couples with small children, the joggers and the cyclists go by. A few people were sitting on the beach, while others had ventured into the water, despite the cool temperature. Seagulls swooped and squawked overhead. At the far end of the bay was a hill with a statue peeping out over the trees. Frank took a deep breath and felt the oxygen ease the tension in his muscles. Life seemed to go more slowly here.

They crossed a busy road lined with tall buildings, with shops and cafés below. Ornate street lights and plant beds ran down the middle, and an endless stream of modern blue and green single-decker buses with a frog logo on them pulled in and out of bus stops, their air brakes making a shooshing sound. On the other side of the road were several restaurants with plastic tables and chairs in front of them. Most were empty. Bored waiters in white shirts lounged outside, hoping to lure in passers-by.

'Never go to these places,' said Nick.

'I know. The best food's always in the back streets, isn't it?'

'Where the locals go. You know what they say. If the loos don't have shit, the food won't be shit.'

'They remind me of that place I worked in Alicante all those years ago. Christ! That was awful.'

'No *passion*, Frank. That's the problem.'

They meandered down a crowded, moody, narrow passage that seemed to be full of tourist shops and small bars with open doors. Nick led the way through more narrow passages, these ones less crowded. Church bells rang out in the background. Eventually they came to a small bar with a black and white sign above the door that said 'Grina'.

Nick took off his sunglasses. 'This is it! Best pintxos in San Sebastián,' he announced, as they stepped inside. It was crowded and bubbling with chatter and laughter. Scrunched-up napkins littered the tiled floor. On a long wooden bar with a brass rail around the edge were dozens of plates – green peppers with octopus in olive oil, fried hake, padrón peppers, anchovies in parsley and olive oil, tortilla, pastry horns with cream cheese and anchovies, Ibérico ham on crusty bread. Most had been speared with cocktail sticks. Hams and necklaces of dried red peppers and garlic hung above the bar.

Frank stood, shaking his head in disbelief. 'Bloody hell, Nick, this is amazing!'

'Told you,' said Nick.

The names of the dishes and the prices were chalked on a large blackboard above a row of tables, which were all occupied.

'I've not got the foggiest what most of this is,' said Nick with a frown as he studied the blackboard.

'Yeah, they're not written in Spanish – Basque's the language here. See all those x's and k's.'

They stood at the crowded bar and waited to get served. Three barmen, each wearing a white shirt and waistcoat, were working flat out. A cheerful barman with receding black hair came over to them. Frank ordered two beers, two slices of tortilla and two dishes of grilled octopus in garlic. He watched as the barman poured the beer, thinking he looked familiar. When the man placed the drinks on the counter, Frank noticed that his left hand looked odd.

Peering closer, he realised that it was artificial. As he paid, he searched the barman's face, desperately trying to remember where he had seen him before. Maybe the man had worked in one of his restaurants, or maybe he just reminded him of someone else.

'You know, I've spent so long thinking about the Golden Pan award,' said Frank.

'Just a few hours now,' said Nick.

'You reckon I'm in with a shot?'

Nick hesitated and took a sip of his beer, 'Yeah, I guess so ... but there's a lot of competition.'

'I mean, even though Concept F hasn't worked out, I did something original,' said Frank as he cut a piece of tortilla.

'No one can argue with that.'

As he and Nick chatted, enjoying the cold beer and pintxos, Frank kept stealing glances at the barman.

'You all right, man? You seem a bit preoccupied,' said Nick.

'That barman who served us looks familiar.'

'Yeah?'

'I can't place him, though.'

'He probably just reminds you of someone.'

'Did you notice he's got a prosthetic hand?'

'Has he? He must have had some sort of accident.'

Frank stared hard at Nick and then glanced again at the barman.

'What's up, man?'

Frank drained his glass. 'Nothing. Come on, let's hit another bar.'

20

The next morning, Frank and Nick boarded a smart blue train for the journey to Hendaye, a small town just over the border in France. As they sat down in the immaculately clean carriage, Frank could feel the fuzzy feeling in his head after their tour of the pintxo bars the night before beginning to evaporate.

When he had woken up, his head was vibrating like a jackhammer and his mouth felt like cardboard. He had sat on the edge of the bed in his boxer shorts, restlessly surfing the TV channels, hoping it might somehow help to shake him out of his stupor. He flicked between news bulletins presented by young women too glamorous to be attractive; silly game shows with grinning hosts even more over the top than Baz Boggins, if that was possible; a football match in Italy with a manic commentator; a documentary about strippers being hired for funerals in China; two earnest men in beards sitting in a studio arguing in French about something or other; a German movie with a car chase and lots of shooting; and children's cartoons. Why was it now that wherever you went in the world, the TV programmes all looked the same? Where was the originality?

The children's cartoons tugged at him and made him think of James. He wondered what the boy was doing, and reminded himself to buy him something before he went back to London. Maybe a T-shirt or a football jersey of the local team. He wondered if he should buy Annalisa some expensive perfume, but then remembered it would have to be vegan friendly. He doubted, somehow, that there were many vegans in San Sebastián.

How many bars had he and Nick been to? He thought it was six or seven, Nick insisted it was nine. But it had been a fantastic night! And, my God, the food he'd eaten had been sensational. Such simple dishes but made to perfection. As he gradually re-entered reality, he vaguely remembered belting out a Bon Jovi song at the top of his voice as they weaved their way along the promenade back to the hotel. He had a faint image in his mind of two stern policemen with peaked caps and guns on their belts standing in front of him, and of Nick raising the palms of his hands apologetically and manoeuvring him away.

It was the face of that barman, though, with the artificial hand, which he remembered most. He couldn't get him out of his mind.

The train hurried along the tracks in the sunshine, calling at small stations, where few passengers got on. Apart from an occasional glimpse of a distant mountain peeking out between a clump of trees, all Frank saw through the window were balconies of modern blocks of flats, walls of endless tunnels flashing past, and a large marshalling yard where rusting engines and carriages daubed in graffiti stood abandoned. After crossing a bridge over a wide river, which marked the border between Spain and France, the train pulled into the single platform at Hendaye.

They took a taxi from the station to the winery. As the driver barrelled north towards the coast, Nick talked excitedly about the txakoli the winery produced, saying it was the best he had ever tasted. Frank, having now put the excess of the night before behind him, was looking forward to trying some.

The sign at the winery's entrance announced, in green and black lettering, Bodegas Zoriontsu. As Frank paid the driver, he asked him what the name meant. 'Happy,' replied the driver. Then he pulled away, navigating his cab around a group of elderly Japanese tourists, who, cameras at the ready, were disembarking from a coach.

Frank stood there, taking in the view. Whichever way he looked, he could see rows and rows of vines. To the north, beyond a line of trees, he could make out the sea, while to the east stood a range of mountains. It was a truly spectacular scene, he reflected.

'You know, man,' said Nick, 'whenever I come to somewhere like this to meet a supplier, I get a thrill.'

'I can see why,' said Frank.

'Yeah, and not just that. I remember why I wanted to be a chef. It sort of takes me back to my roots.'

Inside the stone building, Nick introduced himself to a young woman who was stacking bottles of wine on a glass shelf behind a long, polished wooden bar. She disappeared and returned with a portly man with a shock of frizzy grey hair, under which a friendly, lined face peeped out. He wore a frayed blue denim shirt, work trousers, and thick boots.

'Nick, it's great to finally meet you!' he said in excellent English.

'And you, Xavier,' said Nick, and then introduced Frank.

'Frank, it's an honour. I've watched some of your programmes.'

'You have?'

'Why, of course. I like to keep an eye on the culinary scene in Britain. There seems to be a lot happening in it. I love going to Britain. Last year, I went to Norfolk. Delightful! I had some delicious crab – what do they call it?'

'Cromer,' said Nick.

'Cromer, that's right. Oh, wonderful! Wonderful!' Xavier blew a kiss. 'Nick tells me that you are going to the International Culinary Academy awards.'

'Yeah.'

'He thinks he's going to win the Golden Pan,' said Nick.

Frank shot Nick a disapproving glance. 'I'm just going because I'm an academy member. It's sort of expected.'

Xavier nodded. 'Yes, of course. So, Nick, are we going to see you on TV? There are so many British cookery programmes. It's quite extraordinary. It seems cooking is more popular than football. What do you call those two priests?'

'The Vegetarian Vicars,' said Frank.

'That's right. Very amusing. And who are those two big men with tattoos everywhere?'

'You mean the Lager Louts.'

'I don't really like them. A bit loud.'

Nick wrinkled his nose. 'I've never wanted to be on the telly. I got asked once. But I couldn't see myself talking to a camera. Frank's the man for all that stuff.'

Xavier said he would take them on a tour of the winery. They followed him down a corridor and emerged into a building with a high ceiling crossed by wooden beams. Rows of gleaming stainless steel tanks, some with hosepipes attached to a valve at the bottom, stood on either side. A man in overalls was mounting a ladder leaning against one of the tanks.

'So how did you get into wine?' asked Frank.

Xavier gave a smile of satisfaction. 'You see, Frank, I had a dream. I wanted to create my own vineyard to make txakoli. I wanted to build something.' He chuckled. 'I liked to drink wine, but I didn't understand much about grapes and how it was made. I was working in construction.'

'That's quite a leap,' said Frank.

'It was. My wife couldn't understand it at first. Why do you want to leave a good career, she said. Because I have to, I said. I felt this strong – I don't know what – force, or urge, something, to make wine. I can't really explain it. She was right to wonder if I wasn't crazy. But, look around. Fifteen years later my dream has been realised.'

Xavier led them into another large room, this one with rows of oak barrels stacked one on top of another.

'What kind of oak is it?' asked Nick.

'French,' said Xavier. 'You know, the type of barrels you use is very important. To a winemaker, the kind of barrel is like spices or fresh ingredients to a chef.'

As Frank listened to Xavier talk about the ageing process of the wine, he felt admiration, even envy. There was a look of intensity and sincerity in Xavier's eyes as he spoke. He'd had a dream and he had followed it. And by all accounts he had become successful – but Frank sensed that, for him, making wine wasn't all about money. It was about something else.

They moved on to a smaller room, which had a wide open entrance. A forklift truck lurched in and tipped a large plastic crate of green grapes into a hopper above a vibrating conveyer belt. Several workers wearing blue gloves and baseball caps stood at either side of it, extracting grapes that weren't good enough to go into the crusher machine.

'It's an impressive set-up you've got,' said Frank.

'Thank you,' said Xavier. 'It took passion, sweat, and the support of my family to achieve all this. Producing wine is hard work. But I love it. I'm a lucky man. I'm happy.'

Xavier then took them down several flights of stairs to the cellar, a dark place with cobwebs on the vaulted ceiling and mould looking like cotton clinging to the walls. Stacked at angles on either side were what seemed to Frank like thousands of bottles of wine, some with mushrooms growing on them. Xavier pulled out a bottle, dusted it with his hand, and held it up.

'This is a 2009. A fabulous year. We'll drink some of this at lunch.'

'I look forward to that,' said Frank.

'You know, they say the history of wine is the history of Europe. Wine's been made in Europe since Roman times. But it was the monks in the Middle Ages who really developed wine-making.'

'Never knew that,' said Nick.

'Yes, wine has always been important in Christianity. For Catholics, it's a sacrament, of course. In fact, there are many references to wine in the Bible. Do you know one of the first things Noah did after the flood?'

'No idea,' said Frank.

'He planted a vineyard.'

Xavier's words made Frank think back to what Casper had said about restaurants being the new churches. Before long he would need to contact him to explain that Concept F was in serious financial trouble.

They climbed back up the stairs and went outside into a yard, where plastic crates filled with grapes were stacked high. Frank reflected on Xavier's words. The man was genuinely happy in what he did. And it was that word again. He had passion.

What did it really mean? He wished he knew more about language and the roots of words. Did it come from a French word, or maybe a Latin one? He didn't have a clue. But the word seemed to stab him each time he heard it. *Passion,* he repeated in his head.

Xavier led them along a path towards the vineyard. In the distance, Frank could see a group of workers gathered around a tractor and trailer. Making their way along another path, following a guide, were the Japanese tourists.

'So has it been a good harvest this year?' asked Nick.

'Pretty good, yes. Not like five years ago when we had all that rain. But, as you say in England, life is not all plain sailing, is it?'

'That's true,' murmured Frank.

As they walked between two rows of vines, the branches bulging with clusters of plump black grapes, Xavier explained that he used both manual and mechanical methods of harvesting. A mechanical harvester was more efficient, but he liked to still employ a few locals, as harvesting provided them with an income. It also kept alive the old tradition of harvesting, and he believed traditions were important.

'We keep our tasting notes very simple,' said Xavier.

'I've always liked that,' said Nick. 'No bullshit.'

'We're producing wine, not poetry. Some people in the wine world talk a lot of nonsense. It's a bit like the emperor's new clothes. I always say a bottle of wine is about the success.'

Frank looked puzzled. 'The success?'

'Yes: see, swirl, smell, sip, sense, and savour.'

Frank noticed a building with a tower on the horizon. 'Is that a church or something?' he asked Xavier.

'It used to be a monastery. The community live there now.'

'Community?'

'The Community of the Culinary Brotherhood. I'm delighted to have them as neighbours. They sometimes help with harvesting and work in the kitchen.'

'So what is it?' asked Nick.

'It's a remarkable place,' said Xavier in a reverent tone. 'It's a group of men who have chosen to live what they call the culinary life. It's a kind of college. Most spend a year there, but some come for just a few weeks.'

'Yeah?' Frank had never come across anything like this in England. It sounded very odd. The culinary life? What on earth did that mean?

'They come from all over the world. America, Germany, Australia, everywhere,' said Xavier with admiration. 'In fact, I think an Englishman joined recently. You can visit if you like.'

'They won't mind?'

'Just say you're a guest of Xavier.'

'Tell you what, Frank, you go and have a wander. I've got to discuss a few things with Xavier,' said Nick.

'Yeah, okay, then.'

'We'll have lunch in the winery at one,' said Xavier.

21

Frank set off briskly towards the building in the distance. He opened a wooden gate at the end of the vineyard and then followed a path with thick vegetation either side into a wood. As he ducked the low branches of the trees, he felt he was on some kind of adventure. What on earth was this culinary community thing? It sounded so odd. He stepped gingerly along a narrow plank of wood that had been placed across a small, clear stream and emerged into an area of neatly cut grass, like you would find on a golf course, divided by gravel pathways. In the middle was a fountain and a statue of a man. Beyond was a complex of sandstone buildings with terracotta roofs and a clock tower. The hands of the clock were two chef's knives. An archway led into a garden with rose bushes and well-tended flower beds. Frank walked underneath it and came to another building. A heavy wooden door was open. He paused and looked around, wondering if he should walk in. Then, in the porch, he spotted a bell with a long cord. "Please ring for assistance" a handwritten sign said in French, Spanish, and English. So he tugged the cord. From inside came the delicious smell of bread baking.

A few moments later, he heard the click of footsteps and a middle-aged man with a shaved head and bright blue eyes appeared. He wore a buttoned-up white chef's jacket with a small logo on it, white trousers with a green stripe down them, and wooden clogs.

'Bonjour, bonjour!' he said cheerfully.

'Morning,' said Frank, suddenly worried he might be intruding. 'Er, Xavier suggested I might be able to have a look around.'

'Ah, you are English. Yes, please come in. You are very welcome. I'll find someone who can give you the tour.'

The chef led Frank down a long vaulted corridor with a stone floor and bare stone walls. He reached a door and opened it, motioning Frank inside. The room had comfortable chairs arranged around a low wooden table with a stack of glossy magazines on it. On the wall hung a portrait of a bearded man wearing a medal on a red, white and blue ribbon. Someone would be with Frank shortly, said the chef, and disappeared.

Frank picked up the magazine on top of the pile and sat down, casually flicking through the pages. It was written in French and contained lots of attractive colour photos: chefs at work, the interiors of restaurants, farmers picking crops, a fisherman on a small boat. There was also an article about Auguste Escoffier, and a black and white photo of him working in the kitchen at the Savoy Hotel in London.

Frank had completely forgotten that fact. There had been a time when he would often consult his stained and well-thumbed copy of Escoffier's classic work *Le Guide Culinaire* for ideas, even though it had first been published nearly a hundred years earlier. He couldn't recall the last time he had read it, or even whether he still had it.

He stood up and wandered over to look at the painting, which, he was startled to discover, was of Pierre Limogne. The chef looked older than in the photos of him Frank had seen. Frank studied the painting, as if searching for some kind of answer.

Looking through the window, he saw a man in a green jacket and green trousers pushing a wheelbarrow towards what looked like a barn. Another man, dressed identically, raked over a patch of soil. Why were they dressed the same?

Hearing footsteps and voices, he turned around. The chef with the shaved head stuck his head around the door and said breezily, 'I've found one of the brothers who will give you a tour.'

Frank stared in disbelief. 'Bloody hell! Casper!'

Casper stared back in equal astonishment. 'I can't believe it! Frank! What are you doing here?'

'No – what the bloody hell are *you* doing here?'

Casper gave a faraway smile and came towards him. 'I joined the community a few weeks ago. You're talking to Brother Casper now.'

'What's all this rig-out,' said Frank, gesturing at Casper's green jacket and trousers, and trying hard to hide his amusement. For some reason, the uniform reminded him of those American prisoners he'd seen on TV, wearing orange jumpsuits.

'Oh, it's what all community members have to wear – the chefs wear white, though. Green symbolises new life and nature.'

'I'm still stunned,' said Frank, shaking his head and sitting down. 'I was told there was an English guy here, but I never in a million years imagined it would be you.'

Smiling, Casper sat down opposite him. 'I'm as surprised as you. I have to say, if you'd said to me when we first met at that Gussmann exhibition that I'd be living in a culinary community one day, I'd have said you were being ridiculous. But here I am. So what brings you here?'

'I'm visiting the winery next door. The owner – Xavier – suggested I come here to have a look.'

'Yes, Xavier is a great supporter of the brotherhood,' Casper said with affection.

'I've come to San Sebastián for the Golden Pan award.'

'Ah, I'd completely forgotten about that. We tend to live in a bit of a bubble here. Well, you must be in contention.'

'No, I'm just here as an academy member.'

'Frank, you don't realise what an innovator you are.'

Casper looked different. His hair was cropped short and his cheeks seemed redder. Frank put on a serious face. 'So, come on, tell me what's this all about. I'm intrigued.'

So Casper explained. He had always loved cooking, ever since he was at university, when he would rustle up simple pasta dishes or soups for his friends who came around to the flat he shared in Richmond. He had considered training as a cook, but instead went into the City after graduating. Yet he kept his interest in cooking alive, sometime preparing simple dishes for his wife and children. As his company grew, he found little time to do this, and soon he was eating ready meals at home. His wife didn't like cooking. One day, he wandered into a bookshop and picked up a copy of *To Be Frank*. And that was it. He was hooked on cooking again. He bought Frank's other books and watched his TV programmes, and he recaptured the love of cooking he'd had at university.

Casper paused dramatically. 'And then, Frank, I had what I can only describe as an epiphany. I have to say, there's no other word for it. It was at the opening night of Concept F.'

'Yeah.' Frank cleared his throat. Casper didn't know that it was leaking money – his money. He had convinced Casper that the restaurant would be a massive success. Instead, it had bombed. There were so few customers that, in desperation, he'd even employed the window trick, something he had never imagined he would do.

Casper spoke softly. 'It was at Concept F that I suddenly realised that my ... calling, if you like ... was not to work in property and finance but to become a cook. Seeing your brilliant idea come to fruition, experiencing food through the senses but not actually eating anything, was such a profound moment for me. So profound! When I left the restaurant that night, I said to Dolores: I'm going to become a professional cook. She thought I was joking, of course, but the next morning I talked to her more about it, and she could see I was serious. She said, if that's what you really want to do, I'm behind you.'

'I'd no idea that Concept F had affected you like this,' said Frank, studying him closely.

'It was life-changing, Frank. Life-changing. You see, I came to realise that seeking profit had clouded my search for meaning. I had sacrificed my dream for money. Even when I wasn't at my desk in the Beanstalk, my mind was still there. I started to see my job, my company, as a prison. My suit became a uniform and my tie a chain. I asked myself: at the end of my life, what would I regret? And the answer was clear. I would regret never having followed my passion.'

'But, I mean, how did you end up here?'

'Some months back, I came on what they call a taster weekend.' He smiled. 'Yes, I know. That's where you get to know the community and they get to know you. I had a chat with Chef de Cuisine and told him I felt I wanted to be a cook.'

'Who's he, then?'

'The one you met. He's in charge. He's an absolutely extraordinary man. He gained three Michelin stars at a restaurant in Lyon. Some of the brothers say he used to be in the French Foreign Legion, and led some sort of daring raid to rescue hostages in Africa. Between ourselves we refer to him as Cuis, which, being English, I find funny. It makes me think of *Mastermind*. Anyway, he advised me to go away and think about it, and if I still felt the same way in six months to contact him.'

'Amazing, Casper.'

'It's Cuis that's amazing. He quit cooking in Michelin restaurants to set up this community. He wanted to put something back.' Casper gestured towards the door. 'Right, let me give you the tour.'

As they strolled down a corridor, Casper explained that most of the buildings dated back to the thirteenth century and had been part of a Cistercian monastery. During the French Revolution, the monks were thrown out and the monastery turned into a paper mill. An art collector had bought it in the eighteenth century and spent a huge sum restoring it, adding some additional buildings. Frank had got the impression that the community was all male, and he was right. Casper informed him that there was a similar, all-female community – the Sisters of the Culinary Arts – a few miles away.

Casper opened a door and invited Frank to go in. The room was filled with shelves of books from the floor to the high ceiling

Frank whistled through his teeth. 'Wow! Some library.'

'This was the monastery library and now it's the brotherhood's. I rather like that. I gather there's something like 15,000 books here. Nearly all of them about gastronomy.'

'Incredible,' said Frank, with genuine surprise.

Casper went over to the far side of the room and ran his finger backwards and forwards along a shelf. 'Here we are,' he said triumphantly, pulling out a book and holding it up. 'You see, you're here! *Frank's Secret Service*.'

Frank smiled. Casper seemed a different person, almost childlike. It was very strange.

157

They climbed a steep flight of steps and came to a door marked Development Laboratory. It was a large, brightly lit room with a long steel table in the middle. Lining the walls were shelves containing rows of books in glass cabinets and what seemed like hundreds of jars of ingredients, all labelled. It smelt like a chemist's shop, thought Frank. There were pieces of equipment that he didn't recognise. Two of the brothers, wearing goggles and leather aprons, were pouring a steaming liquid into a tall cylindrical container that stood on the floor, while another brother sat hunched at a desk, peering through a microscope.

'One of the things we are doing at the moment is conducting a big project to grow tomatoes on the moon,' explained Casper, making sure to keep his voice low.

'On the *moon?*'

'Yes, the community is very forward-looking. One day, Frank, there'll be people living on the moon.' Casper let out a chuckle. 'And if there's people, then there'll be a McDonald's.'

Frank had heard about the space race, but it had never occurred to him that it might have a culinary dimension. He had always thought of it in terms of rockets, probes and space stations, not tomatoes.

Casper took Frank down a long corridor to the accommodation block where the twenty-two community members lived. Like all the other rooms, Casper's contained just a single bed, a desk with a chair, a washbasin, and a wooden wardrobe. Frank couldn't see a radiator. The walls were white with no pictures decorating them. It seemed very spartan, thought Frank.

Leading off the room was a small kitchen with a cooker, a sink, and copper pots and pans hanging in a row on the wall. Casper opened a door to reveal a herb garden. Listening to him enthuse about it, Frank wondered why he never bothered going into the greenhouse at home. The showers, baths and toilets were communal, which took some getting used to at first, said Casper.

'So what about the chefs? Where do they live?' asked Frank.

'In another part of the complex.'

'How many are there?'

'Twelve.'

As they continued their tour, Casper explained the day began at 7am when the community gathered in the restaurant to listen to one of the chefs read an extract from a book by a Culinary Master. At the moment, it was *A Culinary History from Antiquity to the Present* by Jean-Louis Flandrin and Massimo Montanari. After the reading, another chef would deconstruct a recipe. Following this, the brothers would sit in silence for half an hour, thinking about what they had heard and concentrating their minds on the day's work ahead. After breakfast, they would go to work in the communal kitchen, bakery, gardens, or farm. Others would work in the laundry or on cleaning or maintenance duties around the complex. There were weekly rotas for all this, as there was for serving in the restaurant, which was regarded as an honour.

All the community met for lunch at 1pm after something called the Service of Spherification. The afternoons were devoted to study and practice. Casper said the subjects on offer were fascinating, and went on to enthusiastically list some of them: From Plato to Pesto; Ancient Herbology; The Culinary Fathers; From Monasticism to Molecularism; The Golden Age of Pimenton; The Ibérico Jamón Wars, 1867–1872; Early Restaurant Décor; The Garlic Restoration; The Radish Revolution; The Coming of the Hamburger.

With growing astonishment, Frank listened as Casper explained that to master various culinary skills, each of the brothers had to spend an hour each morning and two hours each afternoon cooking alone in his kitchen. The formation chef would often carry out unannounced inspections to ensure that the members were preparing and cooking ingredients correctly. On Sunday mornings, each of the brothers had to meet with his personal culinary director for an hour and admit to any errors he had made when cooking a dish or any ingredients he felt he hadn't treated with the necessary respect. Casper said in a grave voice that he had been guilty of hacking a butternut squash apart and of burning a Hollandaise sauce.

The brothers also attended cooking lectures and demonstrations and took part in team cooking sessions with one of the instructor chefs. There was an hour's free time before the evening meal, which was followed by another reading from a Culinary Master and the recitation of the community's Rules for Restaurants. Sometimes on Saturdays, members would travel to a local restaurant, where they would work a twelve-hour shift. They were given Sunday afternoons off. The complex had a squash court and football pitch, which

Chef de Cuisine encouraged them to make use of. They were not allowed mobile phones or computers and were only permitted to watch TV on Sunday evenings. Contact with their families had to be by letter or by the community pay phone.

After Casper had finished, Frank puffed out his cheeks and said, 'It sounds like the bloody army!'

'I won't lie and say it's an easy life,' said Casper. 'And I miss Dolores and the girls. But it's an incredibly fulfilling one. I wouldn't want to be anywhere else. And I've made some great friends from all over the world. There's a great spirit of camaraderie in the brotherhood.'

'So how long you planning to stay here?'

'A year. If I pass my exams, and the Cuis thinks I am worthy, if I'm admitted to the culinary brotherhood, I'll become what is called a cuisinier. That's when, at a special ceremony' – Casper gave a dreamy look – 'I'll receive my chef's whites and white apron, and my knives.'

Before becoming a cuisinier, though, you had to pass through three stages. Each lasted for three months. Casper was still a garçon de cuisine, which is why he wore a green apron in the kitchen. You received a green and white striped apron when you graduated to apprentice and black and white striped apron when you became a commis.

Frank wondered if his old catering college operated such an elaborate and weird system. He doubted it. 'You said something I didn't quite catch about a spherry-something-or-other.'

'You mean …the Spherification,' said Casper in a reverent tone.

'Yeah, what's that all about?'

'It's the most important moment of the day. It's when we remember Ferran Adrià.'

'You serious?'

'Absolutely. The culinary world owes him so much.' Casper looked pointedly at his watch. 'Spherification is being celebrated in fifteen minutes, actually. Would you like to stay for it?'

'Okay,' said Frank, thinking again what an odd place this community was.

Casper led Frank through a cloister to the kitchen, where several of the brothers were busy chopping vegetables or making stocks. The kitchen was modern and spacious, and everything – ovens, ranges, griddles, fridges, work surfaces – gleamed. Frank had never seen a kitchen so spotless. Casper explained that Cuis didn't like food waste, so they tried to use every part of all the ingredients.

'The one chopping celery?' said Casper out of the side of his mouth.

'Yeah.'

'He's going on the missions.'

'What's that?'

'He's going to Colombia to help farmers grow crops. It's a way of trying to combat the drugs trade. And you see the other one?'

'Yeah?'

Casper leaned his head close to Frank and whispered. 'He was a vegan!'

As they came through to the restaurant, Casper put a finger to his lips. Frank nodded in acknowledgement, but didn't know why. The restaurant had a high vaulted ceiling, stone pillars, and simple stained glass windows, which allowed natural light to flood in. Casper leaned close to Frank and whispered that the two long tables near the far end were for the chefs and the brothers, but they didn't eat together. Beyond the tables were four rows of polished benches, and in front, a set of heavy maroon curtains. In between them was a lectern with a thick book open on it, an organ, and a small wooden table on top of which was a single candle in a gold holder, a glass dish, a silver dish, a silver goblet, and a folded white cloth.

Casper, still whispering, told Frank to take a seat on the bench at the back. 'I have to have a quick wash before the Spherification – it's the rules, I'm afraid. I'll be back in a few minutes.'

22

Frank inspected the restaurant more closely. He sniffed the air. It smelt musty, with an undertone of furniture polish. The only sound was that of birds tweeting outside. Under one of the latticed windows were two marble tombs of aristocrats, the features of their faces worn away by the years. Frank bent down to read the Latin inscription, but the only word he could understand was 'Bordeaux'. Nearby were four modern statues of chefs on plinths, all engaged in some aspect of cooking. He read the names Marie-Antoine Carême, Alexis Soyer, Bernard Loiseau, and Ferran Adrià, who was holding up something thin between his fingers. Adrià, he knew about, of course. And he remembered that Loiseau had shot himself following speculation that his restaurant might not keep its three Michelin stars. But he didn't recognise the other two names. He'd never seen a restaurant like this. And this whole Ferran Adrià thing. What the bloody hell was all that about? And Casper. Wearing that funny green uniform and living in a tiny room, and talking with such intensity about cooking. It all seemed so bizarre.

The silence was broken by the heavy sound of bells tolling. Frank sidled onto the rear bench. On a ledge on the back of the bench in front were small blue books. He casually picked one up and opened it. The pages were divided into the four seasons, each section marked by a thin silk ribbon attached to the spine: green for spring, yellow for summer, black for autumn, and white for winter. Most of the text was written in French, but on some pages there were italicised words in English and Spanish.

He heard a door squeak behind him and turned around. The community members began to silently file in and take their seats. Most seemed in their forties or fifties and bore earnest expressions on their faces. Casper came and sat next to him, but didn't speak. Everyone sat there in total stillness, their colourful uniforms seeming to light up the restaurant. The only sound was that of someone coughing or the rustle of pages.

There was another squeak of a door and Frank turned again, this time to see a dozen chefs slowly processing in, one behind the other, in almost military fashion, their clogs making a slapping sound on the stone floor. Some wore tall, white toques on their heads, others white berets. At the rear, carrying a purple cushion with a long silver spoon on it, was the bald chef Frank had met earlier, Chef de Cuisine, with a gold V-shaped sash draped around his neck. The chefs lined up in a row behind the table and stood there solemnly with their hands crossed over their chests.

Frank watched in bewilderment as Chef de Cuisine moved forward to the table and laid the spoon on it. As he did this, another chef, a thickset man, stepped towards him and theatrically placed a gold cape with a white hood over his shoulders. He pulled the hood over Chef de Cuisine's head and backed away. Chef de Cuisine bowed in front of the table and then produced a lighter and lit the candle. He placed a hand inside the goblet and pulled out a slim brown object, holding it to the candle wick before reverently placing it back in the goblet, mouthing something silently. Thin smoke began to rise into the air. Frank could smell the pungent aroma of cinnamon. Chef de Cuisine went over to the lectern, opened his arms wide, and addressed the community. The organ struck up with deep, heavy notes, and all the brothers stood up as one and began to chant in French. Casper nudged Frank gently in the ribs and held out a blue book, hovering his finger over a page. Frank read the words, which were written in English.

> Oh, praise the humble celery
> For the joy it gives to me.
> From the earth it arises
> In many different sizes.
> With onions and carrots
> A base it does make.
> And such deliciousness we all partake.
> Oh, let us praise the celery.

> For being what it is meant to be.
> Praise to the celery.
> Praise to the celery.
> Praise to the earth
> And all its bounty.

Frank had to cough in an exaggerated manner to stifle his laughter. Casper shot him a reproving glance.

The brothers then all sat back down. A chef who looked as if he might be Vietnamese took several paces forward and stood in front of Chef de Cuisine. They bowed to each other, and the Vietnamese chef lifted the tall toque off Chef de Cuisine's head. He bowed again and returned to the line, holding the toque in his hands like you might a priceless object.

As if in slow motion, Chef de Cuisine picked up the spoon, kissed it, and placed it in the silver dish. With intense concentration on his face, he carefully transferred a liquid to the glass dish, which contained a solution. While he did this, another chef moved to the side and pressed a button on the wall. The curtains slowly closed in front of the table, concealing all the chefs. It reminded Frank of the cinema. On one curtain was written in ornate gold lettering 'Practice', and on the other, 'Perfection'.

Frank looked around, wondering what was happening. The atmosphere was hushed. The members all sat there as if in a trance.

A couple of minutes later, the curtains reopened to reveal Chef de Cuisine unfolding the white cloth and laying it on the table. With great care, he placed the spoon in the glass dish and gently tipped a liquid on to the cloth. A bell tinkled and everyone bowed their heads. Frank glanced sideways at Casper. He had his eyes closed. Chef de Cuisine stood there for a moment, his face showing no emotion, staring straight ahead. Frank watched as the liquid, almost magically, formed itself into a tiny sphere. The chefs and the brothers began to chant again, this time louder and with more urgency.

One of the chefs approached the lectern and picked up the thick book, raising it high in the air. He held it there for a moment before placing it back on the lectern. He looked down and started to read aloud in Spanish.

'It's from *The Secrets of El Bulli*,' hissed Casper.

Frank nodded, as if he understood what Casper was talking about, and wondered how long this ceremony would go on. He was expected back at the vineyard for lunch and he was getting hungry. He couldn't wait to see Nick's face when he heard about everything.

After the reading, someone blew out the candle and all the chefs turned to the right and slowly processed back out, with Chef de Cuisine again at the rear. Once the chefs had disappeared through a door, the brothers began to disperse. Casper stood up and slid along the bench, signalling Frank to follow him.

'So you've attended the Spherification,' Casper said with a smile as they left the restaurant.

Frank pulled a face and said, 'Yeah, but I'm not sure I understood what was going on.'

'It's all about paying honour to ingredients and giving respect to culinary techniques. You probably know that Ferran Adrià invented a new culinary language. He brought about a gastronomic revolution.'

'I mean, I know he had a big influence on modern cooking, but I've never thought of him in the way that you do here.'

Casper looked thoughtful. 'In the brotherhood we are taught about the importance of tradition, that something always grows out of what came before it. The problem nowadays is everyone wants something new all the time. You see it in the restaurant scene. If we look to the future, we also need to look to the past.'

Frank murmured, 'Yeah.'

'You see, there's a restlessness today. I used to see it all the time at Canary Wharf. Everyone checking their mobile phone every five minutes, grabbing something to eat on the go, hurrying to the Tube station, buying ready meals on the way home. We're all so busy. Do you know what one of the great things about being here is? I mean, apart from what I'm learning.'

'Tell me.'

'Not having to remember PIN numbers and passwords.' Casper sighed. 'It feels so liberating.'

'Yeah, I get that.'

Casper carried on. 'I have to say, the problem is that for many people, eating's just about filling up. Like putting petrol in a car. It's not about the ingredients or sharing a meal. Cuis – Chef de Cuisine – likes to say that every dish tells a story. And not only that. Every dish carries within it a culture and a history. It's not just a plate of food. When Ferran Adrià performed his first spherification, that was a defining moment in culinary history. That's why we gather together as a brotherhood to remember it.'

Frank had never considered cooking in this way, and he had to admit that he liked the idea that a dish might tell a story. 'Anyway, Casper, I'd better get back to the vineyard. Xavier's expecting me for lunch.'

'Of course. I'll come with you to the door. By the way – I meant to ask how Concept F is going?'

'Yeah, yeah, well,' said Frank evasively.

'And the diners are loving the experience?'

'Definitely.'

'I'm so pleased to hear that. I did wonder if it might sort of fizzle out after the initial novelty had worn off. But, you see, Frank, you were right all along.'

Frank smiled thinly, shame surging through him.

23

In the vineyard restaurant, which was empty apart from a couple of families with teenage children, Xavier had laid on a lunch of grilled sardines, caught that morning by his brother off the coast, a rabbit stew, crusty bread, and a locally made ice cream. Frank sat at the table and watched in fascination as Xavier held one of the 2009 vintage bottles of red wine at arm's length, picked up a knife, and with a single flourish of the blade sliced off the top as if it was a watermelon.

'That's a new one on me,' said Frank with genuine amazement.

Xavier laughed. 'It's my party trick.' He poured Frank and Nick a glass and waited expectantly for their reaction.

'That's bloody good!' pronounced Frank after taking a sip.

'Yeah, fantastic stuff!' enthused Nick.

Xavier beamed back at them proudly and then filled his own glass.

As they all ate, Frank recounted his visit to the Community of the Culinary Brotherhood, still not sure whether to take it seriously or not, and the extraordinary meeting with Casper.

Xavier leaned his head across the table and said softly, 'Frank, you must understand that here in the Basque Country – in Spain – food and wine is like a religion.'

'Yeah, seems like it.'

Xavier paused and said, 'They say that with gastronomy, just like music, you can touch people's souls. Have you heard of Boulanger?'

'Don't think so.'

'Some say he opened the first restaurant in Paris – in the 1700s sometime – I don't know if that's true or not. But what's interesting is that on the window of his shop – he sold broths – he inscribed a line from the Gospels: "Come to me all who labour and I will give you rest." You see, the broths were meant to restore the body.'

'Really?' Frank found himself remembering the man who had set up the Christian pizza company at Hospitality UK.

Nick chipped in. 'The thing is, Frank, in southern Europe they take ingredients and cooking much more seriously than people do back home. Food's a key part of the culture here, isn't it, Xavier?'

'You reckon it's not in Britain, then?'

'Look, you've written all these cookery books, right, but people still buy ready meals.'

'Rubbish. Lots of people cook at home.'

'Some, yeah, but not that many.'

'Why do I sell so many books, then?'

'I don't know, birthday gifts, at Christmas, because they look nice. To stick in the loo. But I bet most of the pages don't even have a stain on them.' Nick turned to Xavier. 'What do you reckon, Xavier?'

Xavier topped up their glasses and said, 'I don't know enough about the food scene in Britain, but I think here not as many people cook at home as they used to. The younger generation can't be bothered.'

'But they like to look at photos of it,' said Nick.

Xavier grinned. 'That's probably true. But you can't eat a photo.'

Frank stared back at Xavier, his remark hanging there in the air. *You can't eat a photo. You can't eat a computer.*

'So what's the restaurant situation here, then?' asked Frank in an attempt to blot out the remark.

'You know, Frank, what we do here is just try to serve good food. Many restaurants do things the same way they've done it for years. And customers love it. Sure, we have all these Michelin restaurants, but most people aren't into fancy dining. And you know what? Many of the dishes that are popular now were once the food of the poor. At one time, people just ate whatever food was available locally. They grew vegetables, caught fish, hunted animals. They made their own cheese and bread. That was how it used to be.'

Frank remembered that he had been blown away by the food he had eaten when he had travelled around Europe in his teens. Even in simple cafés at railway stations, and in dusty bars down back streets, he had been served fantastic meals. It was so different to most places in Britain.

Nick put down his knife and fork. 'The thing is, they're not into making a restaurant like a fucking circus. In London everything has to be about novelty. Why? In Spain or anywhere else where they've a strong food culture, they serve the same dishes they've been doing for donkey's years. It's all about cooking the best version. It's not about fucking deep-fried Nutella burgers or kimchi ice cream on a stick. Christ! I mean, they have festivals in Europe in some places to celebrate local dishes and everyone cooks their own version of it.'

Frank interrupted him. 'Yeah, but, come on, we've got some great dishes and produce in Britain. I mean, think of shepherd's pie, cod and chips, roast lamb with Yorkshire pudding, vegetables, cheeses.'

'I love Yorkshire pudding!' interjected Xavier, licking his lips. 'With your wonderful roast beef.'

'Yeah, course we have,' continued Nick. 'And I'll tell you what. A good Yorkshire pudding doesn't need messing around with. The number of times I've heard one of my guys talk about giving some classic dish a twist! You don't need to give it a twist, I say – you're not a fucking plumber! That's why it's a bloody classic, for God's sake.'

Frank winced in mock fashion. 'I've got to put my hands up. I've said that on TV.'

Nick narrowed his eyes, shaped his fingers into a gun and pointed it at Frank, making a *pow!* sound. Xavier laughed.

'Aagh!' cried Frank, leaning back in his chair and placing his hand over his chest.

Nick grinned and waved him away. 'You know what, Xavier, most of these new restaurants opening up in London are about style rather than substance. Yeah, they've spent a fortune kitting them out, and they do all this marketing, but some of the food is crap.'

'And expensive crap,' said Frank.

Nick continued. 'You know, I went to this new Asian fusion place in Hoxton – it's a trendy area, Xavier. When we looked at the menu it said, you'll experience a true taste of the East.'

Frank gave a little chuckle. 'Did you?'

'Yeah ...' Nick began mopping up the rabbit stew with a piece of bread. 'Tokyo fucking airport.'

'Oh, I love that, Nick!' chortled Xavier, standing up to uncork another bottle.

'The scene's so different from when Frank and I started,' said Nick.

Frank nodded. 'Bloody hell. I can't keep up with it all – by the way, Xavier, fantastic rabbit!'

'Thank you, Frank.'

'And the wine's the dog's bollocks,' said Nick, adding hastily, 'I mean fantastic.'

Xavier grinned. 'I hope you'll be ordering some cases.'

Nick said, 'Too right I will, Xavier. The thing is, in London, everyone wants to be different. It's like a big theme park out there. There's this place that's just opened in Kings Cross.'

'The one serving tinned food?' asked Frank.

'Not that one. You sit in the dark, stark bollock naked, and have to guess what you're eating.'

Xavier's eyes widened. 'Is that true?'

'It's called mystery dining. For Christ's sake! What are these people on? The mystery's how people fall for all this stuff.'

Xavier shook his head sagely. 'People forget that food's about sitting around a table – like us – and sharing a meal.' He paused and took a sip of wine.

'Spot on, Xavier,' said Frank, thinking his father would like Xavier.

'Perhaps if we all did more of that, there might not be so many barriers between people. Food humanises us. Don't you agree?'

Frank nodded. He did.

24

Frank and Nick, both wearing tuxedos, approached the entrance to the Basque Centre of Food and Culture, a low, modern, glass building on the outskirts of San Sebastián. Frank waved his invitation card at a man in uniform, who ushered them inside.

The big night had finally arrived for Frank. And now it had, he wasn't feeling as excited as he had expected he would, but he couldn't work out why. That morning, he had sat at the desk in his hotel room writing his acceptance speech, trying to think of something both profound and funny to say, but it had proved much harder than he'd imagined. But at least he had come up with a list of people he wanted to thank.

After he and Nick had been issued with name badges and a glossy programme, they made their way to the already crowded bar, where photographers and two TV crews floated around. Surveying the smartly dressed people milling around him, Frank wondered how many of them were hoping to win an award and who were the others in contention for the Golden Pan.

As he waited for Nick to get served, he glanced through the evening's schedule in the programme: young chef of the year … best restaurant manager … best hotel manager … best sommelier … services to hospitality … the Golden Pan award. He would have to wait until nearly 10 o'clock to hear the result. God, that meant he would have to sit through two hours of speeches. From previous awards ceremonies he had attended, he knew how dull that would be.

Frank and Nick mingled with some of the other guests. Frank made small talk with several chefs and restaurant owners he had met before, but, for some reason, he found himself feeling bored. Nick, on the other hand, was quite animated, which Frank suspected was because of the attractive female Norwegian restaurant manager he was talking to.

Frank spotted Johnny John making his way through the crowd towards him. His wife, a leggy brunette in a red evening dress, was by his side. Annalisa should be here, thought Frank. It was going to be one of the biggest moments in his career.

'How you doing, Frank?'

'Yeah, okay, Johnny.'

Johnny motioned to his wife. 'You've met Carol, I think.'

'Hi, Carol. Nice to see you again.'

Johnny's wife smiled back demurely, but didn't say anything.

'Sorry to hear about the new restaurant,' said Johnny.

'What do you mean?'

'You know, all the reviews and stuff. Some of it was quite vicious, really vicious, wasn't it?'

Frank shrugged. 'You can't please everyone. You know that.'

'True, mate.'

Johnny scanned the bar. 'So this is the night, eh? I wonder who's going to walk off with the Golden Pan.'

'No idea – I'm just here to support the academy.'

'Me, too.'

Frank felt relieved when an announcement over the public address system, in Spanish, French, Italian and English, invited the guests to make their way to the main hall for the meal and ceremony.

He and Nick filed in with the other guests. At the far end of the hall was a podium with a backdrop proclaiming in large letters The World Gastronomy awards 2017 and underneath the coloured logos of the sponsors, a Chinese luxury hotel group, a Korean mobile phone company, and the airline company Asia Express. Laid out in long rows were tables decked with white tablecloths, silver candelabras, vases of flowers, and expensive glasses.

A woman in a black trouser suit led them to their places. Frank found himself sitting next to a chef and restaurant owner from Japan, while Nick was seated next to a jocular wine writer with a craggy face and bibulous nose, from Germany.

Frank ran his eyes down the menu, his eyes widening at the creativity: griddled porcini mushrooms with truffled egg yolk on a bed of baby onions; Atlantic oysters with citrus caviar foam and txakoli wine; red mullet with seaweed and a pine nut puree with three-way grilled beetroot; roasted lobster with scallop shavings and garlic-infused lemon peel; glazed oxtail with pumpkin seeds and pan-fried apple marinated in pimenton juice; roast loin of venison with pear chorizo and shredded young lettuce hearts; steamed and roasted pigeon with corn dust and cocoa; runny hazelnut cake with frozen goat's milk and frothy prawns; idiazabal cheese with braised edible flowers and honey crackers.

While Nick soon got into a lively conversation with the writer, Frank struggled to make any headway with the Japanese chef, whose English was very basic. The sound of excited chatter rising in volume throughout the hall didn't make things any easier. Soon he found himself restless, staring into the distance. Had he been feeling chirpier, he would have made more of an effort, but he couldn't be bothered. He contemplated the long evening ahead, the nine-course meal interspersed with the announcements of all the winners and the bursts of applause that would ring out. The Japanese chef seemed to think he was in with a chance of winning the most innovative restaurant category, as he had opened one on top of a volcano.

Frank poured himself a generous glass of red and leaned forward over the table, angling his head towards the wine writer, who was explaining in great detail to Nick what made a fine wine.

'You see, any fine wine always reflects its origin,' said the writer pompously. 'In musical terms, it's the instrument by which the score of a place – its soil, its exposure, its climate – is expressed. So the variety must be the right instrument to do it. Then the place, the variety, and the wine are one.'

Frank gave a sarcastic laugh.

The wine writer raised his eyebrows. 'Oh, don't you agree, er ...'

'Frank Darley.'

'Of course. I'm sorry. I should have recognised you.'

'It seems to me that there's a lot of bullshit talked about wine.'

'I beg your pardon?'

'Yeah, like you were saying about musical instruments. I don't buy it. I'm sorry.' Frank was surprised at the combative tone he had taken with the man. Why was he doing that?

Nick cut in. 'Frank, er –'

'Jürgen.'

'Jürgen was telling me he's been a wine writer for forty years.'

'Yes indeed, nearly that long.'

'And he owns his own vineyard.'

Frank snorted. 'I still think there's a load of rubbish talked about wine. Too many people want to make it mysterious and complicated.'

'Producing excellent wine is complicated. It depends on so many factors,' insisted Jürgen, his jocular manner disappearing.

'What a load of cobblers.'

'Cobblers?'

'Look, you either like a wine or you don't.' He held up his wineglass and pointed a finger at it. 'That's it as far as I'm concerned. The language these professionals use to talk about wine is beyond most people. All this stuff about smelling the sea or an old church. I mean, Christ! Come on.'

'Frank's a bit on edge because he's in the running for the Golden Pan award,' said Nick apologetically.

Jürgen looked interested. 'I see. I hear there's a lot of competition this year, especially from the Far East.'

'The Far East?' said Frank.

'I believe so.'

Yes, there did seem to be a lot of guests who looked Japanese, Chinese, or whatever, thought Frank.

The arrival of a team of waiters and waitresses brought the conversation to an end. A balding, middle-aged French man stepped onto the stage and, speaking in heavily accented English, welcomed everyone to the ceremony.

He thanked the sponsors, naming each one, and making exaggerated claims about them, the San Sebastián City Council, and the Basque Government.

Between dishes, the compère read out the shortlist and then the winner for each successive award. As each winner stepped eagerly on to the podium to receive their award from the chairman of the International Culinary Academy, a dour Belgian, peals of applause rang out around the hall. The Japanese chef sitting next to Frank made it on to the shortlist, but the award for the most unusual restaurant went to an underwater hotel in Thailand.

Finally, the compère came to the final award of the evening, the Golden Pan. A hush descended on the hall as he opened the envelope. 'This award goes to the chef who the judges believe is the most innovative, who has done something in the world of gastronomy no one else has done.'

Frank sat there, and ran his hand around the back of his collar. He glanced across at Johnny John, who was looking pensive.

The compère grinned broadly and read out the shortlist: Fan Ju from China, who provides cookery classes in a hot air balloon for elderly people; Rafael Arconada from Spain, for creating self-cleaning cutlery; Namat Ashraf from Malaysia, who has developed a project where professional comedians go into restaurant kitchens and tell jokes to chefs with anger issues; and Ho Lee Fook from Hong Kong, who delivers takeaways by helicopter to charity workers in disaster zones.

That was all.

Frank stared vacantly ahead, doing his best to conceal the blow. Self-cleaning cutlery...a hot air balloon...comedians...But he had opened a restaurant that didn't serve food!

The compère paused dramatically. 'And the winner of the Golden Pan award is... Namat Ashraaaaf!'

Namat Ashraf skipped excitedly towards the podium, punching the air victoriously. Frank applauded lamely, as he watched him raise the golden trophy in the shape of a frying pan above his head, like a footballer at a cup final.

'Never mind, man,' said Nick, patting Frank's back.

'You must be disappointed,' said Jürgen above the noise.

'Not really,' murmured Frank.

'You see, the winner was always going to be from somewhere in the Far East.'

'So you said,' said Frank gruffly.

'No, I mean it was decided in advance.'

'I don't get you,' said Frank.

'The awards are now mainly funded by wealthy Chinese, Malaysians and so on. They call the shots now. They want their people to win. In other words, it's, as you say in English, all rigged.'

Frank stared at him open-mouthed. 'Rigged. You serious?'

'Shit!' said Nick.

The writer gave a satisfied chuckle. 'Oh, yes. I have very good contacts. There was no way the Golden Pan award was going to go to a European. Look at who the sponsors are. What do you English say? He who pays the piper plays the tune.'

25

Frank lay sprawled on his bed, his head propped against a pillow, restlessly flicking from one TV channel to another. After the ceremony, Nick had gone to a bar with two chefs and the Norwegian woman. Frank wasn't in the mood for a late-night drinking session, so he had returned to the hotel. Unable to sleep, he had switched on the TV. He impatiently dabbed the remote again and skated through more channels. 'Jesus Christ!' he said aloud, sitting up suddenly.

On the screen was a young man dressed in chef's whites, his sleeves rolled up, in a steamy, noisy restaurant kitchen. Behind him the heads of other cooks bobbed in and out of shot. Someone could be heard shouting, 'Backs!' The young cook was standing at a metal work surface, a tea towel draped over his shoulder, and wielding a long knife poised over a turbot. He looked assured and at ease as he talked to the female interviewer off camera.

Frank scrambled to the end of the bed and sat on the edge, mesmerised by the image on the TV screen.

'… It's all about fresh ingredients. Take this turbot. It was caught last night off the coast of Cornwall. Shipped here this morning. You know what? This fish is as fresh as you'll get anywhere in London. You can forget Billingsgate.'

You don't like Billingsgate?

'The thing is, some of the stuff sold there's from the other side of the world. That's not what I call fresh. How can it be?' He picked up the flat, glistening fish with one hand, held it up and said, 'Smell it. That's the smell of the sea. Isn't it bloody fantastic!'

Mmm … Yes … So is that the secret to a successful restaurant? Fresh ingredients?

'A good restaurant's about much more than that. It's about having a good team who know what they are supposed to be doing. It needs to operate like an army. It's all about paying attention to the smallest details. Remember, we eat with our eyes. You know, does the cheese board look appealing? Are the flowers arranged correctly? Keeping an eye on the wine cellar. How are people greeted when they arrive? Does someone thank them at the end of an evening? I want people to go away from my restaurant and remember the evening. Yeah, that's what I do. I create memories.'

The camera zoomed in on the hands of the chef as he ran the knife at an angle down the middle of the turbot and then expertly slid it under the flesh to peel it back. With a few swift movements he freed the flesh from the fish and placed it to one side.

Do you think a lot of restaurants don't pay enough attention to the small details, then?
A close-up of the chef's face. 'Yeah,' he said confidently.
Why's that?
He shrugged. 'Easy. Because people don't have passion. You asked me what the secret of a good restaurant is. I'll tell you. It's passion. You can't do this job – not properly – without passion.'
So it's more about business for some restaurant owners?
'I mean, restaurants are a business – and a bloody hard one. But if making loads of money becomes your main goal, then you've lost it. You've lost that passion. You should never lose sight of what's important, the reason you became a chef or wanted to open a restaurant. Some restaurants go in for gimmicks. Look, if you're cooking great food and you've got all the other things right, then you don't need gimmicks.'
Do you think you would still cook if one day you weren't passionate any more?
'When you have a passion for cooking – a true passion – it doesn't leave you. This restaurant – this kitchen – is what gets me out of bed every morning. Yeah, it's hard work and it can be tedious – you know, spending hours trimming green beans or peeling potatoes. But it's more than a job. It's part of who I am.' He paused. 'Do you have passion, then?'
Me? Well ... I like what I do ... Meeting different people –
He looked at the camera with an intense expression, his eyes seeming to grow larger. 'Yeah, but that's not what I asked, is it? I meant are you passionate

about doing interviews? Like this one?'

Er ... I suppose so ... I hadn't thought about it that way. Tell me, where do you think your passion comes from? When did you develop a love of cooking? Was it watching your mother?

He chuckled and shook his head. 'My mother wasn't a great cook. It was my dad. He ran a restaurant, and I helped him in the kitchen. Other boys dreamed of owning a motorbike or becoming a footballer or whatever. Some got into trouble – I grew up in a rough part of south London. But I dreamed about cooking. I found that it was something I liked doing. I felt I could be good at it – that's why I went off to catering college.'

What about fame? You're becoming a TV star. How does that feel?

'Yeah, I enjoy the TV stuff. It's not what I'm really about, though. I'm just a chef.' He gestured around him and grinned. 'This is where I'm really at home.'

So it won't change you? You'll still be cooking in the kitchen?

'Yeah, course I will.'

Frank sat there on the bed, still staring ahead, his mind whirling, churning, spinning. On screen he looked so young, so handsome. He was so animated about cooking, about the ingredients. The way he talked about that turbot. What was that? The smell of the sea. He was so at home in that kitchen. About ... what? ... creating memories. What a great line ... Money? Never lose sight of why you became a chef. And all that talk about passion again.

He sauntered over to the window and gazed vacantly out at the sea, wondering if it was possible to recapture the innocence of those days and the enthusiasm he had for cooking, the joy that it gave him. Somewhere along the way, he felt, he had become a different person.

His father had warned him often about the dangers lurking in the celebrity world. 'Don't get so far into it all so you can't see the wood for the trees,' Terry had said. Maybe that's what had happened. He had got caught up in the whirl of making TV programmes, signing books, endorsing products, trotting off the same old answers in interviews while making sure he smiled all the time, and everything else that went with being a celebrity. And in the process, maybe he had got lost along the way.

26

'How you feeling?' said Nick over breakfast in the hotel restaurant.

'You win some, you lose some,' said Frank quietly, slicing into his egg.

'That's the thing about these awards, man, you never know what's behind them, do you?'

'Yeah, they're never what they seem. I was a bloody fool getting so worked up about it.' He sighed. 'Anyway, you have a good night?'

Nick winked. 'What do you think?'

The flight to Gatwick wasn't due to depart until 8pm, so Nick had suggested they visit the Modern Museum of Gastronomy. On the way there, Frank popped into a sportswear shop to buy James a blue and white striped Real Sociedad football shirt.

The museum turned out to be a circular glass building on the banks of the river Urumea. Above the entrance was a sign depicting a crossed knife and fork circled by images of the flags of a dozen countries. Frank felt proud to see Britain included on it. He and Nick took their place in the queue outside, which stretched halfway down the street. Many of those in it appeared to be from the Far East.

Would there be anything in the museum about Pierre Limogne, wondered Frank. What an amazing coincidence finding Casper living at the culinary community and then seeing a painting of Pierre Limogne on the wall there. An image of the interview at Sticky Lettuce flashed before him. Why on earth had he allowed them to dictate the answers to those questions for *Out and About* magazine? He should have stuck to his guns. In a way, he'd done a disservice to Pierre Limogne, a man whose book had inspired him so much when he was a teenager. This thought still niggled away at him.

Inside the museum, he studied the map briefly and explained to Nick that there were five galleries: The Liberation of the Gourmet, Slow Food to Fast Food, Fashions and Foam, From East to West, and Menus, Manners, and Money.

They entered the first room, The Liberation of the Gourmet, which was dimly lit with glass display cases on either side. In the middle were back-to-back wooden benches, where two young nuns wearing brown habits with headsets over their veils sat whispering to each other. Frank was intrigued by the sight of the two women. They seemed so out of place in the museum.

He went up to a display case containing a waxwork effigy of a Victorian man in a charcoal frock coat and white cravat, leaning on a walking stick and holding a book in the other hand. It was Alexandre Balthazar Laurent Grimod de La Reynière, regarded as the first modern gourmet. He was holding a copy of the first restaurant guide, published in 1803 in Paris.

As they wandered from room to room, Frank became more and more fascinated. He examined old menus written in spidery handwriting, sets of restaurant cutlery, the world's first food blender, a collection of chef's hats and clogs, and a piece of melba toast created by Escoffier.

In a small cinema, they sat and watched a short film about the history of tapas and the bloody Pintxo Uprising. It explained that the origins of tapas were shrouded in fierce controversy. Some claimed tapas originated in the sixteenth century when tavern owners in Castile-La Mancha discovered that the strong taste and smell of mature cheese could help disguise that of bad wine, thus 'covering' it (since the word 'tapa' comes from the Spanish word for 'cover'), and started offering free cheese when serving cheap wine. Others claimed King Alfonso X introduced tapas after recovering from an illness by eating small dishes with his wine, and accordingly decreed that taverns could only serve wine if it was accompanied by a small snack. Another theory held by some was that tapas could be traced back to King Alfonso XIII when he stopped at a tavern by the sea in Cádiz for a cup of wine. The waiter covered the glass with a slice of cured ham before offering it to him, to protect the wine from the beach sand. The king, after drinking the wine and eating the tapa, ordered another wine, insisting it be covered. Another belief was that Felipe III passed a law in an effort to curb drunken behaviour, particularly among soldiers and sailors. The law stated that to reduce drunkenness, drinks had to be covered by a lid with a small quantity of food.

The film included black and white footage from 1932 when owners of bars and restaurants in northern Spain rose up against tapas and declared a new snack, pintxos. The Spanish government's Tapas Ministry reacted by rounding up many owners and imprisoning them. Some owners fled and went into exile in Portugal or France, where they formed the Pintxo Resistance Movement and the Pintxo League. In 1942, following the intervention of the Italian Gastronomic Union, the Pintxo Peace Treaty was signed in Bilbao.

'Bloody hell, Xavier was right about how seriously the Spanish take their food,' said Frank when they came out.

'That's the thing about war, isn't it? It only takes something small to start it,' said Nick.

'You're sounding like a bloody military historian,' chided Frank.

They moved on, stopping to look at a jewelled casket with a tiny glass window. Inside, it transpired, was part of the finger of a chef who had been executed during the Lettuce Wars in Murcia in the 1820s.

In the final room of the exhibition, a stained apron hung from the ceiling. Frank was amazed to discover that it had been worn by Pierre Limogne. He stared up intently at the different-coloured stains, imagining what great dishes they must represent and the hours Pierre Limogne must have spent cooking in the apron.

Turning around, he noticed a room where people emerged excitedly clutching miniature glass bottles.

'I wonder what's in there?'

'No idea,' said Nick.

Frank peered at the panel of text by the door. 'Bloody hell! It's water boiled by Ferran Adrià.' He chuckled. 'You can buy a bottle of it.'

'You serious? Boiled water?' said Nick.

Frank moved his head closer to the sign and read aloud. 'It says you have an opportunity to take home water that had been brought to boiling point in the kitchen at El Bulli by the great Ferran Adrià on 30 July 2011, the historic last day of the restaurant. It says it's not ordinary water; it's water that's been in contact with one of the gastronomic mystics of the modern age.'

Nick frowned. 'Gastronomic mystics! Christ! How much is it?'

'Ten euro.' Frank shook with laughter. 'I've seen it all now. Why on earth would anyone spend ten euros on boiled water?'

'Maybe they think it's got some special powers or something. Like at Lourdes. You know, that place in France where people go to get healed.'

'Hang on, there's a quote from Adrià.' Frank leaned forward to read the small writing. "Everywhere the sky is blue. There are a multitude of cuisines and dishes. I think of them as the languages and dialects of food."'

'That's not bad,' murmured Nick. 'I suppose it's sort of poetic.'

'Or bollocks.'

'That's your problem, you see, man. No appreciation of culture,' jested Nick.

Frank grinned back and silently mouthed, 'Piss off!'

Frank was astonished by how Adrià seemed to be revered in Spain. It was as if he was part of a religious cult. This would never happen in England, he told himself.

27

When they came out of the museum, Frank told Nick he wanted to buy something for Annalisa in a shop he'd seen in the old town, and that he would meet him for lunch in a bar next to the hotel in about an hour. Nick offered to come with him, but Frank insisted he'd rather go on his own. In fact, Frank wasn't going to buy anything for Annalisa. Now she had become a vegan, he had no idea what kind of things were okay. It was all so complicated.

Frank made his way to the old town and threaded his way through the lunchtime crowds of tourists dawdling along the narrow passages. Every now and again he looked up at a street sign on the wall and peered anxiously ahead. He walked around for half an hour before he spotted the black and white sign. He paused outside the bar. The man might not be working, he thought. After all, it was Sunday. What then? He couldn't return to London without seeing him. This was the only person who could relieve of him of this guilt he had been carrying around inside him all these years. Despite the success of his books and TV programmes, and all his other achievements, he could never shake off the memory of what he'd done. It had stalked him all these years.

He stepped inside the bar, feeling anxious. It was busy, but not as busy as it had been when he and Nick had been there on Friday. There were two young guys serving behind the bar. He scanned the room hopefully. No sign of him. Maybe he would be coming on duty shortly. There was still over six hours before he and Nick needed to leave for the airport. He ordered a beer and stood looking impatiently around. Most of the other customers seemed to be tourists, all laughing and chatting.

After a few minutes, he saw the waiter emerging from a door behind the bar, carrying two plates of pintxos. He said something to the other two barmen as he placed the plates on the bar and they both laughed. Frank watched as he served a middle-aged woman in sunglasses. His gazed in a kind of macabre fascination at the artificial hand, wondering what he should say and how the man would react. He had been docile and easy-going when he worked in the restaurant, but he might explode in anger when he discovered Frank was responsible for his disability. If he did, it was something he had every right to do, concluded Frank. José's life had changed forever in that moment, that moment Frank now more than ever felt so deeply ashamed of.

Frank drained his glass and signalled with his hand. 'Another, please.'

The barman came over and smiled at him. 'Certainly, sir.'

Frank hesitated, trying to find the right words. He needed to speak to him now. The bar was getting busier. 'I think we know each other.'

The barman broke off from pouring the drink and gave him a puzzled look. 'Do we?'

'At El Molino,' said Frank nervously.

'El Molino?'

'In Barcelona. A long time ago.'

The barman studied Frank closely and then said, 'You do look familiar now.'

'Frank. Remember. In the kitchen.'

He broke out into a big smile. 'Yes! Frank! Imagine seeing you again. After all these years.'

Frank said nothing.

'So what are you doing know?'

'Cooking. In London.'

'What, a restaurant, a hotel?'

'Restaurant.'

'Is it your own?'

'Yeah.'

'That's marvellous! So you made it. You always said you would. I remember you were always very ambitious. I'm so pleased. I had to give up cooking.' He held up his prosthetic hand. 'You remember what happened.'

'Yeah.'

'Still, I work here, and I love it. It's a happy place.'

'Seems like it. The thing is, José, there was something I wanted to speak to you about.'

'Yes?'

'I wondered if we could go somewhere quiet. I mean, I know you're working –'

'They won't miss me for a few minutes.' José pointed to a door. 'Come through to the back.'

Frank followed his directions and found himself in a storeroom-cum-office. José entered from another door.

'Take a seat, Frank. It's so lovely to see you again! I can't believe it!'

Frank perched on a plastic chair and José sat opposite him.

'There's something that's been on my mind for a long time, José.'

'Yes?'

'You see … the accident … when you slipped …'

José nodded.

Frank gave a deep sigh and looked at the floor. 'Well … it was me who stole it.'

'I don't understand.'

'I took the food from the walk-in fridge … the food Salvador accused you of taking.'

José went quiet.

'Look, all I can say is, I'm sorry.'

José rubbed the back of his neck and then shook his head. 'Frank, you came here to tell me this?'

'Yeah. I came to the bar on Friday. And when I saw your hand I just knew it was you.'

'I'm shocked. I don't know what to say.'

'What I did was unforgiveable. The thing is, I was so driven by ambition that nothing else mattered. I was even prepared to let you get the blame. José, you don't know how ashamed I am.'

José spoke quietly. 'Frank, you were young. It was a long time ago.'

'Yeah, if it wasn't for me, you wouldn't have that and you would have achieved your dream. You wouldn't be working in a bar. I hate myself for what I did!'

'Maybe, but we can't live in the past. We can only live in the present. Frank, I'm happy. I have a good job, a wife, three children. What more do I want?'

'But you wanted to be a chef.'

José shrugged. 'I did. But it didn't happen. That's life. Instead I've found fulfilment elsewhere.' He waved his artificial hand and grinned. 'And I've got used to this now.'

Frank stared at him, not knowing what to say. José's reaction had taken him by total surprise. José was a good man, what his father called the salt of the earth. He was the kind of man Frank wanted to be. 'Aren't you angry? You must have been angry, knowing that you'd been blamed for something you didn't do.'

'I was. And, of course, I wondered who had taken the food. But after a while I realised that anger was no good. If we allow ourselves to be filled with anger, then we suffer. We become prisoners of anger.' José reached inside his waistcoat pocket and pulled out his mobile phone and began to scroll through it.

'My wife, Mariana,' he said, handing the phone to Frank.

'She looks lovely.'

'She is. And do you know where we met?'

'No.'

'At the hospital after the accident. She was a nurse there. So you see, Frank, if it wasn't for you we would never have met.'

Frank smiled weakly. 'I suppose so.'

'Are you married?'

'Yeah.'

'I'm pleased. Children?'

'Yeah. A boy.'

José stood up. 'Frank, I have to get back to work. Are you here for long? Maybe you could meet my wife.'

'I'm flying back to London today.'

'She would have liked to meet you.'

'Next time I come.'

José studied Frank closely and said gently. 'Frank, I get a sense that you have been carrying a lot of guilt over what happened at the restaurant.'

'Yeah, you could say that.'

'I thought so. Well, there's something I want to say to you.'

'What's that?'

José looked him in the eye for what seemed a long time and then uttered, 'I forgive you.'

For the first time in years, Frank felt tears welling up. He couldn't think what to reply. José opened his arms and embraced Frank. Frank could feel the hardness of his plastic hand on his back. And he felt that a burden had been lifted from him.

28

When Frank met Nick for lunch at the bar next to the hotel, he told him about his meeting with José.

'Fuck me, you're a dark horse, aren't you? All the years I've known you and you never mentioned this.'

'Annalisa doesn't even know,' said Frank.

'I thought I knew all your secrets.'

'No one knows everyone's secrets, do they?'

'And it's really played on your mind all this time?'

'Yeah. No matter how much I tried to block it out, it didn't work.'

'And then you come here and who do you meet? This guy. Shit!'

'Incredible, isn't it. I thought I was coming here for the Golden Pan.'

'That's life, man. Always full of surprises.'

Frank shook his head. 'But what a guy! I mean, I don't know if I'd be as forgiving if someone had fucked up my life like that.'

'Same here.'

After they had eaten, Frank suggested they go for a walk along the promenade, as there was still over two hours before they needed to get a taxi to the airport. He breathed in the sea air, feeling relaxed and reflective, and looked out at the greenish-blue water sparkling in the sunshine.

'You know, coming here's made me think,' said Frank as they ambled through the crowds.

'That's a rarity,' said Nick.

'No, seriously. You know, life, restaurants, food, marriage, the lot.'

'That's what going away to somewhere does. You get perspective. We're all so busy.'

'Funny that, isn't it?' said Frank.

'What?'

'One of the things people always ask you is, are you busy?'

Nick reached for his packet of cigarettes and lighter. 'Tell you what, it's been great not to be busy these last few days. So you're over the whole Golden Pan thing now?'

Frank laughed harshly. 'Yeah. What a bloody prat I was, getting so worked up about it.' He paused and wandered over to the wall above the beach and stared out across the bay. A ferry, looking tiny, crawled across the horizon, trailing wisps of thin smoke. Squinting in the sunshine, he wondered if some of the small boats were fishing boats. He remembered the time his dad had taken him out fishing off the coast at Whitstable and the boat had nearly capsized when the wind whipped up. His dad had remained calm, telling him not to worry, and that they were safe.

'The restaurant business is crazy. Why the hell did we go into it, Nick?'

'Because we love cooking.'

Frank went quiet and said wistfully, 'Yeah, that's what got me into it, but I'm not sure that love's there any more.'

'Remember what Alfie used to tell us when we worked our bollocks off at the Majestic?'

'What?'

'That being a chef was like being married.'

'Yeah, I remember.'

'Forget relationships, marriage and all that stuff, he said. You're now married to the kitchen.'

'I suppose I got divorced, then.'

'Listen, man, you've got to get your passion back, that's what it is.'

'I mean, you've never lost your passion, have you?'

'Cooking's what I do. It's who I am. If I can't sleep at night, sometimes I think up new recipes. Shit, I don't know what I'd do if I wasn't a chef. I'd be working in some boring office, or in a supermarket or something. Or maybe I'd have turned to crime.'

Frank slapped Nick playfully on the back. 'Yeah, you've always been a bit of a dodgy bugger, haven't you?'

'Get out! You know what, Frank?'

'What?'

'What I'd really like to do is open my own little place, by the sea somewhere. Maybe down in Sussex or Kent.'

'Sounds good.'

'Yeah. Nothing fancy. I'd serve fresh fish and seafood. You know, lobster, crab, turbot, hake, squid, sea bass. There's so much fantastic stuff in British waters, but the crazy thing is we export most of it. People come here and eat langoustines caught in Scotland.'

'Hey, you're making me hungry.'

Nick became excited. 'Imagine it! The menu would be what had been caught that day. I can see myself down on the quay arguing over the prices with a fisherman. I wouldn't be bothered about pleasing Michelin. I'd only be bothered about pleasing the customers.'

Frank smiled. 'Like it. Yeah, I could see you doing that.'

'And I'd name it after my father. Antoine's. It's got a ring to it.'

'You still planning to take your mum to Lebanon?' asked Frank.

'End of next month. She's not been back since she left. She probably won't recognise it. When I was there last year, I couldn't get over all the restaurants in Beirut. Wow! Some great places, man.'

'Maybe I'll go one day.'

'You should.' Nick looked into the distance and took a long drag from his cigarette. 'I spent years chasing a star. And then I got one and then, bugger me, I got a second one. So I thought, what now? You know when you're cooking good food. So why do you need a Michelin inspector or anyone else to tell you? Why go through all the pressure of trying to impress some guy from a fucking tyre company, just to get a restaurant listed in a book?'

'I gave up on the whole Michelin thing years ago,' said Frank reflectively. 'People have high expectations when they pay top dollar at Ambience. And it looks bad if you lose a star. That's happened to a few guys, and they were devastated. Remember Dave Knight?'

Frank shook his head. 'Yeah, poor bugger. Jumping off Blackfriars Bridge.'

'What was he? Thirty-two or something?'

As they walked on, two giggling young women came towards them. Nick elbowed Frank in the ribs and said out of the side of his mouth, 'Hey, I wouldn't mind giving either of them a portion.'

Frank grinned. 'You've a one-track mind, that's your problem ... You know what?'

'What?'

'The truth is that I don't know if I ever wanted to be a chef. Maybe it was because of my dad, and I just followed in his footsteps.'

'You reckon?'

'Yeah, I think what I always wanted was recognition, which meant being famous. I don't need that recognition any more. You know what, being a celebrity chef isn't about cooking. It's about personality. I know who I am now. I'm Frank. Not the Frank on TV and book covers. But Frank the ordinary guy. I've been all about self-promotion. Frank the brand. The problem is, self-promotion's not the same as promoting your self.'

He remembered James's visit to a large branch of Tesco with the Beaver group he attended. Tesco had invited the children to visit the supermarket to learn about where food comes from and how it gets to us. In the letter sent out to parents, the initiative was called From Farm to Fork. Frank hadn't paid much attention to the visit at the time. It was just another event in his son's busy social diary. Now he asked himself why the children hadn't gone to a farm. He knew why, of course. The marketing people at Tesco were clever. They wanted the children to associate Tesco with the source of their food, not a farm or anywhere else where food was actually produced. It was a way of building brand loyalty, just like what Zoot had always talked about. He realised now that he, Frank, was like a supermarket chain.

'You've lost me there, Frank,' said Nick.

'You need to try and become a better person, more true to who you are. That's what I mean. Basically, I sold out. I chased after fame and left behind the thing that I had always wanted to do.'

'That's what you reckon?'

'You see, fame's intoxicating – it's like a drug. It does something to you and you want more. You lose touch with reality. You know it's all an act, but then you forget this and think it's real. All these people telling you how wonderful you are, buttering you up and all that. It goes to your head. At least it did with me. Listen, cooking isn't about doing TV shows and all that stuff. It's just about taking some ingredients and doing something fantastic with them. Cooking's a way of showing love.' He paused. 'It's a way of creating a memorable moment.'

'I remember you used to say that.'

'Because it's true. The thing is, Nick, cooking and business are two different things. People start off with a passion for cooking but then want to be successful in business, write books, do TV, become famous, all of that. They go from one restaurant to two then three, then four … They stick their name above the door to try and convince customers that they, the master chef, are in the restaurant. But it doesn't work. It can't work. Do you know why?'

'Go on.'

'You lose your passion. Your passion for ingredients, for the magic you can work with them. That's why. Xavier's someone with passion.' Frank blew his cheeks out. 'I've become ridiculous. A chef who doesn't cook. And then what do I do? I open a restaurant that doesn't have food. Have you ever heard anything like it? I'm a bloody laughing stock.'

'You know what, man, don't give up on the thing you love. It sounds like you need to get back into the kitchen. Forget all this TV and other shit. A professional kitchen's not a TV set. If someone had said to you back when we first met that they were going to open a restaurant with no food, you'd have said they were taking the piss.'

'I probably would have.'

'Course you would. You loved cooking then. The thing is, you bought into all this celebrity bullshit. We're chefs, Frank, not fucking rock stars.'

'You sound like my dad.'

'Well, he's right. When he was in the kitchen, there was none of this celebrity bollocks like you get nowadays.'

'Yeah, you're right.'

'I get young guys rocking up at the hotel asking for a job. After a week dicing carrots and chopping onions, they're complaining. Part of the problem's the fucking catering colleges. Because they charge students an arm and a leg, they pass them whether they're any good or not. Some of these kids just aren't up to it. They can't cope with the pressure of a busy kitchen. They just want the fame, not the graft and long hours. They think cooking's like fucking X Factor. You know what, a guy started work the other week and he came up to me on the first morning and said, "Chef, don't I get my name on my whites?"'

'What did you say?'

'What do you think I said? I said, this is a fucking kitchen, not a fucking primary school. If you want your name on it, go and ask your mum to put it on.'

Frank laughed.

'Listen, man,' said Nick. 'Did you really believe Concept F would work?'

'At the time.'

'I've got to be honest, I couldn't get it.'

'I was being clever. No one had ever come up with an idea like that.'

Nick chuckled. 'Yeah, and you know why?'

'Go on.'

'Because people go to a restaurant to fucking eat.'

'They want an experience as well. You should know that. Michelin's not just about the food, is it?'

'Yeah, but you have to have food. That's what a restaurant does. It serves food. I prep it, cook it, people eat it, they pay for it. End of story.'

'You reckon I lost the plot?'

'To be honest, yeah. I mean, I thought old Johnny's idea of customers cooking their own food was bonkers, but, fuck me, you took it a stage further. You've got balls, Frank, I'll give you that. It would take more than the window trick with what you were doing.'

They walked on in silence, with gloomy thoughts circling in Frank's mind. Nick was right. He could see that. It was bonkers to think that you could have a restaurant where people didn't eat. How on earth could he have really believed in such an idea? James had understood this. A bloody child! He had lost his way. That's what had happened. He had allowed the fame to seduce him, and he had ended up believing in his own publicity. And, to his shame, he had persuaded Casper to stump up money for the restaurant without telling him the real reason behind it.

Frank stopped and looked at his watch. 'Listen, Nick, there's something I've got to do.'

'What?'

'I need to go and see Casper before we go back.'

'You can't, man. That's miles away. We've got to be at the airport by six.'

'Yeah, I know. You go ahead and I'll meet you there.'

'You'll miss the flight.'

'If I don't go, I'll miss something else.'

29

Frank jumped out of the taxi, telling the driver he would only be a few minutes, and hurried towards the main door of the Community of the Culinary Brotherhood. He impatiently tugged at the rope to ring the bell and waited. One of the brothers appeared, looking flustered, his hands covered in flour. Frank explained that he needed to see Casper. It was urgent, he insisted. The brother beckoned him in.

As he led Frank down the corridor, the brother explained that things were hectic in the kitchen, as a large group of boisterous children were having a baking class. They emerged into a farmyard. Another brother was making cluck-cluck noises and scattering handfuls of corn to the chickens scurrying around. Ahead, down by an apple orchard, Frank spotted the unmistakeable figure of Casper. He was dressed in white overalls and painting a gate to a field where sheep grazed. As Frank approached, Casper looked up.

'Frank! I didn't expect to see you here again,' he said, putting the tin of white paint on the ground.

'Yeah, you know, I just thought I'd come and say goodbye before flying back.'

'How lovely to see you.' He wriggled his brush playfully. 'As you can see, they keep you busy here. Cuis doesn't believe in idleness – just like my father, actually.'

'Listen, Casper, there's something I have to tell you,' began Frank nervously.

'Yes.'

'How can I put this? ... Well, Concept F hasn't been doing too well.'

Casper nodded. 'I see. That's most disappointing.'

'To be brutally honest, it's turned out to be a total bloody disaster —'

Casper put a hand up. 'Frank, it wasn't a disaster. How can you say that?'

'Yeah, but Casper, the problem is, you're not going to get your money back.'

'Well, some business ventures make money and some don't. That's economics for you.'

'Yeah, but you invested so much.'

'I did. And I don't regret a penny of it.'

Frank hesitated with a pensive expression. 'The thing is, I've got to come clean with you. I only really opened it to try and win the Golden Pan award.'

Casper pursed his lips and cocked his head. 'Is that true?'

'Yeah.'

'Oh, I hadn't realised that.' He sounded disappointed.

'I'm sorry, I should have told you.'

'I have to say, you should have, really. It never occurred to me that you had an ulterior motive for the restaurant.'

'I mean, you've every right to be bloody furious with me. I deceived you, Casper.'

Casper assumed a thoughtful expression and put his brush down on top of the tin. 'It doesn't really matter now. Frank, the truth is, I owe you so much.'

'How do you mean?'

'Concept F brought me to the brotherhood. My father used to say, you only have one chance with a second chance. This is my second chance.'

Frank didn't know what to say. He was astonished by Casper's reaction to the failure of Concept F. How could he be so casual about it? It was just like when he'd admitted to José about the incident in Barcelona. He wondered briefly if he was actually dreaming.

'I'm gobsmacked. I thought you'd fly off the handle.'

'Why would I?'

'So what happens when you leave here?' asked Frank.

'Well, if I'm admitted to the brotherhood, I will simply start applying to join a brigade back in London. Part of me would like to go on the missions for a year, but that wouldn't be fair to Dolores.'

'What about the business, though?'

'Oh, I sold it. To a Malaysian company. I'm done with property now. The thing is that most of the people in the Far East I was involved with just saw properties in London as commodities, like gold or iron. They would buy places without even seeing them. I began to wonder if this was a good thing.'

'Yeah, it's bloody crazy, isn't it?'

'It's as though the city's been sold off to people who have no feel for it. That can't be good for its future, can it? Anyway, I've found my passion. And do you know what?'

'What?'

'I believe that if you find your passion and pursue it, you become a better person. This might sound a bit twee, if you like. But it's what I believe.' Casper paused. 'Frank, an idea has just occurred to me. You can say no if you like.'

'I'm listening.'

'I was wondering ... What about if we turn Concept F into one of your regular restaurants?'

'You mean another branch of Frank's?'

'Precisely.'

Frank brightened. This would be a huge weight off his shoulders. 'Yeah, brilliant idea!'

'And we could say to the press that ... well ... Concept F was only meant to be an experiment. That way, it doesn't look as if it's failed. And, just as importantly, your reputation doesn't suffer.'

Frank laughed harshly. 'That would make a nice change.'

'I have another idea.'

'Go on.'

Casper hesitated and chewed his lip. 'How would you feel about me working for you. Being in one of your brigades.'

'What, in the kitchen?'

'In one of your restaurants. Maybe Concept F.'

'Come on! You want to work in one of my restaurants? Listen, Casper, I'm not trying to be funny or anything ... but you're not exactly a spring chicken, are you?'

'I'm fitter than I've ever been.'

'Yeah, but cheffing's a young man's game. On your feet all day, working quickly, long hours. You don't want that.'

'Of course, I know I've still a lot to learn about the culinary arts – I'm still only a garçon de cuisine – but even in the short time I've been here I feel I've made huge strides, if I say so myself,' babbled Caper. 'I can dice carrots and onions, make stocks, bone a chicken, fillet round fish, and I'm learning all about the differences between frying, steaming, braising, and so on.'

'That's great.'

Casper continued. 'And I've even done some baking – still trying to get the knack of pastry, though – and I'm learning how to make cheese.'

A brother driving a tractor chugged into the yard and waved at Casper. Casper smiled and waved back.

Frank looked with affection at the figure in the ridiculous green outfit standing in front of him, who talked with such awe about cooking and chefs, about passion and dreams, and that whole spherification thing. This was a man who was much wealthier than himself. A man who made millions from a single property deal. And he was going to give it all up – to cook. The costume might be ridiculous, but Casper wasn't. Frank felt a deep respect for him. And envy. I was like this once, he said to himself. What the bloody hell's happened to me? What was that his father had said about not seeing the wood for the trees?

'Casper?'

Casper looked anxious. 'Yes, Frank?'

'Listen, if you really want to work in one of my restaurants, you've got a job.'

'Do you really mean it?'

'Yeah.'

Casper broke into a beaming smile and put a hand on Frank's arm. 'You don't know how happy you've made me.'

Casper walked with Frank to the front of the building, where the taxi was waiting.

'It's such a shame you're going back today,' said Casper, as they walked past a row of beehives.

'Yeah, I know,' said Frank with genuine regret.

'You could have come and seen our Loaves and Fishes project.'

'What's that?'

'We run a centre in San Sebastián, providing meals – and I mean good food – for people on the streets.'

'That's impressive.'

'Yes, we get all sorts: Africans, Poles, chefs who've hit the bottle, people on drugs. You name it. The centre's near the main railway station. Sometimes the culinary sisters also help out.'

Frank reflected again on what an extraordinary place this culinary community was, what an atmosphere of peace it exuded.

As he was about to get into the taxi, he said, 'Casper, there's something else I wanted to tell you.'

'Go on.'

'You remember when we met at that fish restaurant.'

'The Fillet of Fish. Of course. How could I forget.'

'Well, my fish was bloody good.'

'It was?' A smile slowly spread across Casper's face. 'So you were … pulling my leg, as they say?'

'Yeah, you could say that.'

30

Frank tore off a docket from the printer, briefly glanced at it, and shouted above the noise, 'On order! Casper! Three sea bass! One turbot!'

'Yes, chef!' called back Casper at the grill station through a haze of smoke.

As Frank attached the docket to a rail along the steel shelf that ran above the pass, the restaurant manager came bustling through the swing doors.

'Chef, table ten's complaining about the wait,' she said.

He quickly scanned the dockets and let out a sigh. 'Two bread salad, one calamari, one meatball picante. For ten. Guys, come on, come on, let's step it up!'

It was early Thursday evening two weeks before Christmas at Frank's restaurant in Marylebone, and the kitchen team were working flat out to keep up with the orders flowing in, many from groups of office workers having their annual get-together.

Frank had been working in the kitchen since seven that morning. He had written prep sheets, emailed orders to suppliers, checked inventories and equipment, written the staff rota for the following week, interviewed candidates for a kitchen porter vacancy, prepped vegetables, made sauces, and filleted fish.

One of the lessons he had learned working at the Majestic Hotel was that a restaurant kitchen had to be run like a military operation. It was all about timings and precision. There were so many things that needed to be got right and so many things that could go wrong. The day before, the pizza oven had packed up, a drain had become blocked, and a new supplier had failed to deliver a batch of olive oil on time. This afternoon, the dishwasher had broken down and the engineer couldn't come until the morning. So Frank had had to bring a table from the restaurant into the kitchen, on which to stack the dirty crockery and cutlery. It was already piled high.

He wandered over to the cold food section, where Giles, a black teenager he had recently hired, was plating up salads. Frank stood there for a moment, watching.

'Don't forget to always wipe the edge of the plate,' he said, wiping the rim of the plate with a section of kitchen towel.

'Sorry, chef,' said Giles.

Frank patted him on the back. 'Hey, listen. You're doing well. Your mum was right. You're a hard worker.'

'Thanks, chef. She really likes your dad. She says he's her favourite resident.'

'Oh, he can be a real charmer when he wants. Just remember presentation when you're plating.'

'Yes, chef.'

'You know, someone once told me being a chef's a bit like being an artist.'

Giles looked up. 'I've never thought of it like that.'

'Yeah, it's true. We're creating a picture on a plate.'

'Chef, can I ask you something?'

'Go ahead.'

'Someone said you're not doing any more telly.'

'That's right.'

'Oh.'

'This is where I belong, Giles, not in a TV studio. If you want to become a top chef, then focus on cooking, not on becoming a celebrity. That was my mistake.'

After returning from San Sebastián, Frank had found that he no longer had any desire to be part of the media circuit he had lived in for so long. Something had changed inside him. He wasn't sure what it was, but he knew that what he really wanted was to be back in the kitchen.

Since then, he had been cooking at his restaurants three or four days a week. He would usually spend a week in each one. He had closed Concept F and reopened it as a regular branch of Frank's. And Casper, after leaving the Community of the Culinary Brotherhood, had begun working there.

The rest of Frank's time was spent working at his head office, meeting suppliers and others involved with his businesses, helping out at his café, training staff, or taking classes at his cookery school.

It had surprised him how quickly he had adapted to his new working life, and how he didn't miss doing interviews or promotions. He felt happier and more content than he had done in a long time. No one had been more surprised by the way Frank had changed than Annalisa.

The restaurant manager reappeared with a big smile on her face. 'Chef, table fifteen says compliments to the chef. They said the food was sensational.'

Frank grinned. 'That's what I like to hear.'

'They asked if they could speak to you.'

Frank hesitated, wiping his brow with the back of his hand. 'Yeah, okay. Give me a minute.'

A plate of seafood spaghetti and another of pork belly porchetta arrived at the pass. Frank pulled a spoon out of his back pocket and tasted the spaghetti and, after wiping the spoon with a kitchen towel, did the same with the porchetta. 'Service! Table twenty-three,' he shouted.

A waitress swiftly picked up the plates, turned, and expertly shouldered her way through the swing doors.

Frank wiped his brow with the back of his hand and surveyed all the heads bobbing up and down. Everyone was working fast and in unison. He called to Matt, his sous-chef, that he would be gone for five minutes. Matt nodded and gave him the thumbs up.

When Frank entered the restaurant, a number of the diners looked up in surprise. With a smile, he made his way towards table fifteen, at the far end of the restaurant. He suddenly stopped halfway. Annalisa, James, Terry, and Jill were sitting there.

'Bloody hell, what are you all doing here? You never told me,' he said when he reached the table.

Annalisa laughed. 'We thought we'd surprise you.'

'You can say that again.'

'It was my idea, Frank,' said his father.

Frank was taken aback by this. 'Yeah?'

'I thought it was about time that I came to try your food.'

'I've been telling him he should go,' said Jill. 'I tried to persuade him to go to your opening … but you know how stubborn he can be.'

Terry shook his head and beamed. 'Frank, I can't remember the last time I had a meal this good! It was perfect.'

Frank stood there, lost for words. And then he noticed that his wife had eaten grilled salmon. Hang on. 'Annalisa, you've had salmon.'

'Mm. It was delicious.'

'But you're supposed to be vegan.'

'Daddy?' interrupted James.

'Yes, Little Man?' replied Frank, sitting down at the table.

'I want to come here for my birthday.'

'You like it?'

'I had a burger.'

'Was it good?'

James nodded. 'Can I come here for my birthday?'

'Of course you can.'

'I've decided, well, veganism's not for me,' said Annalisa.

Frank chuckled. 'That's a bloody relief.'

'I mean, a lot of what they say, you know, it sort of makes sense and that … but I can't really just eat tofu and hemp seeds all my life.'

Frank didn't say it, but he wondered if Annalisa's abandonment of veganism was also to do with the scandals surrounding the Vegan Mary. She had been accused of using funds from the charity she had set up to fund a luxury lifestyle. And, even worse as far as vegans were concerned, she had been secretly filmed tucking into a huge steak at a rodeo in Texas.

'Frank, I take my hat off to you,' said Terry, pouring himself a glass of Pinot Noir. 'You've got a great place here. The staff are so friendly.'

'Thanks, Dad. You know how important it is to make people feel welcome.'

'That's what I always tried to do with the bistro. You'd have liked it, Annalisa.'

Annalisa smiled. 'Frank's told me about it. You used to have a singer sometimes, he said.'

'Oh, Charlie Spencer. He was a real character.'

'That's one way of describing him,' said Frank, breaking into laughter at the memory of Charlie speaking in a fake American accent.

'Daddy, can I see the kitchen?' asked James.

'You want to see the kitchen, do you? Okay, come with me.'

Frank got up and took James by the hand.

When they entered the kitchen, the boy's eyes widened at the sight of all the cooks rushing around. 'Daddy, I thought you cooked all the food.'

'No, I have people to help me.'

James went silent momentarily and frowned. 'I can't see the computers.'

'The computers? Oh, there's no computers here. Just food.'

'But I thought you ... cooked computers.'

Frank laughed. 'I never cooked computers, but I used them in another restaurant.'

'That was a silly idea, Daddy, wasn't it?'

Frank crouched down, put an arm around James and said gently, 'Yeah, James, you are absolutely right. It was a silly idea. You see, sometimes in life we can forget what's really important. And that's what Daddy did.'

James nodded.

'The thing is, we all want to ... impress people ... to look clever. We shouldn't do that. We should just use our talents, work hard, and –'

'Be nice to people.'

'Yeah, of course. And be ourselves.'

James looked around the kitchen and pointed. 'Daddy, who's that old man?'

'Old man? You mean Casper. He's not that old.'

Casper smiled and waved a ladle in the air.

'He looks like grandad.'

Frank laughed. 'Don't tell him that. Listen, you know what, Casper's a very clever person.'

'How?'

'Well, you know what? Casper used to work in an office in a big building, the Beanstalk. I've pointed it out to you. Remember? And then he decided he didn't like it. What he really wanted to do was to learn how to cook.'

James frowned. 'How's that clever?'

'He's clever because he realised that life isn't just about money and that you must follow your dream.'

THE MAN BEHIND THE MENU

Greg Watts is an author and journalist. His previous books include *Ole! Ole! Passion on a Plate: The Rise of Spanish Cuisine in London* (2016) and a memoir, *The Long Road Out of Town* (2015). This is his first novel. He is married and lives in south-east London, and enjoys cooking at home.